THE PROMISE

BETHANY-KRIS

Published by Bethany-Kris

www.bethanykris.com

ISBN 13: 978-1-989658-47-5

Editor: Elizabeth Peters

Cover Design © Mignon Mykel

For all those Russian Guns fans ... you've waited long enough. XO.

CONTENTS

ONE

The mind was a messy thing.

A *fickle* thing.

Karine's was even worse. Her hair blew in the breeze coming through the rolled down window, while she kept her face turned away from Roman because she didn't want to meet his eyes. The intensity she always found staring back from the striking blue gaze distracted her in ways she couldn't explain, and the last thing she needed was to drown in them.

Hell.

She was already drowning in herself, after all—in her mind, the hellscape was a dying carcass circled by the vultures that were her thoughts. Things she didn't want to see, others that she's worked so hard not to *know* ... she couldn't possibly deal with an overwhelming man, and the violent currents inside her mind at the same time.

Karine also didn't know what to say to Roman without it sounding like an attack. Instead, she remained silent, her

1

stare locked beyond the window at the passing scenery whether she was actually seeing it, or not.

So did Roman.

The only sound came from Masha's soft, rhythmic inhales and exhales from the backseat. She seemed content to sleep, probably the longest stretch of rest she had for the first time in decades. It was also entirely possible that she had helped herself to the pills she used to ply Karine with—they did say what was good for the goose was good for the gander.

Every time Karine glanced in Roman's direction, she found him glaring at the black patch of road stretching on ahead of them. A hardness had set into his handsome features that made her pause with each glance she stole his way. He gripped the steering wheel tight until his knuckles turned white, and his mouth *shut*. The entire drive had been that—it felt like.

Unbearable silence.

Unexplained anger.

She didn't know how much further they had to go—never mind where he planned for them to end up. He rolled into her life at the worst possible time, seemingly unaware but too curious and interesting for his own good, and she barely knew him at all.

Except she wanted to.

A dangerous thing for someone like her.

Karine almost had to wonder what was broken inside Roman Avdonin that made him do the things he'd done. What he still was doing, even. It would have made sense— *maybe*—if the other woman who hid within herself was one who had lusted after and seduced him, and then spent the night with him.

Karine would be lying if she said a part of her didn't blame him. That didn't change how she felt sitting beside him, not knowing where they would go—*safe*. She had no choice but to trust him now.

What else could she do?

"Are you scared?" Karine suddenly asked, breaking the silence that had become something else that was just *too much* for her to handle. Yet, it was also something she could control.

And maybe if he talked, then that loudness in her head might quiet. If only for a moment … *God*, she'd take a single second.

Roman didn't have a particular reaction to that question— almost like he had been expecting it. "Scared of what?"

The way he grumbled the words had her blinking back in response. His rumbling annoyance didn't seem to be directed at her asking, but she still shrunk subtly back like it might be. Roman chanced a quick look her way, his shoulders gently rising at the tilt of her frown, before he continued to concentrate on the road ahead.

"Sorry—I'm just tired," he said.

Karine let out the breath she'd been holding and nodded. From the corner of her eye, while she stared at his chiseled profile, she noticed the New York State sign zoom past.

"I meant them—back in Chicago," Karine replied, softly. "Are you scared of them?"

That was all she needed to say for him to know exactly *who* she was talking about. She didn't really think he needed a clearer picture.

"I didn't realize I had any reason to be afraid of them," Roman murmured.

Karine swallowed the lump that formed in her throat, promising to keep her fears locked tight in her chest, thumping there with every beat of her heart. He didn't know what he was talking about—he still said it with enough confidence to convince someone else he might.

But not her.

Even if she wished he could.

Maybe he genuinely didn't know how things operated in Chicago, but Karine's entire life had been an unfortunate lesson in the topic. Her father might be distracted with the plot to assassinate him, but it was only momentarily. She was supposed to marry Dima in two days—agreements like those weren't broken without someone answering for it, too.

Last night, the risk had seemed worth the choice, but as the sky cleared with the light of the morning breaking through the dark clouds, she sat in the passenger seat unsure of herself.

Of her decisions.

Of his.

She had grown up around those men—she doubted the ones he came from were the same. Even though there were times of her life that she couldn't remember, she didn't wonder at all about this. Those men weren't going to let her simply escape into the sunset. A deal had been made, and there were men who would make sure she kept her end of the bargain, one way or another.

Karine hadn't gotten away with anything in her life—she certainly didn't think the universe was going to start now.

Despite a sheltered life, she had in fact lived long enough to see a woman face the consequences of not seeing an arrangement through. Her wedding to Dima might not happen when it had been originally planned, but that didn't mean it was anywhere near *void.*

Roman hadn't even mentioned the wedding.

How could she trust this man?

What did he have to gain by saving her—or was it *keeping* her? Was it possible that he would do all of this just because they slept together once?

Same body, different girl, came a cackling glee from somewhere in the recesses of Karine's mind. She blinked away the taunt, but it lingered all the same.

She forced herself to talk so that voice *wouldn't.* "I'm supposed to get married tomorrow. Do you realize that?"

Roman said nothing, but his narrowing eyes while he continued to stare straight ahead said he was listening. That didn't mean he liked what he heard.

"I don't think you truly understand what that means. They're going to come looking for me," Karine said, the steady stream of her thoughts tumbling out in fast sentences she couldn't control. "It's not like they'll sit back and file a missing persons report with the cops or something."

A dark cast washed over Roman's face while he acted as though the feverishness of her rambling wasn't concerning. He was so good at doing that, she'd noticed.

ᵀᴴᴱPROMISE

Already.

It only urged her to continue.

"Dima expects his bride to show up, to get what he wants, and if he doesn't—"

"The wedding isn't going to happen," Roman interjected, the calm in his tone belying the coldness that settled in his gaze. "Not too many people know about it, anyway. I don't think most of the Yazov bratva even knows, only those involved directly within the city limits. They had only just started delivering the invitations. By *hand*, mind you. There's time for them to make a decision that doesn't include returning you."

But not likely.

Karine wasn't *dumb*.

A mess, yes.

Dazed, at times.

Not stupid, though.

"Everything was set up," she whispered, picking at her fingernails to soften the sound of her own voice saying things she *hated*. "We were going to exchange vows in the rose garden. The wedding dress was picked out for me, I didn't even have to think about it. Masha was going to do my makeup."

Karine spoke mechanically, aware of how she sounded but unable to stop repeating everything that she had been told by others. Her father. *Dima*. Even by Masha. Over and over again.

She had spent a lot of time preparing herself for her marriage to Dima. There was no real choice presented to her, she couldn't stop the wedding—it was out of her hands.

Karine had already been sworn to Dima, and there was no escape from that. No matter how far she ran.

"I'm going to say it again," Roman said, turning to meet her gaze with a clenched jaw and expressionless. "Know it will be the last time I say it, Karine. There will be *no* wedding tomorrow. You're not marrying that motherfucker. Not ever."

She swore every muscle in his body tightened and coiled in the seat next to hers—like a snake ready to spring. If the

5

conviction he spoke with couldn't convince her, his anger that flared at the suggestion certainly *might*.

Karine sucked in a sharp breath, shaking her head as she told him, "I don't know what you're doing, I don't understand it at all."

Roman didn't even blink when he replied, "Neither do I."

• • •

"Why did you do this?" Karine asked, well-aware that some time had passed since she last said a word. Within the city limits, everything was new to her. Each building, every block ... she tried to take it all in, and Roman said nothing while she did so. She'd never been anywhere but Chicago. Yet, even there, she hadn't done much exploring of her own city. At Roman's questioning glance, she added with a shrug, "Take me, I mean?"

It was a question that wouldn't leave her alone—the problem was that she could come up with a million answers of her own, and none of them were *good*. He didn't answer straightaway, but he didn't seem like he was trying to come up with something just to say it, either.

Was he ignoring her—changing his mind about bringing her with him, maybe?

She couldn't decipher this man. His mind was a place she couldn't reach, but she suspected it was nothing like her own. Her belief that he wouldn't hurt her, not for as long as he assumed responsibility for her, did nothing to assuage the other questions she had.

Like what if he woke up tomorrow morning, and decided he didn't want to deal with her anymore?

It was then, as she tried to avoid his gaze that kept slipping her way, that she noticed the bruising on his wrists. The blackened-blue marks were too fresh. She'd been thinking he kept holding tight to the wheel because he was angry—those grimaces and hard stare was further proof—but suddenly, she didn't think that was the case at all.

Karine couldn't help but ponder if those bruises were in anyway connected to what caused him to walk into her

ᴛʜᴇPROMISE

bedroom in the middle of the night, and take them away. She had a feeling he wouldn't tell her even if she asked him.

"I don't remember any protests when I suggested this plan last night," Roman replied, arching a brow her way as he rolled onto a bridge behind a line of taxi cabs.

She didn't miss it.

How *careful* he was—how he posed each word as to not suggest something that might set Karine off. He clearly hadn't forgotten that breakdown in her bedroom the night they spent together.

Karine chest tightened all the same—she didn't have the words, or maybe the vocabulary, to explain to him how overwhelmed she was. At everything, *constantly*. He didn't make it better, even if he might sometimes make it easier. He had offered an opportunity that couldn't be refused, but now she wanted to know the truth.

What did it actually mean?

Before she could ask; Roman continued speaking. "You could ask me about your father, about—what he's done or is going to do. You could ask anything, Karine, but what you do is question my intentions. What makes you think I had a choice in any of this—that even this car that isn't mine is somehow part of *my* plan?"

He didn't look at her while he spoke that time, but she was suddenly grateful for that. Not even the obsessive, undeniable attraction she felt for the man was enough to soothe the way his words stung her skin.

She *had* asked.

At least he was honest.

Karine tried to find an appropriate response, but the words were lost to her murky mind as Roman pulled the vehicle off the road, and into the underground parking lot of a tall apartment building with windows that looked like panes of chrome, and high, black brick walls. A thrill ran down her spine at the sight.

She didn't know much about New York, but at the very least—well, the movies had been right.

It was glamorous.

7

• • •

The lobby of the building had clearly been designed with the outside in mind. Chrome accents twinkled in the tile under their feet while black brick made up the walls, and even the face of the reception desk that they passed in a hurry. Roman walked like he was, anyway. It took two of Karine's steps to keep up with his one.

Masha trailed far behind them, still as quiet as ever. All the years that she'd served the Yazov household taught her how to make herself invisible, and blend into the background when not required.

Karine stared up in awe of the rows of hanging chandeliers made from twisted chrome along the high ceilings of the lobby. She barely even cared that their bright lights made it hard to see what was ahead of her when she looked away.

Roman definitely had good taste.

And money.

The man and woman at the reception desk greeted them with smiles as they passed—Roman didn't offer a reply as he headed straight for the elevator. Karine, at least, returned their smiles with her own, but couldn't say it felt very true.

He carried one bag in his loose grip—*hers*. It was the only one he'd been able to pack in a hurry. *Only what you'll need for a couple days, I can replace everything else,* he had told her earlier as they drove into the state. She'd already noticed how he had no bags of his own. Did he really have no belongings in Chicago—nothing that he held dear enough to bring back with him?

They stood at the elevator doors until they spread apart with a loud *ding*. It was clear by the size and available space that it wasn't made for more than a couple people at a time.

"Which floor, Mr. Avdonin? I'll take the next one," Masha said, making her voice heard before they entered.

"Fiftieth," Roman replied without a glance over his shoulder. "It'll open right to it."

Just as fast, he placed a hand to Karine's lower back and urged her inside with the pressure of his palm. The doors slid shut behind them, and she caught sight of a quiet Masha before they closed. Alone with him in the confines of the elevator, she clutched her stomach, the wave of claustrophobia starting the second the floor seemed to jump under her feet.

Maybe then would have been a good time to point out to him how she didn't enjoy closed spaces. Her anxiety went through the roof, forcing her to ramble or babble nonsense for nothing more than the distraction it provided.

She said the first thing to come to her mind, but she wouldn't pretend like the thoughts hadn't been bothering her for a while. "You said you had no choice—so you didn't want to take me with you? Is that what you meant?"

The elevator lifted faster than she expected it to. She was able to watch the numbers change on the digital screen over the doors rapidly while the pressure and speed vibrated underneath her feet.

Roman didn't look at her, not even once, keeping his hand firmly stuffed in the pocket of his pants while his other held tight to her bag. Instead of answering her question, he simply asked, "You talk a lot when you're nervous or scared, huh?"

Karine chewed on the inside of her lower lip, muttering only, "Sorry—I can't stop it."

"That's okay. Didn't say it was a bad thing, did I?"

Wasn't it?

Before she could mull the question—or his words—over, the doors slid open again and welcomed them into what appeared to be another lobby. Only *much* smaller, with one entire side of the space being dedicated for floor-to-ceiling windows that overlooked the buildings across the block, and the street below. They passed leather bucket chairs placed on either side of a electric fireplace on the way to the door at the other end of the small corridor.

"The whole floor on this side of the building is the apartment," he said, making Karine realize he was paying more attention to her than she thought.

How much did a place like this cost?

"It seems—"

"Modern," he filled in when her words stopped forming altogether. "And the deed to this side of the floor was a gift to me from a family friend involved in the development when I ..." For a moment, his gaze slid to her as he seemed to consider the words he wanted to say. Then all at once, he just decided to apparently say them when he shrugged and said, "They gave it to me as a gift when I joined the family business. Some people tried to make a game out of it—who could get the best gift. Got three cars out of that, too, so *hey*. Not too bad."

Karine blinked, unsure of how to respond. Roman seemed to enjoy her stunned silence, the grin stretching across his lips making her heart race a little faster. It screamed wicked—all sorts of fun. It didn't seem like the time, but he could probably make her willing without even trying. And she liked it.

Roman pulled a keycard from his wallet, and slid it through the electronic lock at the end of the small entry. The door unlocked and opened on its own as he nodded a head toward the dimly lit space that greeted them. His voice was kinder than she expected when he said, "You should have a look around, make yourself at home. Might be here for a while, right?"

She stared at him, considering that—would it be such a bad thing?

Instead of waiting for her mind to come up with its own answer, Karine pushed open the door and stepped inside the apartment. Roman made his way in behind her, reaching beyond her shoulders to flick on a row of switches that lit up the open-concept floor of space to her view. Black marble pressed into the soles of her shoes while high, vaulted white ceilings waited overhead. She could see through the main floor of the space to where a long, glass dining table welcomed guests into a kitchen full of stainless steel, white marble countertops, and more black brick.

Roman remained at the door while she took slow steps further beyond black marble pillars to see the living space and entertainment section overlooking more floor-to-ceiling windows, but these were different than the ones in the entry. Curved outward in a domed shape. The life and buzz of an unknown—but strangely beautiful—city stretched out in front of her.

This high, it was like she was floating in the air above it.

"You still didn't answer my question, Roman," she said, enjoying the view but knowing he'd left something unsaid. Karine didn't like that. Turning away from the windows, and forcing her stare up from the shiny black marble under her feet to meet his gaze, she couldn't allow herself to get carried away. Not in anything. Not even in him until she had an answer. "You didn't want to take me with you, did you? You were forced to."

If he was shocked at what she asked, Roman didn't show it. Lucky for him that he didn't have to answer her question, either, because the approaching footsteps from the entry they had just come from had Roman turning away.

Masha didn't seem at all aware that she had interrupted them. Karine hated to admit that she was relieved at the sight of her—she wasn't sure if she wanted to hear what Roman's response would be.

She had a habit of doing that. Asking, but not wanting to know.

Karine was fine to let Roman busy himself with showing Masha where things were and disappearing with her down a back hallway where he said one of three bedrooms and the main bathroom could be found.

She remained standing where she was—quiet by the glass wall where she could see the hustle of a city. Where she really didn't have to *think*.

Of course, she still did.

*Over*thinking.

Entirely numb.

Who was Roman?

Who was he *really*?

Despite being told to explore, she didn't do much as Roman and Masha's voice carried out from the back hall. She did marvel a bit at the touchscreen panel on a pane of the glass that controlled everything from the automatic blinds covering the glass dome-shaped walls to the massive, curved flatscreen television next to the oversized, squared leather sectional. There was even a full-fledged bar at the corner of the living space, melding between there and the dining space.

The apartment seemed fit for a man who had priorities for a good time, and few responsibilities. A bachelor's life. There she was, ready to disrupt it all.

She still couldn't come up with a single *good* reason why he would have willingly done this—taken her.

"*Hey.*"

Roman's firm, but not unkind tone, had Karine jumping in her skin. She hadn't heard him come back into the room. Spinning around, she found him standing at the entry of the hall, his shoulder pressed into another one of those black marble pillars as he looked her over.

Masha was nowhere in sight, clearly having chosen to stay out of focus. Maybe *wisely.*

Karine licked nervously at her bottom lip, determined not to blurt her thoughts, and making a conscious effort to keep the words inside the longer he stared and said nothing.

"*What?*" she eventually asked.

A little too sharply.

Roman still gave her a crooked smile—it was just as tempting as everything else. Then, he told her, "Just because I was forced in to taking you doesn't mean that I didn't want to."

She hadn't expected that.

"Why?" she asked.

Seconds ticked on as he took in a deep breath, and his shoulders rose and fell from the effort. His reply wasn't what she was looking for. "I don't really have an answer for that, Karine."

"That's a lie."

If he could say he wanted something, then he should be able to say *why.* Besides, everything else about her life was a lie. It wouldn't even hurt her feelings if he lied about this, too.

"The real question is whether you want to know the truth," Roman returned just as fast, never once breaking her stare. "Because that requires accepting certain things, you know? I think we've both established you have—just a bit—of a problem doing that in different aspects. Think about it."

That truth was cold.

He also wasn't wrong.

Karine chose not to reply, and that time, it wasn't hard to keep the prattle of words induced by her anxiety and fears inside. Maybe he understood her better than she was willing to admit.

She still thought he shouldn't.

TWO

Roman woke up already tired the second he opened his eyes. Back in a familiar bed, in his own apartment, he could almost believe for a second that it had all been a bad dream. The sounds of a city he knew well told him he wasn't in Chicago anymore, and that only meant one thing.

There was a beautiful, troubled woman sleeping in one of the other bedrooms. He really didn't have the time to enjoy being back in his bed, considering that little detail.

Swinging his legs off the bed in a rush to start his day, a splintering pain pierced through his ribcage. Reminding him all at once that *nothing* was a fucking dream. He groaned, pressing a palm to the most tender rib as he straightened up.

One breath.

Then, another.

It really didn't get easier.

Hell, a bad dream would have been better than the reality. Maxim Yazov certainly made sure Roman had no choice but to remember that baseball bat. For days, likely.

ᴛʜᴇPROMISE

Fuck.

It took all of his energy to not wince with every step he took. He had to make a conscious decision to not limp as he crossed the room to head for the bathroom. The pain hadn't been so bad yesterday because he kept going on pure adrenaline. Nothing more. Too damn much had happened in the span of twenty-four hours for him to even process, let alone physically.

Now that the adrenaline had worn off, and what he was left with was a torn and broken body. Covered in dark bruises that ached at the sight alone, especially around his wrists where Maxim had notched the rope and chain, he eyed his reflection in the bathroom mirror.

It looked as bad as it was.

But *hell.*

He'd looked worse.

However, his injuries were the least of his concerns. Nothing was bad enough to keep him in bed currently, and he certainly wasn't *dead.* That counted for something. It was almost noon when he caught sight of the clock in his room. Half the day had already passed with him prone on his back. He needed to make sure Karine was okay more than he needed the aches and pains to settle.

Splashing his face with water in the connected bathroom, he surveyed the current version of his reflection. At different angles, he hardly recognized himself. Between the bruises, the exhaustion in his eyes, and even his beard that was becoming more unkept by the day, he looked sick.

More than tired.

Getting himself involved in this shitshow was taking its toll—physically and mentally. And yet, there was no way for him to untangle himself from it when the more prominent concern on his mind revolved around the woman sleeping somewhere in his apartment and less on the pallor coloring his skin.

Karine didn't have a single clue about what was really going on here—at least, not the full scope of it. Her father had forced her on him, yes, through an agreement Roman really couldn't back out on, all things considered. But that didn't mean she understood any of it. There was no turning back now.

Maxim made the bed.

Roman laid down in it.

• • •

It didn't take long for Roman to find Karine. She apparently hadn't bothered with a bedroom, instead opting to sleep on a chaise in front of the glass wall. The shutters hadn't even been pulled to keep the bright afternoon light from pouring in on her face. Not that it mattered. Nothing disturbed her sleep.

One thing to be thankful for, he supposed.

Given that Masha was nowhere in sight, he assumed that she had utilized one of the bedrooms unlike Karine.

At least, she had found a pillow and a blanket to make herself comfortable on the chair. Although, could she really have been comfortable spending the whole night there? It wasn't like the firm chaise had any kind of *give* to it when it came to rest.

If she had spent the night there, actually. He supposed the events leading up to their arrival at the apartment would be enough to keep anyone up for a while. God knew he hadn't heard a fucking thing to say otherwise once his head hit the pillow.

Masha assured him Karine would be fine before he went to bed. He'd trusted her only to say she wasn't comfortable enough with New York City to do anything but stay right where she was, and keep an eye on Karine.

Which was all he needed.

Just long enough to sleep …

Roman didn't want to think about what else Karine might have done to pass the time if she hadn't slept the night and morning away like the rest of them. That would just end up fucking with his head, and she was *there*.

Right there, in front of his face.

Fine.

That's what counted.

ⅎPROMISE

Roman, ready to turn on his heel and head back to the bedroom where he could at least do something productive—*like fix the way he looked*—but something made him pause. A notebook peeked out from underneath the pillow where Karine rested her head. His spine straightened. It wasn't a sketchbook, but that didn't mean anything. He bet Katee could draw on anything she found to do the job.

His next breath came slow, and deep.

What had he got himself into?

What's it fucking matter—here you are.

Yeah.

Standing next to the large metallic slab at the other end of the room—the counter to his kitchen islands—he turned his gaze away from a sleeping Karine and that notebook. For a second. Long enough to clear his head and *attempt* to appreciate the fact he was home. He'd been very specific with his interior decorator when he knew the place would feature the marble and black brick. He wanted an industrial vibe where it could be fit in. Something to suit what he did for a living, to make him feel like he was back at the loft over the garage.

His first home that he kept—one that actually felt like *his*. In a way he couldn't really explain. Call it nostalgia.

From his position leaning against the counter, he could still see Karine's slender body gently rising and falling underneath the blanket in the corner of his eye. Even *making* himself stare elsewhere did nothing for what his mind seemed to want. He was struck by how innocent she seemed while she slept—how vulnerable and fragile she was to anyone who might want to do her harm.

As she slept, she reminded him of the Karine he first met. The lost, beautiful woman who carried a starry daze in her eyes and confusing words on the tip of her tongue. The one who had instigated their night together, her cheeks flushed with embarrassment and courage. All at the same time.

Roman was only starting to realize *that* Karine was just one part of her—the one he initially felt an urge to protect, the one he wanted to keep safe from Dima. He didn't think it was by accident that he came upon Karine as she was first, and not the versions of her that came out to play with people she must have known she couldn't trust.

Not that he was in any way educated enough to understand what was happening in her mind—because he didn't. Wouldn't pretend to, either.

Yet, he wondered …

Was there a connection there?

A reason?

He had to turn away from the sight of her altogether, knowing he needed to keep the part of him in check that seemed to grab hold of the idea that it was his responsibility now to do what she needed—*anything* she needed. If only because he liked it, and he wasn't ready to deal with that.

Roman still had to figure out how he was going to fit Karine into his life—in New York with his family, and business. It wasn't like he could just show back up here without some kind of an explanation about the chick that came along for the ride. The agreement with Maxim got her here, but he wasn't exactly sure what he was supposed to do now, either. Not that he really had an option but to make it work.

That was the thing about choices.

Once made, it was done.

Besides, he wasn't sure here was where Karine wanted to be, anyway. She was suspicious of him—didn't trust his intentions. And why should she?

At most, he'd given her a good lay. At worst, he'd taken her away from a man that wouldn't take kindly to a missing bride on his wedding day.

He bet she was so used to the illusion of a choice—or none at all—that Roman demanding she do as he told her, even leaving with him, was just another thing Karine *did*. What happened when she learned she could do things for herself—be her own voice?

Roman figured that was for Karine to work out—however she wanted and needed to. Grabbing a bottle from the bar, he headed back to his bedroom with quiet footsteps. He had to make a phone call, and quickly.

ᴛʜᴇPROMISE

In the privacy of his room, Roman still didn't feel like it was enough. He slipped between the sliding glass doors that led to a small veranda where two chairs sitting between a glass table faced outward. On the table, he sat down the bottle of vodka he'd grabbed from the bar.

It was the only thing that was going to help the pain that was beginning to spread everywhere. It didn't matter what time of day it was; he didn't need a fucking excuse to drink. He still had a pretty good one.

He dropped into one of the chairs and dialed his father's phone while working the top off the vodka bottle. Nobody could say he wasn't capable of multitasking when life got tough—*right?*

The last time he'd spoken with Demyan was a few days before the shit went down in Chicago, but that felt like a hot minute now. His father had no idea what had happened, or just how much had changed. The advice he'd given Roman to keep his head down, stay out of trouble, and to get the job done was entirely fucked at this point. He couldn't have screwed that up any worse than he did.

"Roman," came Demyan's calm greeting the second his father picked up the phone.

If only he felt the same.

What was it like to be unaware—*blissfully*, so, even?

"We need to meet up," Roman said.

His father's answering silence said a lot, and even though he couldn't see him, he was fully able to imagine Demyan's furrowed brows. Or even the disappointment cloaking his father's stare.

He had to give Demyan credit, though. He didn't ask Roman to repeat himself, or even confirm that his words meant he was in the city—*home.*

In fact, all his father asked was, "Where?"

• • •

Roman eventually wandered back to where Karine was still asleep. Only to find she had moved slightly, making the

19

notebook—secured under the pillow earlier—fall to the gleaming floor.

He knew better, but he also couldn't help himself. Getting close enough to kneel beside her without a sound, he reached for the notebook but doing so faced him directly with her. She slept peacefully, not even a knot between her brows to say her dreams were unpleasant. Like this, it was hard to imagine that she was the same troubled soul who had been in the passenger seat when he left Chicago.

The walls were up during that car ride.

All the way up.

If she regretted coming to New York with him, by her own choice or otherwise, could Roman really blame her?

No, he knew it wasn't her fault.

Sighing in her sleep, Karine's eyelids fluttered as she shifted a bit on the chaise. Roman straightened up and backed away with footsteps that weren't exactly quiet, but at least put some distance between the two.

She didn't wake up.

Roman let out the air he'd been holding as Karine rolled to her other side. Her shoulders lifted with a loud exhale, but that was it. She seemed to fall into a deeper sleep, unbothered with her surroundings. Her dark, sleek hair tumbled over one side of her face so he couldn't see her, but the rhythmic rise and fall of the blanket said she was fine for the moment.

Roman resisted the urge to just carry her to a bedroom where she would sleep comfortably, and not be in the way. That really didn't seem like the brightest idea. He didn't need to wake her with a startle because he was touching her, or whatever.

Fuck it.

She could sleep where she wanted—for today.

With the distance between them, he felt safe to flip through the notebook. One he recognized. She must have discovered it in the kitchen junk drawer where everything that didn't have a specific home found a place. Random doodles and angry marks from a pen filled the first couple of pages. Nothing he could decipher as important. On the third page, he found a sketch of himself.

Roman studied the pen strokes that made up an image of him asleep on his bed. It was a precise and artistic representation, including the peek of the tattoo on the back of his neck while he laid on his stomach, and arm stretched under his pillow to offer more support. It captured the same thing in his sleeping expression that he had found in Karine's.

At first glance, the sketch seemed like a crude job done by a kid. It was only upon closer inspection that it became clear the messy strokes that repeated around the main lines of the sketch were only to distort the more perfected image beneath. Like the hand of the artist had been taught to hide what she was drawing ... *or seeing.*

More surprising was what he found written at the bottom of the page. A single sentence written and addressed to him, confirming what he'd already known the second he saw the notebook.

*

Thank you, Roman.
-Katee

*

So, even though Karine had slept her night away, a part of her had not. The morning was sacrificed because of it, apparently.

He was less concerned with the fact he had been watched for probably hours the night before as he slept, and more that he wondered how often she did get a full night's rest. Adding that on top of the medication constantly shoved at Karine, and a world filled with people who either couldn't stand the sight of her or only wanted to hurt her, he was no longer asking why.

Roman thought the better question might be *why not.* And fuck, he couldn't afford to be any more invested in this than he already was—it was already too much for him to handle. He wasn't equipped for this.

There was a lump in his throat that he quickly swallowed because it didn't matter what Roman *couldn't* do—there was still a lot he could. He wasn't exactly the type to lose, and the first thing he had to handle before anything else was his father.

He owed Demyan that.

• • •

Demyan arrived at the apartment in record time—he always did have the best drivers who knew exactly how to fight their way through city traffic. One of the most unfortunate parts of being the boss, Roman knew, was the fact they were rarely behind the wheel themselves.

Roman barely had time to make it halfway through the bottle of vodka on his veranda before the people from the front desk in the lobby rang him to say Demyan—and another guest—had arrived.

Demyan wasn't made to wait in the downstairs lobby until Roman came down to get him like the rest of the guests for the building—policy bullshit unless the front desk was told ahead of time. That happened to Demyan all of one time before his father made it very clear it had better *never* happen again.

At the door of his smaller lobby, he waited to greet his father when he emerged from the elevator. A minute later, Demyan stepped out followed by the bull who was never too far away from his boss. The man kept his distance from the two as Demyan came closer to his son, and also his eye on the boss at all times.

Even in his son's home.

The man was never safe.

Demyan strode past the leather bucket chairs in the small lobby with not a hint on his face that he was surprised his son was back in New York. He hid it well, but Roman still found the concern his father tried to hide in the way the man's gaze roamed over him from head to toe. It was a hard pill to swallow to know he was bruised and battered, and there wasn't anyway to hide it.

Roman stood back, tipping his head at his father in one quick acknowledgement. "Papa."

"You look … sore," Demyan commented. "Why?"

Where did he start?

Maybe the reason he didn't know where to begin was because his father most likely wouldn't even understand. He couldn't start with Maxim and the agreement without going through the lead-up, and that was just as messy. Things that were simple for other people—black and white things like *rules*—were a lot more complicated for Roman.

Always had been.

"I'm fine," he replied.

Demyan came to a stop in front of his son where Roman stood in the half-opened apartment doorway. He could have walked right on through to the living area, but he didn't. It was the scrutiny of his gaze that focused on the blooming bruises crawling around Roman's wrists where he had shoved his hands into the pockets of his baggy sweats. He had bothered to put on a shirt, but that was only to hide the worst of the bruises.

The bull took his position in the hallway where he could keep his sights on his boss, but still closer to the elevator than the two men.

"Those marks don't scream fine," his father murmured.

"You should see my ribcage."

His sarcastic joke flew right over his father's head because Demyan didn't even blink. The arch of his brow said he wasn't entirely pleased, though. It was then that his father moved beyond him in the doorway to step inside without waiting for permission, and Roman was fast on his heels.

It took everything in him to keep from tensing up or crushing his molars from the pressure of his clenched jaw while his father walked into the brightly sunlit space. Not *because* he was there, but what Roman expected his father to immediately notice.

Or rather, who.

Demyan spun around on his heels fast, his earlier calm façade gone. He hadn't even spotted Karine—didn't give himself enough time to before his concern overweighed his need to keep up the image. "So, are you going to tell me what the fuck is going on, Roman, or will I have to embarrass you by asking specific questions?"

Right to the point, as usual.

It wasn't even the tone—that *you will listen, you will hear me* tone—his father used that made Roman's spine straighten and his hackles raise. He didn't even think Demyan could help it; authority coated everything he did because it had to. That didn't mean his son was any better at dealing with it than he had been as a fourteen-year-old troublemaker with a serious disrespect for anyone in power.

That hadn't gotten better.

Except this time, it wasn't so much the tone Demyan used as it was the decibel he spoke at. He had no idea Karine was sleeping mere feet away, or that he even had a reason to lower his voice.

That didn't change the fact that Roman didn't want to wake Karine. She clearly needed as much rest as she could get. He seriously doubted the coming days were going to be easy, for different reasons.

"We can talk," Roman snapped, his own words hushed but not hiding their warning, "but you need to keep your voice down."

Demyan tipped his head a bit to the side, saying only, "Excuse me."

He didn't even ask it.

A clear *try that again.*

Roman didn't bother, glancing in Karine's direction instead, letting that do the work for him. His father followed the action, and finally, he found the sleeping form on the chaise near the windows. At least, the light had shifted just enough to be off Karine's face. Not that it had seemed to bother her, but he didn't think that would be comfortable. Sleeping, or not.

It took Demyan a few seconds.

Then, *more.*

⁵⁵PROMISE

He blinked once, turned his head back to Roman like he might say something, but then his gaze narrowed just as fast, and he stared at Karine again. He counted the seconds—a full two minutes—it took before his father finally responded. Every single one of them was absolute hell.

"Roman," Demyan muttered, careful now to keep his voice down as he eyed his son with that *don't fucking lie to me* gleam in his eye. "Roman, son ... I'll ask once. Just the once, and I want a truthful answer. Who in the hell is that?"

Well, *that* was an easy answer.

"Karine."

Demyan's lips pressed together in a grim line as his gaze passed between the woman on the chaise, and his son again. "*Karine*—the Yazov girl?"

Roman's silence must have said enough for him.

Demyan shook his head, the disbelief lighting up his face as he struggled to find the words. Or maybe he just couldn't form all the questions he suddenly wanted to ask. Then, he pointed Karine's way, but didn't take his eyes off his son, asking, "That's her?"

"Yeah, that's her," Roman replied with a nod. "That's Maxim Yazov's daughter."

That should be clear.

She was who she was. No matter who had tried to hide it. Whatever their reasons, it still didn't change that important fact.

Demyan's curiosity—though Roman didn't understand why—couldn't be contained, and he stepped in Karine's direction. Just to have a look, maybe. His muscles tightened painfully with the urge to block his father's path, to give Karine her privacy.

Even if Demyan didn't know all her vulnerabilities, and the very reason why she was sleeping there on the chaise out in the open to begin with, Roman *did*. The protective surge came from nowhere, but he tampered it down.

His father didn't mean any harm.

That didn't make it easy.

Demyan stood close enough to Karine to watch her sleep. She didn't move, not even her eyelids fluttered, for the few seconds he spent surveying her tucked under the blanket. Roman hoped that meant even despite her worries about him and being in New York, that some part of her was also at peace—even better if she trusted him and her surroundings. She probably wouldn't admit it to him, if that even was the case, but it was still his hope all the same.

Demyan let out a low groan when he spun around to face his son again—two of his fingers pressed into his forehead as if he was willing away a sudden headache. His next question hissed out between clenched teeth, "What is going on?"

Roman considered that, but the answer wasn't as simple like before. So, he went with that—*honesty*. At the very least, his father would respect that. "I want to be truthful, but because I'm missing details and facts, I don't think you'll believe me."

Demyan fumed as he stepped closer to his son. "Are you fucking with—"

"No."

That didn't make it better. Demyan obviously couldn't fathom what Maxim's daughter—the daughter he kept practically secret and locked away from the entire world— was doing in Roman's apartment. He didn't blame him.

Unsurprisingly, it didn't fill Roman with confidence about how this situation was going to play out with his father, either.

"Well, you're going to have to—*try*, Roman, and explain this to me. Start somewhere. Anywhere."

"Not here," Roman replied, lifting one shoulder in a shrug.

With his hands clenched into balls at his side, Demyan's face darkened with a deep red—that anger was barely in check. "I don't care if you want us to go stand in the middle of the damn street. I just want some fucking answers. *Now*."

"My office is open."

He didn't offer a different alternative, spinning on his heels to lead the way to the office he kept in the apartment. As he did, Roman looked over his shoulder at Karine who was still fast asleep.

ᴛʜᴇPROMISE

He would've loved to sleep as soundlessly as her—except he was quickly reminded that her peace in the moment was caused by a greater chaos she couldn't seem to control. And *that* ... well, that checked him back into his place fast.

THREE

His wasn't as grand of an office as his father's, but it was Roman's, nonetheless. His place of business, and a space where *he* was the boss. To find his father standing on the opposite side of a desk was practically unheard of; something men in his position often took special care not to do lest it make someone think they were the lesser man in even something as simple as a conversation.

He wasn't accustomed to this reversal of roles, even though his father didn't make note of it—he blamed that on the situation at hand, and nothing more. The only thing that concerned Demyan was the fact Karine Yazov happened to be sleeping in his son's apartment, and he wanted to know why.

Roman pulled the rolled up notebook out of the back pocket of his sweats, and dropped it on the desk. Still, his father didn't bat an eye. He wasn't about to be sidetracked from his answers when he said, "Start talking."

So, Roman decided to give him something.

ᴛʜᴇPROMISE

Carefully, he removed the simple white T-shirt he had pulled on with the sweats earlier. Another time, he might have opted for the slacks and jacket, even jeans and leather to get dressed and start his day. The pain meant he went for comfort, and nothing else.

His father's eyes roamed over the bruises that were hard to miss, still fresh, and tender to the touch. They had turned a deep purple color, the very edges a sickly yellowish-brown, and it was obvious that they were fairly new without him needing to say it. For that, he was thankful.

Demyan nodded once—as if to say, *enough*. Roman was then quick to hide the evidence that he had been beaten to damn near a pulp.

"That hurt?" he asked.

Maybe because he had nothing else to say.

"I've been better," Roman replied with a chuckle.

A painful one, yes.

But also *real*.

"And you've been worse," his father returned with a fleeting, easy smile.

That was true, too.

"Except those times I was high on coke, and didn't feel a fucking thing."

Roman would be a liar if he tried to say he hadn't considered getting his hands on some snow as soon as he got into town, but that meant possibly putting Karine in one of two situations. One where he couldn't be close to her—or where she was with him in a situation that might be even worse.

And really …

Did he need to be high right now?

The dull eight on his pain scale of one to ten said yes, but the rational, *sober* part of his brain that remembered sweating the coke out on a cell floor said no. He wanted to listen to that little, bitchy voice.

For now.

Demyan let out a testy sigh before sliding his hands into the pockets of his pants. "If you see your mother, you better keep those bruises out of her sight."

Roman grunted in response and sat down in his leather swivel chair, suppressing a groan from the pain of the bruises. At least, the plush back of the chair cradled his sore muscles and bones that gave him a bit of comfortable pressure to take off the edge. The vodka was starting to hit, too. That shit made all the difference.

All the same, the pain taunted the edges of his mind and nerves. A constant reminder of how fucked up his life was.

Demyan remained standing, asking, "Let me guess— Maxim and you had a friendly chat?"

"He did this *himself*, too," Roman said with a nod at his father's widening stare. "Shit, yeah, he didn't even bother handing me over to one of his men for it."

"I did not expect that. You pissed him off, then."

That obvious?

Roman kept the comment to himself.

Barely.

"You have no idea," he muttered instead.

Finally, Demyan gave a shake of his head and decided to take a shot of the vodka on the desk. Roman wasn't even sure how that bottle made its way into the office—it wasn't the same one he'd been drinking out of, but liquor served a purpose everywhere. He watched his father closely because he'd asked Demyan there purposely.

For something he'd never done. Or rather, *cared* about, in a way. This wasn't quite the same. He needed his father's opinion. Now was the chance to come clean—about most of it at least.

He wasn't sure how much about Karine's disorder he was willing to share with even Demyan. Not now. It was too soon. Superficially—it would obviously look like a bad idea. Nobody else seemed to get Karine the way he did, and even he knew this was a mistake.

Roman took in a deep breath and continued to speak. His father wiped his vodka laden mouth with the back of his forearm.

"Maxim has been hiding his daughter from the world. She is...troubled, and has not received the proper care she needs."

ᴴᴱPROMISE

"What do you mean, troubled?"

Roman shrugged. That was as much as he was willing to tell.

"Let's just say Maxim has no patience for a daughter like her. A girl who never fit the bill. Instead of nurturing her as a parent, he agreed to marry her off to Leonid's son. Dima. You know Dima. We all know Dima here."

Demyan grunted under his breath.

Yeah.

How could they forget?

"I still don't get what any of this has to do with you."

"I wanted to help her—or shit, just *figure it out*, what was wrong there because something clearly was," Roman said, waiting for his father to comment on that. When he didn't, he decided to continue, but he couldn't meet Demyan's gaze when he admitted, "And so, I kept digging."

"And you found something you shouldn't have?"

Roman let out a slow, aching exhale before saying, "As one does."

"Jesus, son. *Jesus Christ.*"

That was enough to make Demyan roll his eyes, and rake a hand through his hair. The frustration was written in every action, but he had news for his father. That wasn't even the best part of the story. Already, it wasn't headed in a favorable direction for Roman.

"I stumbled on a plot against Maxim's life. Leonid was directly involved. When I informed Maxim about it, he decided he was going to let me come home. Can't remember if he used the words *spare my life* or not."

"Spare your—what do you mean *spare your fucking life?*" his father asked, each word getting progressively louder until he was just roaring it. "For what?"

Roman's throat bobbed with a swallow—that line he'd been walking just got a hell of a lot smaller. It didn't matter that he was a grown man, he wasn't so disassociated with his shitty behavior and lack of self-control that he didn't know when he truly crossed a line. This was definitely that.

"What the fuck did you do, Roman?"

"I slept with Karine," he said, the truth coming out easy even if it was hard.

Demyan stood like a statue, glaring at his son. The silence coated the room until he reached for the bottle of vodka again, the liquor sloshing against the glass. He tipped two shot glasses on the silver tray where the bottle had also been sitting over and poured them both a drink.

Roman took the shot and drank it, never once breaking his father's heavy stare. Demyan did the same, but he thought that was more so his father could consider his next words. He was good at doing that—making sure not a single word was wasted when he wanted every one of them heard.

"So, to be clear, you fucked the young woman who has been promised to Dima?"

Roman didn't bother defending himself, knowing he didn't have one for that. His actions against Dima were always selfish, and he wouldn't pretend otherwise. Those were the facts.

He did, however, correct his father with, "*Was* promised."

"*Is*, Roman," Demyan countered swiftly. "Until all parties agree otherwise in one way or another. When an arrangement is made for a marriage, it is not over until it's *over.*"

Well, those were semantics.

Right?

Roman never did well with those.

Demyan started filling in the blanks all on his own which made things easier for Roman. "Let me guess, Maxim was about to make you answer for sleeping with his *spoken-for* daughter—that's how you earned your proper beating. And then, you told him about the plot, so he let you live."

"Essentially."

"But," Demyan said, wagging a finger his son's way, "somehow you ended up bringing the girl back here with you. That … I'm lost."

Sadly, that was the clearest part for Roman.

"He wanted to get rid of his daughter. Made it known he never wanted to see her again—to me. Besides that, I don't know what is going on in Chicago now that I'm gone, and he's aware of what his man was planning. You want to know why she's here, but I don't have a specific reason beyond what was put in my hands. I just did what I thought was the only option."

Demyan let out a noise that voiced his irritation. If it wasn't his son in front of him—chances were, things might have taken a more violent turn in the room. "And here she is, right?"

"Well—"

"I told you to keep your fucking head down. To mind your *business!*"

"You also sent me to Chicago to get me off your hands— let's not forget that, Papa. I certainly haven't."

"That's not what I did."

"*Bullshit.* You wanted to teach me a lesson. Let me assume responsibility, whatever the fuck that even means."

"Wrong, Roman," Demyan snarled with enough venom to quiet his son. For a second, anyway. "You assume I *wanted* the Yazovs to do anything—the only thing I did was remain ignorant. If someone interferes with your affairs, what problem is it of mine? I didn't plan anything, and I didn't stop it, either. Make sure you understand that the next time you decide one of your stupid decisions is my fault."

Demyan's fists hit the desk with a bang making a pain shoot down Roman's torso again when he flinched. "It doesn't fucking matter now, son. You've brought home a girl who is promised to a bratva man. Do you realize what that means?"

"That this could cost me my life? Yeah, I'm aware. Trust, it's crossed my mind a few times."

It was only as Demyan scrubbed a palm down his jaw as he tried to make sense of the mess in front of him that Roman felt the pangs of guilt tugging at him once more—the ones he experienced when disappointing his father. A familiar feeling as it happened more often than he cared to admit, but he'd never found a reason to do anything different. He knew this probably wasn't the same.

"If a marriage is fixed, it has to happen, those are the rules," Demyan said, repeating his earlier sentiment like it made a difference.

Roman shrugged, murmuring, "It's not going to happen. It's impossible since the bride-to-be is missing and the only people who know where she is are the ones in this apartment, and the dead man walking in Chicago."

Demyan eyed his son, the silence stretching on the longer he assessed Roman. He could feel his father trying to get into his head, to pry the secrets he kept there right out of his fucking skull.

"But for how long, Roman?"

He didn't reply.

His father continued on, saying, "I'm not sure if you sound happy about all of this, or ... not. Is there something else in this equation you're not telling me about—what am I missing?"

Roman almost wished they continued to silently glare at each other. Anything except that damn question. Thinking it might give him a bit of time to gather his thoughts, he said, "I'm not sure what you're asking."

Demyan lifted his brow high. "Are you in love with her?"

That was not the question Roman expected. The words hung between them, filling the room with their weight and girth. It sounded ridiculous coming from his father's mouth—even Demyan couldn't hide his incredulous tone.

Roman, in love.

That was ...

That was crazy.

Still, Roman didn't reply. Love was a strong word for something he didn't understand; an experience he'd never had, really. He also didn't think it would be fair to say he had no emotional attachment to Karine, even if that was also something he didn't comprehend. None of those things really mattered, either.

Too much time passed between them without either of them speaking, and Demyan quickly lost patience for it when he said, "That's the only possible reason for you to act this way—do something as *stupid* as this. And not just yourself, no, you're risking everyone. *Everything*, Roman. Your life, your family, and the rest of your own bratva, because don't be mistaken about that, son. They're going to come after all of us. Until they get to the one they want."

Roman still refused to speak.

His father tipped his chin up, then, looking down at his son sitting in the chair. "Well, there better be a damn good reason for it. And I'm waiting to hear it. If not love, then *what?*"

If only things were simple.

Demyan pointed a finger at Roman, telling him, "It better *mean* something—all you've done … There better be a good fucking reason. At least lie to me."

Except he couldn't.

"I wanted to help her. I didn't say anything about love."

Demyan opened his mouth to retort, his lips already twisted in his anger, but the loud shouts of a man echoed down the hallway. It stopped them both in their tracks. Then, glass shattered, too.

Shit.

"Karine," Roman muttered, already off his chair and rounding the desk.

His father was fast on his heels.

• • •

Andrey, the bull who followed Demyan everywhere, was the one who had shouted loud enough to rattle the walls. As it turned out—he had a good reason. Karine had backed him into a corner of the kitchen, right next to the island. He didn't think her one-twenty soaking wet frame was enough to scare the muscled, brick wall of a man, but the chunky kitchen knife she had thrust against his neck could certainly do the job.

She even made him bleed.

The drops of blood dribbled down from a slice in the man's neck, soaking into his silk dress shirt. Andrey's wide gaze darted wildly around the room, looking for a way out. Karine must have grabbed a knife out of the block that was on the island. It was almost comical—if it wasn't so fucked up—that such a petite woman with nothing more than a knife against the bull's neck was enough to terrify the man.

Had she caught him by surprise?

Masha came barreling down the hallway a few seconds after Roman and Demyan entered the kitchen. He wondered how long she had been awake, and where the fuck she had been, but there wasn't really time for that discussion.

"Karine, sweetheart, put the knife down," Masha said, her voice a soothing whisper.

However, it did nothing to calm Karine or persuade her to put the weapon away. In fact, she paid Masha no mind.

She leaned harder into Andrey, glaring at him with her jaw clenched tight, and hooded eyes nailed into the pinned man. "Who are you—what in the fuck are you doing here?"

That voice.

It froze Roman to the spot.

That wasn't Karine at all.

Still, to be sure, Roman called to her, "Karine, let him go."

She didn't move a muscle, except for the look she threw over her shoulder that met his eyes. It was fast—*wild* and fleeting before her gaze was right back on the threat she had to deal with. She was on high alert; every move someone made, even to inch closer, caught her attention. Yet, not enough to allow Andrey even a split-second to act against her.

That look was enough.

Roman had seen it. The viciousness in her stare. There was a tension in her brows and a sneer on her lips.

Katina had arrived.

Apparently, just in time.

Roman tried not to be taken aback at how the switch between identities could happen without any warning, if only because he didn't have the time to be distracted. Exactly how this situation was triggered—well, he didn't have a clue. Maybe she was startled awake and saw Andrey. A face she didn't recognize—and instead of Karine or Katee, it was Katina who chose to be present.

THE PROMISE

"Please, *Karine*," Masha said, keeping her distance and gentle tone, but continuing to at least *try*. "Look at me, huh? It's fine ... everything is fine."

Her efforts were for nothing. Karine wasn't listening, and Katina didn't care. Andrey didn't move, but one of his hands twitched on the island counter like he might make a move to grab something.

"Who the fuck is this? I was just trying to get a drink, man," the bull said, his words cracking at the end. At his voice, Katina leaned in again. "Easy—*shit*, take it easy, girl. I wasn't doing shit to you."

Glass, shattered into sharp shards, had spread across the floor in a puddle of water. Roman followed the pink-stained water to where it ended at Katina's bleeding feet. Despite the cuts on the soles of her feet, it was one more thing that didn't seem to make her radar.

"You need to tell me what is really going on here," Demyan muttered at Roman's side. "Right now, son."

When shit hit the fan, it *really* hit. Now just wasn't the time. Roman had to take care of the situation at hand first, and then maybe he could clear some things up for his father.

Roman kept a firm tone when he said, "Katina, I'll only say it once more. Let the man go."

That time, she looked at him for longer—and he knew why. Roman addressed her with the right name. It was that same viciousness he'd found in her stare earlier that concerned him the most, though. He wondered if anyone knew the kind of violence this woman was capable of when she was Katina. It took balls to hold a knife to a man's throat and not even blink about it.

"You weren't here when I woke up," Katina said suddenly, throwing the words at him like a slap over her shoulder. "You were supposed to be *here*. But no, this guy was. I don't know him." Strained, her words hissed lower as Roman got closer. "*I don't know him.*"

Yeah.

He got it.

Holding his hands up where she could see, Roman hoped that would assure she wouldn't think he was coming at her with anything. He didn't want her to make any sudden movements that could fatally hurt Andrey—the guy hadn't exactly asked for this. Karine wouldn't want that on her conscience, or hands.

"I was here the whole time. I didn't go anywhere, just to the other room," Roman said fast, inching forward slowly with every word. "I spent the night in my bedroom. You know that. Katee even knows it—she saw me, drew me."

He only stated facts.

Katina tipped her chin up, the tense line of muscle working hard in her neck as her stare stayed locked with his. And just like that, water started to well in her eyes until the tears fell when she finally blinked. Roman took the opportunity to pull the knife out of her hand, and she didn't resist. He tossed it across the counter out of reach. Then, he tugged her in his direction with a gentle pull of her hands in his.

She came easily, falling into his chest and hiding in his arms.

Andrey grunted under his breath, giving Roman a nod when he met the bull's gaze. A silent *thank you*, but he didn't linger near the counter for long before scooting further down.

"Katina—*Karine* ... who are these—"

He decided to ignore his father because Katina prattled on against his chest, muttering words he wanted to hear.

"I'm sorry, I didn't mean to fuck up, Roman. I didn't."

Slipping his hands under her chin, he tipped her head back to make her look at him. "Hey, *hey*—chill, huh? Nobody fucked up, all right? It was just a—"

"I didn't mean to hurt anyone."

The tears came harder, clouding those big blue eyes while her voice cracked, too. Every word coming out at a different cadence. Each blink she made, he realized the cloudiness *wasn't* her tears, but confusion.

Karine.
Katina.
Back and forth.

^{THE}PROMISE

Softly, a whimpering Karine told him, "I really didn't mean to hurt him."

"Yes, you did," Roman interrupted her. "You did, and you don't have to explain why."

His hand curved around her jaw while his thumb caressed her cheek. Her face turned into his palm, and touch.

"I'm just—*sorry*," she whispered.

"It doesn't matter, it's okay. Masha is going to help you with those cuts on your feet right now. She knows where the first aid kit is."

He glanced over at Masha who nodded.

Karine still had her hands on him, bunching his shirt in her tiny fists. "What about you?"

The weakness that welled without warning inside his chest was a punch to his heart that he couldn't afford. He didn't want her to feel alone or vulnerable.

"I'll be right there ... I just need a minute, yeah?"

Masha came close enough to begin prying Karine away. Eventually, she gave in and allowed herself to be led to the hallway. She looked over her shoulder at Roman repeatedly, and he nodded. Just to reassure her. Until she couldn't see him anymore.

Once Karine was gone, he could finally focus on the other problem—his father. If only that proverbial small-fist shaped hole in his chest wasn't bleeding with every beat of his black heart.

Andrey had already left the room by the time Roman turned back on his father. Presumably to go take care of his wounded neck, and he sincerely hoped the man took the hint and stayed gone.

Demyan stared hard at his son, his expression stony when he said, "There's a lot of shit you're not telling me. And I want to know all of it."

"You shouldn't feel too bad about not knowing," Roman replied, shrugging, "because I've only just started to figure it out myself."

And fuck it.

His father could wait.

39

Roman had something more important to handle first—
someone, rather. He headed for the hallway and said nothing
more as he followed the bloody footprints on the marble
floor that led all the way to his bedroom.

FOUR

The most disconcerting thing for Karine was when she didn't know where she was—fully awake, *feeling* aware, but unknowing all the same. She couldn't say how long it might last, but sometimes it happened more often than it didn't. A few moments ago, she'd found herself in Roman's arms, but it had been hard to focus on what he was trying to say. Were there other people there—other men? She kept going in and out of the scene, sometimes looking down from above, almost blacking out from the dizziness making nausea swell inside her.

Even though it was hard, she listened to what the only recognizable face in the sea of confusion kept saying. Over the rushing in her ears, and the vomit threatening to spill, she heard his words.

Roman, that was.

It'll be okay.

He promised to be close by—to not leave her alone. So, where was he?

It's going to be alright.

The thing was—Karine still couldn't make sense of it all. She didn't know what he meant. What was she apologizing for? Why did he keep insisting it would be fine?

Was it?

Was it really fine?

It didn't seem like it, and the sudden, heavy cloak of fear that hugged every inch of her trembling frame in a cold grip only made it worse. The screaming in her mind, every racing beat of her heart, the piercing ring in her ears ... all of it.

She just wanted to run.

Drift away.

Hide.

The disturbing words that came out of her mouth weren't her own. The whispers cutting through her thoughts sounded foreign, and *wrong*. Every blink brought with it strange images that she couldn't place and only left her more afraid.

It was the loss of control that terrified her the most.

Karine couldn't ignore the blackening in the corner of her vision no matter how hard she tried. The more she willed it away, the worse it became. She blinked rapidly until it started to clear just a little bit, but even that didn't stop the hissed *stop it, stop it* coming out of her mouth. Waving her hands in front of her face, she couldn't see them. Couldn't tell which way was up or down.

That darkness—it threatened to close in on her again if she couldn't pull herself from the depths of her own mind.

She knew she was in a room but didn't know which it was or how she had gotten there. Some things looked familiar, the only sense of safety she could pull from her current situation, but most of all—it *smelled* familiar. Like *somebody* she knew.

Someone who made her feel safe.

Roman?

Karine wanted to call out his name—call for *him*—but her voice didn't want to work. She couldn't speak, only keening cries falling from her trembling lips even as she tried to suck in gulpfuls of air to calm the raging currents of her emotions. The only thing she could do was *breathe*. Though it didn't help to make her feel like it was enough, she was still able to do it.

So, she did.

Rapidly filling her lungs with air as much as she could, it at least kept the black smog from filling her vision entirely. If only it did something for ... *everything else.*

The crawling on her skin.

The noise in the room.

Any of it.

All of it.

But it didn't.

She weaved her fingers through her hair before dragging them down her face.

Karine was sure she'd been standing up, but now it was as though she couldn't stop from sinking. Her knees bent without permission. It was more than just gravity pulling her down.

Then, there were the voices.

Clearer than ever.

Scared, and *vicious.*

She didn't know where they came from except that they were inside ... inside her. They were a fading echo. A younger voice, a girl's—she was sweet, her words kind, but she sounded desperate all the same.

It's okay, Karine. We're okay here. It's okay.

She could almost imagine the small hands of the girl stroking her arms and back every time she tried to comfort her.

Overlapping that voice was someone else's. An older voice—still female—that she couldn't place, and didn't feel like she knew quite as well. *She* was snappy. Angry. *Get a hold of yourself, Karine.* A commanding voice.

One she *should* listen to.

Except Karine couldn't do anything.

The voices filled her head, their words too sharp in her ears, and she couldn't think straight while they battled for attention. Even covering her ears and asking for them to stop didn't help.

Why was this happening?

On the floor, fists shaking against her head, rocking side to side to soothe how overwhelmed she was, Karine found at least there, it didn't feel like she was falling. Nothing else helped. The voices just kept getting louder, bouncing off the walls and filling the room.

Who are you ... who are you ... who are you?

Why wouldn't they leave her alone?

Worse, was that they spoke like she did know them—or that she should. They apparently knew her.

She no longer recognized the elements of the bedroom. Where did all the furniture go? Even the walls disappeared when she tried to look up.

Sometimes, in intervals, searing pain ravaged her feet. Once, when she looked down, the bloody mess smeared across her ankles and legs finally brought the floor into focus. She couldn't quite comprehend the pain, or why she was feeling it, though. The reason for the blood barely even registered.

None of it settled in her brain long enough to *understand*— as fast as the thought landed, it would soar away. Her ears, filled with those voices, rang again until she was begging for it to stop.

"No. *No*. Please ... *stop*."

She kept muttering to herself, repeating a mantra that felt safe and loud even if it didn't help the problem. It was the only thing she could think to do because even the idea of unraveling from the ball she'd tightened herself into on the floor where she sat was too draining. She wished they'd stop—those *voices*—that they'd go away, but they didn't.

Or *wouldn't*.

She was helpless and trapped in a body and mind that was battling to be occupied by two other voices. They sounded nothing like her.

They weren't her.

And she didn't want them *out*.

"Karine, hey, look at me." The male voice broke sharply through her thoughts like metal falling through glass. Shattered fragments fell away. It was his hands curving under her tucked chin, tilting her face out of where she'd buried it in the darkness that sucked away everything and brought his face into clear focus. *All at once.* Roman stared back at Karine through the wetness of her tears, and asked softly, "Can you hear me?"

Yes.

Yes, she could.

The relief was instant, the silence in her mind bewildering, and Karine couldn't help but launch herself away from the pit she'd fallen in and into the promise of safety Roman offered to her. Springing up from the floor and into his arms, open for her, her cheek hit his chest when she landed against him. His strong arms wrapped tightly around her body, and she heard the whoosh of air leave his lungs the second he held her.

"I know you heard me say to get the first aid kit—what are you standing there for?" asked Roman gruffly.

Karine looked around the room to find it had come back with walls and all. Masha stood only a foot away, deathly pale with worry writing heavy lines in her forehead. Had she been there all along?

"Yes, sorry, I know," Masha whispered, wringing her hands together, "but I just wanted to calm her down a bit first, but she wouldn't listen. She refused—it was like she couldn't even hear me."

The tearful strain in Masha's hoarse voice drew Karine's gaze to hers where she found the woman's silent pleading staring back. *Please be okay,* she seemed to say.

Softly, Masha told Roman, "I'll be right back with the kit."

He didn't reply, and Masha was quick to flee the room, closing the door behind her as she left. Karine pulled away from Roman's arms, and he released her without argument. But only because it allowed him to bend down and survey the damage done to her feet. Cuts that she couldn't explain marred the soles of her feet that were now throbbing with the same searing pain from earlier.

"Fucking hell," he muttered, sucking air through his teeth before adding, "This looks bad."

It wasn't the cuts that bothered her the most, but the *blood.* She'd forgotten about that. Soaked into the large carpet where the bed sat and smeared across the floor, the stains had been violently dragged around where she'd seemingly walked in circles. Not that she could remember walking anywhere let alone in the same place.

The sight of all the blood made her nauseous, and without warning, Karine started to sway on the spot. Before she could meet the floor in a useless heap, Roman curled his arms around her and had her cradled in his hold like a child. The blood was gone from her view as he carried her over to a bed.

His bed, the younger voice whispered. *See?*

The image of Roman sleeping in that very bed flashed into her mind while hands that looked like hers sketched the image of him doing so at the same time. Karine shook her head wildly to rid the voice and the memory that didn't feel like *hers*.

He must have gently put her down on the edge because she didn't notice she was even on the bed until after she already *was*. Another blackout—the hardest part was the fact Karine had started to become aware of those minute-moments she couldn't explain or stitch together in her own mind.

The next thing she knew, Karine stared down and watched Roman crouch between her legs. In his hand, he held her left foot while he examined her sole. She tried to be still, even the crinkle of her toes sent pain shooting through her feet.

If only she cared about the pain, then.

Karine was more concerned with the man touching her. She bit down hard on her lip at the sensation of his fingertips pressing along the side of her heel and then the arch of her foot, too. How could a man like him—who talked as harshly and cold as he sometimes did, who could silence her with nothing more than a look—also caress her so tenderly?

Carefully.

A thrill ran down her spine, the memory of his hands and those fingertips exploring her body filling her mind without warning. Heat spilled hot in her belly until she noticed the blood staining his hand. Roman muttered under his breath to himself, too low for her to hear.

⁜PROMISE

"H-how did that happen?" she managed to ask.

Her voice was barely a whisper, her throat aching like she'd been screaming for hours.

Roman looked up with blue eyes as dark and as dangerous as a raging storm. There was something else reflecting back at her, too, something she couldn't decipher.

He just seemed ... *tired.*

"What?" she asked, words shaky.

His silence didn't help Karine to settle her nerves.

"Why aren't you talking? Why won't you tell me what happened—I don't ... I don't remember, I'm sorry."

His cheek worked like he was chewing on his words, and just when she thought he was about to stand and walk away from her, Roman pulled in a deep breath. Then, he said, "You were asleep in the living room by the windows on a chaise. I was in my office, talking to my father. His bull—the bodyguard, Andrey—came in for a drink of water, and when you woke up and saw him, you attacked him with a knife in the kitchen. He dropped the glass of water, and you stepped on the shards."

His words were accompanied by white noise in the background of her mind—he said things like *you attacked* and *you stepped* but she couldn't find those memories. She almost couldn't hear him at all.

It only made Karine *angry*, and that served to turn her irrational. She rocked while she sat on the bed, picking at the tips of her own fingers to keep herself from jumping up off the bed altogether. "N-no, that didn't happen. You're wrong," she argued weakly.

"Karine, that is exactly what happened. I have no reason to make up stories. I'm not lying to you."

But then her mind flashed with the image of Roman in the kitchen, hands on her arms as he said her name—*Karine*— before it was black again. *She didn't know.* It was like the memory jerked her back and forth, everything going still, and the colors fading to black and white for a split second before she was staring at Roman still holding on to her foot with the most careful hands.

She didn't know what to believe.

Or *why* this was happening.

"Don't you think I would remember something like that?" she snapped.

Roman released her foot, then, letting it hang and not quite reach the floor. The look she saw on his face was one she knew all too well. She'd become well acquainted with it whenever someone had just had enough of *her*.

Whatever that was supposed to mean—she'd never quite understood it when someone said it.

It was the same look her father gave her—or Dima, even, sometimes Masha, too. Anyone who stumbled upon Karine during a particularly bad spell where she was losing more time than she was keeping, and the blank space in her mind was more of a comfort than reality. A look that said she didn't know what the fuck she was talking about—and neither did they.

It made her feel *crazy*.

She hated that look.

Maybe it would've been easier to handle coming if she was still taking the pills she'd become best friends with over the years. They had a way of numbing her to other people's reactions and opinions. It didn't hurt to know someone else thought she was a little odd or even … *off.* They softened the edges of her brain so all that chaotic, erratic energy was contained even if it did leave her feeling like a shell of who she should be.

Without them now, she could feel the force of Roman's stare like a slap across her face. That *oh, Karine* he was thinking in his mind.

Poor, pity little Karine … crazy, crazy, *crazy*.

She turned her eyes away from him, and saw the flashes of images. Black and white again, snaps of memories like a strobe light inside her brain. A man's back turned to her, a glass of water at his lips. Then, he was staring over his shoulder at her directly. Surprised, but scared, too. Why would he be afraid of her? He was a hulk of a man—*big*, and unknown, and there. He shouldn't have been there. The next blink came with the glint of metal—there was a knife in her hand.

THE PROMISE

"Are you remembering it?" she heard Roman ask.

All those nerves snapping inside of her finally lifted her off the bed, sending Karine running away from the words she didn't want to hear Roman say. She paced on the spot, determined to get those memories and what he asked out of her head.

That wasn't her.

It wasn't.

Roman didn't make a move toward her, but he followed the path she paced with his guarded gaze. It was like he knew exactly what she was thinking just by staring at her, and Karine couldn't quite stand that feeling.

A bug under a microscope.

Even if it was *his.*

"I don't know what you're talking about," she snapped.

Roman sighed, scrubbing a hand over his unshaven jaw. His shoulders squared a bit, then. "Okay, I'm going to go to my bathroom and find what I can for your feet, all right? Masha is taking too long with the first aid kit."

He turned to go, and the fear gripped Karine instantly at the idea he was going to leave her alone in the room. Would the voices come back—*the darkness?* She lunged at him, gripping his elbow tightly, and with a little gasp for air, she breathed, "Please don't leave me here."

Roman stopped in his tracks, turning back to her with an assurance at the ready—not that it helped. "I'm just going in there, Karine—the bathroom is *right there*," he said, pointing at the opened French doors that led to a dimly lit bathroom attached to the bedroom. "You'll be able to see me from here. Do you understand? We need to do something about those cuts before they start bleeding even worse than they already are."

It took seconds for her to unfurl her fingers from his arm. Too many seconds, really.

She gulped down the lump in her throat but eventually nodded.

"Promise?" she asked.

Roman stilled when he started to turn away again. "What?"

"I'll still see you—promise?"

That was the only way she was letting him go anywhere. It felt better like that—everything was better, then.

Roman nodded once, his gaze softening for a brief moment. "Yeah, I promise."

• • •

Karine hadn't been given the chance to see her reflection in a mirror, but she was sure she looked like a complete fucking mess. Maybe under different circumstances, she would have cared, but the state of her appearance was the last thing on her mind as Roman worked carefully on her feet to clean and bandage the wounds.

For starters, those voices were still in her head. Even if Karine pretended they *weren't.*

They weren't as loud anymore now that he was there, tending to the wounds on her feet and giving her something better to focus on, but she was acutely aware of their battling presence in the recesses of her mind, trying to override the fading echoes of her very *present* and aware thoughts.

What were they saying?

The man in the other room—drinking water. He deserved to be knifed, one said, *being there like that,* she spit right after. The younger one insisted everything would be fine, *it always is with Roman.*

Karine chewed on the edge of her pinky nail, gaze locked on a freckle on the back of Roman's hand while he worked on her feet, willing the words away. Pretending like they weren't *there*, as she tried to make sense of them at the same time.

Why is this happening?

Her voice—the only one she thought mattered—went unheard, and unanswered.

Of course.

Masha had looked in with the first aid kit in hand, but Roman sent her away. He could handle it. Apparently, the wounds weren't as bad as they seemed.

On his knees at her feet, working away with his gentle touch, Roman said nothing. No, he simply took care of her.

^{THE}PROMISE

She was still a little too enthralled with that fact—how careful he was, that he took care of her at all, really.

The silence stretched on between them while he finished wrapping the bandages around her heels where she'd gotten the worst of the cuts. But it was only silent to him. Inside, she was screaming.

"It wasn't me," Karine whispered suddenly, the words bursting from her softly, but oh, so loud all the same. Roman's head jerked up, those eyes nailing into hers when she said, "It wasn't me. With the knife. That man—I-I didn't attack him."

Roman put her foot down and straightened up, replying, "Except it was you … it just wasn't you, too. I know, Karine."

He didn't give her time to argue, or deny anything.

"Their names are Katee and Katina," he murmured, rubbing his hands together like he was trying to work kinks out of the muscles and didn't have an issue at all with the things he was saying. It was something that just *was*. That's how he offered the information to Karine, he just said it, and she couldn't tell if he felt any certain way about it. "Katee is a little girl—she draws, hides and watches people, I think."

That didn't mean Karine wanted to admit it.

Or believe it.

"You're lying," she said, shaking her head fast. Pointing a finger at him, Karine muttered, "Stop it, I don't want to hear this. You're lying to me."

Roman leaned closer to Karine, his brow lifting as he said, "No, *you listen to me.*"

She stiffened at his tone.

He took that as permission to continue. "They're there— you're going to have to accept that because you don't seem to have very much control of them at the moment. Maybe you manifested them for a purpose, but now they protect you when you can't deal, you know? I'm not sayin—"

She cut him off with her hand slicing wildly between them in the air. It was like there were hands pinning her to the bed with every word he said, and she just needed him to *stop*. She fought against the urge to run and let those words sink in, but failed when she ended up running for the bedroom door after flying off the bed.

Roman was faster than her, though. He stood in her way, blocking the door with his impressive size and hard stare.

"Let me go."

She raged against him.

Pushing.

Crying.

Begging, too.

He didn't even touch her—didn't move, either. Not once did he stop her from hitting him, those emotions of hers tumbling out in the worst way.

"I can't let you leave, Karine," he told her softly, "You could be a danger to yourself. To others. We gotta get this figured out first, huh? Come on, sweetheart."

She heard him.

Karine simply didn't *want to.*

"You don't know me," she sobbed, her strength and desire to run depleting fast. "*You know nothing.* You have to let me go. I don't care what happens to me."

"Karine, I care about what happens to you."

It all stopped, then.

Her crying.

The fighting.

Even the way he positioned himself in the doorway to block her loosened a bit as those words fell between them. She parted her lips, testing the words she wanted to shout back to protect herself from the hope that dared to grow in her heart. They stuck in her throat instead. He refused to look away.

Roman wanted her to see he meant it—every single word.

Then, he reached for her and she let him. His arms wrapped around her, and despite the feelings trapped inside her that she fought to ignore, she sagged in his embrace because it was fucking *easy.* He wouldn't let her fall, but he also wouldn't let her pretend, either.

"It's okay," she heard him say. "We'll get it figured out, Karine. We will."

ᵀᴴᴱPROMISE

She wished she could walk away now. She didn't want to hear any explanation he had for the voices in her head, or who they were. Maybe her life *was* better caged behind the walls of a mansion that didn't quite feel like home with a constant flow of medication at the ready to make everything bad go away.

Maybe.

"I'm not crazy, Roman," she whimpered, the words muffled as she dug her face into his chest. She didn't want him to see how hard she cried, or that she couldn't control the flood of tears. "*I'm not.*"

He held her tighter.

"I know you're not crazy. You're just a little unwell, babe, and I'm the only one trying to help right now. You have to let me help you, Karine. Please, let me help you."

FIVE

Karine needed help. That was the whole truth, plain and simple. Technically, it didn't matter what the other facts were about her current situation, and Roman wasn't even sure if it was up to him to dig into the past and uncover all the secrets the Yazovs were keeping as to why this had happened to her. What he needed to focus on right now was keeping Karine safe … and stable.

At least until someone could help her.

This meltdown had not been like the first. If anything, it was worse. He thought he was prepared for another one, but he wasn't. The calm Roman kept throughout explaining facts—*as he knew them to be*—to Karine about Katee and Katina was nothing short of a miracle. Self-control he didn't know he possessed, until he realized she wouldn't give him a choice.

The woman was a hurricane.

She didn't need more chaos.

ᴛʜᴇPROMISE

Roman hadn't asked Karine what exactly was going on inside her head—he wasn't sure he should, or if she would even tell him. Not yet. But he noticed every single one of her tics, like how she glanced to the side like she was hearing something there, though he chose not to point them out. But he'd seen the look of realization in her eyes, too.

When he said things she couldn't deny—when she *knew* things he said to be true. Two and two together always made four, even if at first, it didn't seem right.

He didn't know where to start when it came to helping Karine, though. It was so fucking obvious he was in *way* over his head. Was he expected to be an expert on how to handle all of this?

Hell, he didn't even *know* an expert to deal with this. But he sure as shit was going to try. Who else would do it for Karine?

That was the sad thing he had already realized. If not him, then she had no one.

He'd spent some time consoling Karine, only to get her back sitting on the bed where he found a cut on her heel had reopened to bleed through the fresh bandage. It was then that Masha heard the loud sobs, and returned to suggest that Karine might like to have a bath.

If he agreed, that was.

Masha's words.

Not his.

Even though they weren't in Chicago—or under the demanding, watchful eye of Maxim Yazov—it seemed that Masha had already placed herself on a lower rung of an imaginary hierarchy. He wasn't sure how he felt about that, to be honest, but there were bigger issues on his plate. In fact, he wasn't even technically attached to Karine in any way that gave him control over her, but Masha was willing to treat him like he was.

Without question.

The burdens of his responsibilities were never more apparent to Roman. And he couldn't say that he had been ready for it.

He took the opportunity to step away when Karine was led out of his bedroom by Masha. She kept glancing at him over her shoulder, and she wasn't crying anymore, but she looked completely broken—one step at a time, he supposed. Roman nodded at her, and stayed where she could see him in the hallway until Masha directed her into the bathroom down the hall.

She still threw him one last, fleeting look that made his chest ache.

How was he supposed to do this?

How *did she*?

That was the better question.

By the time Roman finally was able to step back into the living room, he found his father by the bar, pouring a glass of vodka.

The broken glass on the floor had magically been cleaned away. Not a shattered shard in sight. Even the bloody tracks, droplets, and smears all over the marble floors had been cleaned, too. The bull was nowhere to be seen, either, and Masha had been busy with Roman and Karine.

The only person left who could have cleaned the mess was now sipping from a lowball glass of three-hundred-dollar a bottle vodka.

The very best Roman had.

Top shelf.

Demyan—his father.

He didn't seem to want a thank you from his son, and didn't appear to care if Roman mentioned it one way another as he approached. Hearing his steps, Demyan turned with a sigh and a quiet, "This deserved the *good* vodka, son. I hope you understand."

Roman only shrugged.

What else could he do?

He had expected a lot of different reactions from his father after everything, but instead, Demyan remained calm. He eyed his son carefully, considering each one of Roman's steps until he finally came to a stop in front of him.

"I don't understand how you've found yourself in this position," he began in a murmur around the rim of his glass.

℡PROMISE

Fair enough.

Roman raked a hand through his hair, then grabbed the bottle right off the bar altogether. Even a stiff drink wasn't going to cut it this time. He might as well take the whole damn bottle at this point.

"The girl I just saw back there," Demyan said, his gaze darting to the hallway that he had a decent view of from his position, "… she's fragile. Cotton candy, Roman. Just the hint of contact is all that's needed, and she'll disintegrate into nothing. Yet, she'll cling to you like a life raft."

Yeah.

He didn't need the reminder.

Roman drank straight from the bottle, gulp after gulp of vodka that burned, until he felt the warmth spreading in the pit of his stomach. Demyan didn't even tell him to chill—the biggest surprise of all. When he looked at his father again, after dropping the bottle back to the bar, he shook his head.

"You're right, she's fragile," Roman agreed, his tongue swiping nervously across his bottom lip. A tell he couldn't bother to hide from his father. "She needs help. Like *real* fucking help. A medical professional, kind of help, Papa."

Demyan's face twisted—the very mention of a shrink never went down well in their world. He didn't say a thing one way or another about the topic, instead replying to his son, "It doesn't sound like you have any intention of explaining yourself or the girl to me."

"What's to explain, or haven't you seen enough?"

Demyan stared hard at him.

Roman waved one hand, tired. He was over it. "Like I said before, it's not like I have all of the answers to make everything make sense, either. I was dropped into this situation—I'm trying to figure it out as we go along."

"*We?*"

"Me and her. Right now, I'm basically what she's got. Fucking great, huh?"

Because she needed more.

Even he knew it.

Demyan's jaw tightened at that statement. "And you want to stick to your previous answer, then? Saying what you just did, you feel nothing for her?"

Steely eyes studied Roman, and while it made him uncomfortable, he let his father do it. He didn't have an answer, and when he didn't reply, Demyan shook his head.

"Unbelievable. This is a strange hill you've decided to die on, let me say."

Displeased, Demyan let out a harsh exhale before downing the rest of the vodka in his glass. He'd always wanted what was best for Roman, even if that meant letting him destroy his life with choices of his own making. They were his to make, or so his father liked to say. In the past, they'd clashed as Demyan learned the more he tried to fix and control Roman, the worse his behavior became. There were times he sincerely believed his father just wanted to be rid of him. Then, he became older—*maybe* wiser—and had an opportunity to observe his father from the lens of a grown man.

Albeit, still a troubled one.

That didn't change the truth.

Nothing was more important to Demyan Avdonin than his family.

Roman took another swig of the vodka.

"A *very* strange fucking hill," Demyan added in a dark mutter.

Well …

"Yeah, I guess you could say that," Roman replied.

"I plan to say more."

He nodded.

"I figured that, too."

Expected nothing less, really.

• • •

Eventually, Roman and Demyan made their way to the large, glass dining table. His father sat at one end, and he remained at the other. In the silence that stretched between their conversation, the occasional sound echoed from the large bathroom down the hall.

Roman couldn't help but wonder if Karine was giving Masha a hard time—he doubted it wasn't anything she couldn't handle. Otherwise, he would have known about it by now. For a second, he dared to relax.

"Has she settled here?" Demyan asked, drawing Roman away from his thoughts.

"We've been here a single night. She's as settled as she can be, considering."

"Who's the other woman with her?"

"Masha, she's … Karine's caretaker. As far as I can tell, she's one of the Yazov slaves who had been assigned to her. I get the impression they've been together for a while—so they're close. Masha is probably one of the few people who can actually handle her, no matter what condition she's in. She's not scared of her, and Karine usually responds well to her most of the time."

"*You* handled her pretty well," Demyan remarked.

Roman's gaze darted away to hide the thrill racing through his veins. It was disturbing that he could *like* the way Karine clung to him and depended on him—but since he didn't pretend to be a fucking saint, there it was.

Demyan still watched him closely, searching for all those signs that would give away the truth about Karine. All the things that Roman wasn't telling him.

"You can't stay here," he said abruptly.

Roman's head snapped back at that. "What? This is *my*—"

Demyan was shaking his head. "You can't stay here, or in any of our properties in the state. Those are the first places they'll look, Roman. And they *will* look."

"Maxim made the deal. He wanted Karine gone, and she is. He never said anything about telling anyone else."

"But he broke a more important agreement with Leonid and the man's son. And we're saying this while ignoring the fact one of those men were plotting against him. Who's to say they didn't still want *her*? What if Maxim was too late to get a handle on his problems? *You* are the one who has the bride. She was promised to him—why do I have to fucking explain this to you? They're going to come for your head, and then drag her right back to where she rightfully belongs."

Roman's rage was instant.

Hot in his gut.

Like poison.

Demyan lifted a brow when Roman grinded his teeth before muttering, "Karine's safety *is* most important, I know."

"Then, you need to figure out a way to keep her in one piece. This is not the place for it."

The frustration was building inside him. He knew his father was right, but habit and stupid pride meant he didn't want to admit it. It was yet one more thing that he didn't have under control.

Karine needed to be kept safe, and he didn't know how— so, wasn't this bigger than him, now?

"Asking for help isn't a sign of weakness, son," Demyan spoke up, reminding his son in an instant how easily he could read Roman. "Especially not when you ask it from someone who understands. Who doesn't consider feeling something as a weakness. I don't need to know the whys around what you've done to understand what you must do now. Those are different things. And regardless, I'll get my answers eventually."

He breathed in deeply, leaning back in the chair and pushed his hands into his pockets, eyeing Demyan from across the table.

"So, does that mean you're going to help me?" he asked his father.

Demyan shrugged lazily, smirking. "I guess so."

• • •

"How is she today?"

Roman hid the smile daring to creep across his lips as he slipped into the chair across from his father's at the table. Four days ago, Demyan encountered Karine for the first time, and already, had developed a soft spot for her. Not that

^{THE}PROMISE

he would want his son to point it out, but the fact he asked about her before even saying hello to Roman said more than he needed to.

Maybe it was her helplessness, and her dependency on the people around her—those she trusted, her *innocent* aura. He had no idea how her own father could spend even a second degrading her, nevermind keeping her locked away from the world. He could also better understand why Masha was so devoted to her—he swore the woman didn't know anything *but* watching over Karine. She was her first thought in the morning, and seemingly the last at night.

Even if Karine didn't always like it.

"You hungover?" Demyan asked.

He glanced up to meet his son's eyes, but Roman had them covered with a pair of dark aviators. He chuckled in response, and pulled them off his face.

"Not even close. In fact, I can't remember the last time I was actually drunk. These bloodshot eyes are because I haven't slept in four nights."

Demyan grunted as he took a sip of his coffee.

They were seated across from each other in the private dining room of his father's favorite hotel. Demyan called to ask him to meet for breakfast. For the first time in his life, Roman didn't give a shit about an early morning meeting. He didn't have to wake up at the crack of dawn because he hadn't even fallen asleep.

"How is this hotel working out for you?" Demyan asked, piercing a sausage with his fork.

Roman heard the underlying question in his father's words. He wanted to know how Karine was. If there had been any other incidents.

That first night when they moved out of Roman's apartment and into a hotel across town—well, that had been eventful.

To say the least.

Demyan assigned two Avdonin bulls to watch over them. Karine had encountered one of them in her suite in the middle of the night which led to another altercation. She was quickly going to start developing a reputation amongst the

61

men if she kept attacking the bulls one by one. The last thing they needed was *that.*

"We're fine there. I'm keeping a close eye on her."

And that was one of the most significant reasons why Roman hadn't slept in several nights. Not since they left Chicago. He wasn't sure when he would sleep again.

"I'm looking into a safehouse," Demyan continued, lifting his coffee for another sip.

It reminded Roman to do the same with the cup that had already been poured and waiting for him at the table. A strong cup of black coffee ... or two—would hopefully do the trick of keeping him up.

If he was lucky.

Ever since he returned to New York with a car stuffed full of problems, Roman had increasingly felt the urge to indulge in his favorite vice. Cocaine. An easy way to stay *up*, he made a conscious effort to ignore the fact he knew it would help him get through the current shit storm.

He also couldn't afford to fuck things up. This was a matter of life and death, for Karine and himself. He needed clarity. His mind had to be sharp, and while coke certainly made him believe he was on top of a mountain, unbeatable, that didn't mean he actually was. At least, sobriety taught him that.

"What's happening in Chicago?" Roman asked, taking the conversation where he really wanted it to be. "Do we still have time to make other shit happen, or what?"

Demyan didn't look away from his plate, careful in his reply when he said, "I'm in talks with people. Things are moving, but it'll take time as these things usually do. I'm going to figure it out."

He didn't add—*for Karine's sake*—but Roman knew there was a part of his father that meant just that. Through his limited interaction with her, he had started to see that his son was right. She needed professional help as much as she needed people to keep her safe.

It was a lot.

"For now, worry about not letting your mother see you while you're ... like this," Demyan reminded Roman, pointing the sharp prongs of the fork in his direction. "You hear me?"

Despite the warning, the two still shared a smile. His father wasn't wrong—the last thing his mother needed was to get involved with Roman's problems. She would only want to help, and there wasn't a soul who loved her that could tell her no.

Roman, included.

• • •

Back at the new hotel suite, Roman tossed and turned in his bed again. He predicted another night of staying awake. It was the only way he felt *completely* positive that Karine was safe, and wouldn't get herself into any trouble while everyone else slept. Other than the bulls ... and really, he was trying to keep *them* out of her line of sight, too.

This was not the way he'd pictured his return to New York. He would have liked to jump straight back into the chop shop scene—pick up where he left off, and pull in some easy money. He still had a few jobs up in the air when he left for Chicago which he could return to, as he had time, but for the moment, he needed to stay out of sight.

Which was bad for business.

Someone was always willing to pick up someone else's slack on the streets. Time away from New York affected his client list and contacts—his business was going to take a serious hit. All things that pissed Roman off, and for good reason considering how well he'd been doing in a new city.

His list of wrongs was all too clear to him, and at night in bed when he was alone and *awake*, his mind liked to run through all of them on repeat.

He should have stayed out of the Yazov business when he had the chance. Most importantly, he shouldn't have fucked Maxim Yazov's daughter—no matter how gorgeous and curious she was. Then, he wouldn't have found himself beaten black and blue with a baseball bat. He could still feel that pain every time he moved. It wasn't healing fast enough, and had turned into a morbid, *constant* reminder of the agreement he made with Karine's father.

Was he in a better situation now?

Debatable.

It was the click of the door that pulled him from his thoughts, and Roman sat up in bed with a jerk, immediately reaching for the weapon he kept under the pillow. The room was dark, but light spilled in from the hallway, illuminating him in the bed. It was the shadow of her that stopped him from pulling the gun out from its hiding spot.

Karine's petite and slender shape was outlined in the doorway. She stood there in silence, her hands clasped together, *trembling*—peering in on him like she was trying to discern if he was awake.

Maybe if he was a better man, then he would have told her to leave. Or he could have just pretended to be asleep. They shouldn't indulge in nights together. He didn't need to get more involved with her than he already was.

But …

Well, Roman wasn't a better man.

Goddamn.

He wasn't even sure if he was a good one.

"Come in, but close the door behind you," he said to her in a murmur.

Karine did as she was told.

SIX

Maxim Yazov proudly admitted to being many things, namely, an asshole. He never pretended to be anything less than exactly what and *who* he was because he refused to change what made him, *him* simply for the acceptance or pleasure of someone else. But he was more, too ... more than a monster. A man—criminal, ruthless, and cruel. Smart and quick, dangerous, many would say.

He would agree.

Maxim was aware that most people wouldn't view those things as positive qualities. If only the opinions of others had ever been enough to sway how he felt about himself, but here he was. Nonetheless, they were qualities that were integral for a man to survive the life he lived.

Essential, even.

His position demanded it.

The world he'd claimed as his taught fatherless boys like him who hoped to one day be men bearing eight-pointed stars that sinners made their own heaven. And often, that heaven was born from someone else's hell. That world had raised and shaped him, he could not afford to be someone else.

Never even considered it.

Perhaps the qualities that made up his person were not what an average man would take pride in, but they were the skills and the disposition that made him successful as a bratva boss with rivals on all sides.

And it bothered Maxim more than he cared to admit that, those same traits that allowed him to be untouchable, were the ones that also meant he had never been a good father. Lately, it had been more obvious and not something he could justify away with the heaven he'd created for himself in power and wealth. If there was someone who cared to listen to his secrets, he would even admit he felt shameful that his surviving child wouldn't have many fond memories of him when he was gone.

Of course, there was a period of time when he had shown some positive qualities of a father—when he'd been foolish enough to think that a man like him could *be* the kind of father his children actually loved. *Young*, and dumb. Then, life happened and the events that unfolded led him down a path where love was weakness, and weakness was pain.

It started with the death of his wife—not the mother of his children—and the ball just kept rolling. The fatherless boy Maxim had once been assured that he'd rather be a bad father than no father at all, and so that's what he became as he buried every mistake and heartache from his past with money and control.

He wasn't the father his children deserved, and for that, he would always have regret.

The past was what it was, though. And he couldn't change it. His only hope now as a father, was that he'd done something—no matter how small—to change the future. At least for one of his children.

His most precious child.

Once, a long time ago, one of the mothers of his children told him something he hadn't been able to forget. And while he flaunted his sins without shame, he'd never been able to get her words out of his head. It had become a constant reminder that even if he didn't care what kind of man he was, people who loved him *did*.

None of these babies have asked to be born into the world they live in—they didn't ask for us, Maxim. They didn't choose this life, but you did. Don't they at the very least, deserve to be loved?

He'd laughed at her that night when she implored him to show even an inkling of affection towards her child. He'd just accepted his life for what it was, then—and he hoped his kids would do the same because he'd never believed there was another way. After all, everything he did was to keep him, and *them*, alive. He had to be a boss before he could ever be a father.

Now, regret for those choices and beliefs filled him like bricks weighing down his body as he slowly sunk to the proverbial death of his own making.

Standing in his office, only the moonlight rolling in through the windows illuminating the rest of the space he felt *most* at home, Maxim rolled up the sleeves of his silk shirt while a cigar burned between his teeth. He'd already spent too much time pacing, and thinking. Overthinking, maybe.

His laptop was open on his desk, spilling a glow of light across the items scattered there. He continued the strides back and forth in front of it, keeping his eye on the screen, trying to decide his next move.

Demyan Avdonin had been calling for days. He'd even sent emails, and a text, putting a record on paper in a way men like them usually wouldn't. Maxim ignored all attempts the man made to contact him either way. He knew what his next steps for the night were going to be, but he hadn't figured Demyan into his plans, too.

Until time ran out.

Calling him back was not a part of the program, in fact, things would be a lot cleaner on his end if he just burned that bridge without even watching it go. And yet, he couldn't do it.

His foolish sense of duty to the only man he had actually considered a *real* friend kept his gaze locked on that screen, his conscience demanding him to call. Just to tie the loose ends. He owed it to Demyan, didn't he?

The mess he must have …

Karine, and Roman.

Surely.

He had never been the type who valued friendship—until a man who should have been his rival, and was, expected nothing except respect and good conversation whenever the two managed to get together. So, fuck it. He knew he was running short on time, and he owed Demyan a phone call.

What more did he have to lose?

He clicked on the video call link that took him to a blank screen. For a split second, he nearly ended the call. What were the chances the man would even answer? It was past two in the morning over in New York, and Demyan had always struck him as the kind of man who didn't work late.

A family man, Leonid had once told him about Demyan. As if it was a bad thing, and at the time, Maxim might have agreed.

Maxim grunted, displeased, at the thought, just as Demyan answered. The screen filled with a view of Demyan's office. Sitting at his desk and looking tired, his friend stared back at him as if he wasn't at all surprised.

Maxim reduced the volume on his laptop, and immediately resumed his pacing. At least, he felt like he was doing something, then.

"Looks like we're both working late. I've been waiting to hear back from you."

"I've been busy," Maxim replied, shooting a grin his friend's way. It was a genuine excuse—there were a lot of things he needed to handle in the last few days since Roman and Karine left. "Tends to happen when you have an entire plot unfolding beneath your feet, yes? And a wedding that didn't happen, of course."

The bride disappearing was simply the cherry on top of an already *messy* cake. It certainly put a kink in the other plans that he had found out about a little too late. Heads were going to roll, and Maxim had been busy trying to keep things under control within the bratva. Well, for as long as he could.

The inevitable was still … inevitable.

Demyan didn't seem to care to reply to the excuse, but his gaze followed Maxim's pacing form on his own screen.

"Something on your mind, comrade?" he asked.

Maxim stopped and turned to face the laptop. "Isn't there always?"

"You could have just called me instead of this video chat nonsense. I fully intend on this being an official call. I don't know if you've been reading my emails, but I even offered to fly down there and talk to you face-to-face. If you need men or—"

"You don't need to come down, and this is *not* an official call," Maxim interjected, wanting both of those things very clear between them. "I am going to delete the records of this phone call, and you should do the same once we're done."

Demyan dragged in a heavy breath, exhaling loudly. He didn't commit to Maxim's demand, but he doubted the man would risk the blowback he might face otherwise.

Then, Demyan said, "If you called to start this conversation with anything except exactly what's going on there, I don't care to hear it, Maxim. When we first spoke about Roman's situation, we didn't decide on him returning to New York with an unstable girl in tow."

Maxim showed great self-control by not flinching when he heard his daughter described as *unstable*. He really had no right to be pissed about the way others portrayed Karine since he had never treated her with the respect she deserved, but it still stung. And she had never been so lost that she didn't know what she was missing in her father, either.

"That's my daughter," he said in a murmur. "My last living child, Demyan."

Still.

He had to.

Demyan remained silent, but the way his features softened briefly said that he wasn't opposed to the idea that there was more to Karine.

"I'm sure since you've met her, you know this already, but Karine is much more than just an unstable girl. She's confused, *troubled*, sure—but none of it is her fault. She's a very fragile flower in the meadow of giants, and it's very difficult to keep someone like her safe in a world like ours."

As Maxim finished, Demyan nodded. He had never offered his friend a true look at his personal life or the feelings he had for the people in it, but the lack of judgement staring back at him on the screen encouraged him to continue.

"And there are a great many things I have to apologize for," he said, shrugging. "To you, I mean."

"How so?" Demyan asked.

Maxim sighed, his gaze traveling back to the windows where he could see the inky sky—the picture-perfect backdrop to his life. Black. Nothingness. Soulless.

"I should apologize to you for not showing you the same respect you showed me," Maxim said, glancing back to the laptop and the man on the screen. "You shared a lot with me over the years. About your family and such. You even opened up your home and welcomed me into it—I sat at your table, and ate with your wife. I never did the same to you, and for that I'm sorry. I just didn't have the same things to offer, Demyan. The life you have doesn't exist in mine."

Demyan took a sip of drink from the glass that was by his side, seconds ticking by in silence before he finally replied, "There's still time for that. Maybe this is just the start."

Maxim nearly laughed at that, but instead, only a dry chuckle escaped him. "Actually I don't have much time at all," he replied, glancing at the other frames that were open on the laptop screen.

There, the feed from the security cameras showed that one by one, they were starting to flicker off. Pitch black squares dotted the grid of cameras now, and it didn't surprise him. He expected it to happen, and knew exactly what it meant, too.

Even though people assumed he didn't have security cameras—no criminal wanted their crimes recorded by their own hand, after all—he did have a few. A very select few

that were not easily noticed by guests. Only a handful of
people knew the cameras existed.

Maxim reached for the glass on his desk, lifting the golden-
hued liquid to take a whiff of it. Harsh and strong, the scent
filled his lungs, but he didn't take a sip. That was not what he
needed tonight. Instead, he put the glass back down and
took a long drag of his cigar, letting the smoke fill his lungs.

If the snakes in his grass didn't kill him, cancer surely
would someday.

"Chicago's on fire," he finally said.

Demyan, quietly waiting for whatever Maxim decided to
surprise him with next, only narrowed his eyes at that
statement. A boss didn't need an explanation for that kind of
observation.

Chicago was on fire, and his whole world was collapsing
around him. Because this was his world. Or it was supposed
to be.

"About your boy," he added before Dmeyan could
comment, "I would have given him the time to grow into his
role—if I could have—but he'll just have to do it himself,
now. It'll probably be quicker than you would have liked.
Expect that he's going to stumble a bit because of it, those
growing pains hurt, Demyan."

Demyan opened his mouth to reply, but Maxim was too
fast to interrupt with, "And my girl—the thing is, I never did
right by her. Not when I had the chance, you understand?
So, I had to do it now. I had to do something that could help
her, but I was trying to keep my word to you, too. I wanted
to return your boy to you in one piece. A lot of my years
have been spent being selfish. Turns out, it's not so hard to
do the right thing."

"Max—"

"Not that I know what the right thing is," Maxim uttered
under his breath.

Demyan grunted, falling back into his chair on the screen
as he absorbed the rambling that even Maxim didn't truly
understand. He didn't have the time to edit his words or
thoughts, but if the man honestly wanted to know ... *there it
was.*

Everything that was important, anyway.

Narrowing his eyes, Demyan leaned closer to the screen. "You realize very little of this makes sense to me, right?"

"I know," Maxim replied.

More cameras had turned off in the open security frame. Simultaneously, he could also now hear the footsteps approaching his office doors through the long hall. Each step echoed in the darkness.

"I could help if you would just tell me what's happening there," Demyan muttered, unaware.

Maxim ignored him. Those were answers that Demyan wouldn't get from him.

"Do me a favor, comrade," Maxim murmured, a hint of a smile curving the edges of his lips when he glanced back to the screen. "Tell my daughter I did love her ... I just wasn't very good at it."

"What the fuck are you talking about?" Demyan stood from his seat on the screen, but Maxim was already reaching for the *end call* button. "Maxim, what are you—"

He smirked at Demyan, and nodded once. "It's a good night to die, old friend."

That was all he said before he took another puff of his cigar, and ended the call. Automatically, the settings would delete its record.

At the office doors, the shadow of a figure fell on the frosted glass. He knew exactly who it was and why they were coming. He also planned to make them work for it, too.

Maxim tipped the glass filled with gasoline at the edge, spilling the caustic liquid across his desk, drenching everything it could touch in its spread. He couldn't make mistakes, he didn't want to leave any evidence or a chance of survival.

"Maxim!"

The voice echoed as the door opened, but it was already too late. He dropped the cigar with the brightly-burning ash on the desk, sparks igniting the first licks of hot flames.

It spread fast, and *brilliant*. The fire reached high enough to touch the chandelier hanging overtop the desk in seconds. Enthralled, he couldn't look away.

ᴛʜᴇPROMISE

Maybe that was his only mistake.
It was through the flames that he saw the gun.
Pointed right at him.

SEVEN

The loudest voice in Karine's mind made herself known with a sharp hiss—*what are you doing?*

She recognized the voice well, now—Katina no longer cared when interrupting Karine's reality—always putting her on edge. That was filled with anxiety and panic every time Karine dared to make any decision on her own.

She didn't trust her choices. Didn't believe she could make the right ones, and smothered her with the fear of falling, crashing, and burning.

Yet, she ignored the hissed question, and the loud *Karine!* Pretending she didn't hear it at all spurred on the courage she had only experienced once before—the night she asked Roman to come to her room.

"Karine."

That time, the voice wasn't in her head. Roman's murmur of her name also didn't feel like a question—he wasn't *asking*, not again, but he also wasn't telling her, either.

ᴛʜᴇPROMISE

Karine stepped into the room, and shut the door behind her.

The only light in the room came from what the moon provided in the windows. It wasn't much. Her eyes didn't adjust well to the darkness, so she focused on only the shadow of his form lounging in the bed.

Her courage had been enough to lead her into the room, but she couldn't actually step any closer to him once the door was closed. The war raged inside her head. A battle between the urge to just leave—run out of the room again—and the desire to stay because she wanted to be close to him.

This time, it was only herself she fought with, though. Karine was starting to learn those were actually the hardest fights for her.

Roman was far too quiet for Karine's liking, and the silence started to get to her in the worst way. She resisted the compulsion to twist her fingers together to ease the anxiety. If he would just say something, then she wouldn't have to, and she might know what he was thinking.

"Nightmares?" he asked suddenly, and Karine breathed her relief out in a whoosh. "Have you been having them a lot recently?"

Forcing the lump down that had formed in her throat to keep her quiet, she finally found her own voice again. .

"Yeah, I think so," Karine whispered.

She couldn't be sure because she never remembered what happened in the nightmares. Instead, she often woke up with a racing heart, airless as she gasped to catch her breath, and a *heaviness* weighing down her very soul. Still, with absolute certainty, she knew that she had seen something in her sleep that had made her afraid.

And *sad*.

That heaviness was always sad.

"What was the nightmare about tonight?" Roman questioned.

Karine blinked, trying to clear her mind and will back the images that had scared her awake simply because he asked her to, but it was pointless.

"I don't know—I don't remember," she admitted, shaking her head. "But I couldn't breathe. When I woke up, it felt like I was choking. I was gasping for air, but it was like my lungs were empty. I couldn't tell if I was drowning or suffocating."

Roman said nothing when she continued, saying, "I jumped out of the bed, hands around my throat, but—" Karine stopped short, sucking in a gulp of air and forcing her hands to stay at her sides instead of covering her throat again like she had when she woke up alone and scared in her room. "I didn't know where I was, so I went running for the door."

"Oh?"

"I almost fell over Masha."

That interested him.

"Masha?" Roman asked.

Despite the drips of fear still falling through her bloodstream, his voice was heavy and warm in the darkness. It wrapped around her like a hug, tight and secure.

"She was sleeping at the door of my room," Karine explained.

Roman's form shifted, the shuffle of the sheets echoing before a *click* sounded, and the room flooded with light. His hand fell away from the bedside lamp that he'd turned on, and back to the bed.

The warm, yellow glow was more than enough for her to be able to see him clearly now. And he *was* a sight to see.

Naked, save for the black boxer-briefs he wore, Roman rested comfortably on gray sheets seemingly unbothered that she openly stared. Karine couldn't stop it, taking in the black roses tattooed on his upper chest and how the ink only served to draw someone's gaze to his body.

Right now, *hers*.

And the sight of him made her weak in the knees.

His sheets were kicked off around his feet, leaving the rest of him on display for her to admire. The ropes of muscles that made up his muscular thighs. The dark dusting of hair that trailed from his navel to the waistband of his boxer-briefs. Even the way his hand rested against the defined track of abdominal muscles was tempting to her senses.

She'd rather her head be lying there, and his hand stroking her hair. It wasn't lost on Karine that before Roman, she hadn't even *admired* the sight of a man, never mind wanting one to touch her. Then again, she had certainly never been as close to a man as she allowed herself to be with Roman, either.

For the first time, she wasn't opposed to the idea of letting someone in.

Just a little bit.

As long as it was him.

Roman's left brow cocked high as he watched her fidget. It felt like he was constantly trying to figure her out, and she wondered what he saw when he looked at her.

Did he see someone broken?

Lost?

Or maybe just her?

"Does that happen often?" he asked.

She'd lost the trail of their conversation in her distraction, and the furrow of her brow made Roman chuckle.

"Masha needing to sleep at your door," he clarified. "I assume it's to stop you from wandering off in your sleep, yeah?"

Right.

The nightmare.

Masha …

Karine's cheeks flooded with heat, and she no longer wanted to meet Roman's gaze. "I … well, it's not … it's only—"

"You don't have to answer," he added quickly, saving Karine the embarrassment of continuing to stumble over her words. "You don't have to explain anything you don't want to."

Her silence grew the longer she considered what he said, and *asked*. Because she didn't know how to answer his question truthfully without the shame eating her alive. It wasn't that she didn't want to answer.

She had some idea of what he thought of her. He'd suggested it already—that she needed professional psychiatric help to figure out and understand what had happened and was happening in her mind. Now, with Roman probing and away from the influences of her father's control, she had no choice but to hold the stark reality in her hands.

Like a morbid offering for the man in front of her—*here's this mess they've made of me.*

He didn't take his eyes off her, and Karine couldn't decide if that made it worse or better for her when it still felt like he could see right through her.

"I've not really had time to deal with … all of this," she said lamely, waving at herself. "That makes it hard."

"I get it," he replied quietly. "It's fine, Karine."

It wasn't, but she wanted it to be.

Things like that were a lot sharper and clearer without the constant supply of mixed medications at the ready. Everything had become just a tad more difficult to deal with because she wasn't so numb anymore. She couldn't spend her days in a haze, walking around dazed, her time and thoughts and choices controlled by everyone around her as she certainly hadn't been in a state to do anything for herself more often than not.

Mostly.

She was actually feeling things—*real* things, not manufactured by pharmaceuticals and a situation that was entirely out of her control. The universe seemed to enjoy playing cruel jokes on Karine because she hadn't been at all ready for any of this.

No one cared to ask about that little detail, though.

She wasn't sure she could do this, stand there in his room and be scrutinized by the intensity of his gaze. This was a bad decision. Katina had been right—what *was* she even doing here? She shouldn't be there at all.

"I'm sorry. Maybe I'm just thirsty—I'll leave now," she muttered under her breath.

Even her excuses weren't good enough to her own ears, but it was all she had. When she swung around to leave, she caught the sight of Roman shifting straighter in the bed from the corners of her eyes.

"Wait, I have water here if you're thirsty." His voice stopped her in her tracks. He had to know she really didn't want *water*—it was just the excuse to use to get away. She was tempted to look over her shoulder and say exactly that, but she couldn't meet his eyes. "But I'm not sure you are, babe. Thirsty, I mean."

"I could be," she replied shakily.

Why did her heart thunder like that whenever he was near? Better yet, why did she like it so much?

"Except you came here—*in here*. You wanted something, right? That's why you came to my room."

She shook her head in response to that. The last thing she wanted him to think was she *needed* him. Karine didn't want to be only someone that he took care of. As it was, she relied on him—and others—far too much.

At least, that's how it felt.

Karine wasn't in Chicago anymore, she was surrounded by strangers here. Not that being engulfed by her father's people and his world made any difference. Everywhere she looked, as far back as she could remember, she had been under threat.

Call it instinct.

Or force of habit.

Either way, running always felt better.

Right.

"I don't want anything, I just—I-I should go," she insisted, reaching for the doorknob. "Sorry for waking you up."

"You didn't. I couldn't sleep, either."

Her hand froze before it could turn the knob. He couldn't possibly know how he made it even more difficult for her to talk simply because she wanted to hear him more. That voice in her head commanded her to leave while she still had the chance to do so, but there was also a part of her too tempted to look back at him and ask *why.*

Except she didn't need to.

"Karine, you're here. You obviously wanted something. Do you know what you want?"

God.

Why did he have to be like that?

So, *matter-of-fact.*

Black and white.

It kind of pissed her off because when he offered her statements like that—so clear, no options but yes or no—she felt like she was lying to him if she didn't answer. That didn't mean she always *had* an answer, though. Or rather, one that would make sense.

"I don't know, okay?" she snapped, throwing the words over her shoulder. Karine didn't mean to let the irritation bubble over—it wasn't *his* fault she had trouble dissecting her own wants and needs—and was quick to add, "You should know this about me by now, Roman. I never know what I want because it feels like I don't even know *myself.*"

Roman hadn't reacted once, not even when she raised her voice and snapped at him. She wasn't sure if it was because he'd been expecting her outburst, or was trying to *provoke* one when he replied, without inflection, "And yet, you're here in my room right now."

Right.

He wasn't wrong.

So, fine.

Turning and letting go of the doorknob, Karine raised her face up, thrusting her chin out in his direction—finally, she found that courage from before to meet his eyes. She had to tell him something.

"I'm here because I feel safe."

"You feel safe here?" he asked.

"With you," she clarified. "Like my feet are on steady ground, the rest doesn't really matter when I feel like that because I never do. Except with you. I like it, I'm not sure I should, though."

The admittance had Karine's cheeks burning even if she had willingly told him the truth. Not that her secrets seemed to bother him as his gaze roamed over her where she stood a nervous mess. She became hyper aware of her night attire the longer his gaze lingered. An old oversized T-shirt, and a pair of tiny cotton shorts. Roman gave no indication that he even noticed what she was wearing, or *cared*, for that matter as his gaze crawled back up to meet hers.

"I think you do know what you want, Karine. Maybe it's become easier to distinguish your wants and needs without everyone else constantly plying you with whatever *they* wanted or needed at the time to serve their purposes, but either way ... you *do* know yourself. And you're allowed to. No one's taking that away from you here. I promise."

She couldn't look away from him, then, her reason for being there undeniable as that urge to run diminished to practically nothing. The hunger pooling low in her belly as Roman leaned his gorgeous form toward the edge of the bed took center stage for her focus instead.

Karine didn't even try to hide the way she swallowed hard, or how she couldn't stop her tongue from sweeping along the seam of her lower lip like she might find the taste of him there. Or the memory of it. Roman didn't miss the actions either, his attention drawn to her mouth and back up to her wide stare.

"If there's something in this room that you want, Karine, you should take it," he told her, hesitating after he'd swung his legs over the side of the bed. A sensual grin tugged at the corners of his lips. Despite herself, and how in over her head she was with this man, she grinned, too.

Just moments ago, she'd been lost, her mind dark, at war with herself and the people inside her head fighting for attention—*for presence*. And now, it was just her and him, a single moment between them, and she wasn't going to waste it.

"Even if what I want is you?" Karine asked.

"Especially if what you want is me, Karine. You wouldn't be here if I didn't want you, too."

"Good," she said in a whisper. "Because I do."

Roman slid out of the bed, bare feet touching the floor for only a second before he moved toward her, making Karine drag in a shaky inhale of air that left her body on fire. He was a sight to see, coming at her fast, eyes drinking her and hands clenched into fists that he released only when he reached for her.

Every hard line of his body, each chiseled muscle, flattened to her soft curves when he scooped her into his arms, and pressed his mouth to hers. The fire he'd ignited inside her was nothing compared to the way pleasure speared through every one of her nerves at his kiss, bruising and unforgiving against her own.

But she liked it.

And how that bliss melded with the heat spreading through her limbs at an alarming speed. Karine sighed into the kiss, her lips curving into a smile when his tongue teased the seam of her mouth for a taste.

"I like the way I feel when I'm with you."

The words slipped out before she could stop them, but Karine didn't regret saying it all the same. It was the truth, and he should know.

"All you had to do was *say so*," his voice rumbled with her next kiss.

Good to know.

Not that she could say anything at the moment. But it was fine. *More than.* Roman sucked on her bottom lip, his teeth dragging along the plump flesh until she was gasping for air. Feeling his fingers tease her shorts, daring to dance beneath the waistband, she stole his next kiss before he could take it, parting her lips for his tongue to dart deeper, finding hers.

She didn't even care that her arms were folded against his chest, trapped while his kiss pulled the air straight from her lungs. That hungry, harsh kiss turned softer, suddenly deciding to take his time with her. There was no rush as her back flattened to the door when he pushed them forward, never once breaking the kiss.

Karine's heart stuttered when she realized she could spend the rest of the night with him. Tangled up in him, *again.*

If that was what he wanted, too.

And it certainly seemed like he did.

Roman only pulled away from the kiss to spin her around. The change was so abrupt, the room became a dizzying blur before she came to a stop. Her back molded into his chest, her ass tight to his groin where she could feel the hardness and length of his cock between his thighs. His strong arms crossed over her front, engulfing her, pinning her to him while he grabbed a fistful of her hair. Tugging her head to one side, earning a soft moan from Karine, he pressed featherlight kisses along the column of her neck.

She couldn't quite understand how his gentleness mixed so perfectly with the roughness—or better yet, how it made her body sing.

"How good do you wanna feel?" he asked, his words drifting along her sensitive skin and making her shiver. And then, more demanding came his dark, "Tell me."

Karine rushed to say, "*So good.*"

Still slow, his mouth moved over her skin, coaxing those flames licking under her surface even higher, and Karine floated higher with each one. His tongue lapped at the curve of her shoulder, then sucked after his teeth dragged over the same spot.

One of his hands shoved quickly down into her shorts at the same time she turned to catch his mouth for another kiss. His grunt of approval when he found she wasn't wearing panties pulsed against her breathless whine; those deft fingers of his had found her already tender clit, and he rubbed her alive with fast strokes .

Karine jerked away from his kiss, the broken cry bursting from her lips as the air ripped from her lungs. He showed no mercy in the way his fingers played her body, making every one of her breaths come faster and harsher than the last. She pushed herself into him even more, and his cock fit right between her butt cheeks.

It was almost *too much.*

She had to fight the urge to attempt to bat his hand away when it felt like her knees were going to give out from how intense the rolling waves of sharp pleasure were ravaging through her shaking body. Except she didn't—it was also *too damn good.* Too good to make him stop now. She rolled her hips to the rhythm of his fingers, earning herself his low moan of her name when her ass grinded harder into him.

He grew stiffer.

So big.

She could feel how damp she was, slick between her thighs and *hot*, ready for his cock to fill and stretch her open again the way he had that first time.

Fuck.

She'd needed that.

Missed that.

"Is this what you wanted—why you came to my room, baby? *Admit it, Karine.*" His voice came out harsh, but sinful, too. As tempting and wicked as the rest of him. He had his other arm tightly wound over her breasts, keeping her in place against him while he made her wild.

And she was.

So crazy like this.

The more noises he invoked from her, the harder he rubbed her. Then, three of his fingers slipped Karine's soaked, but clenching, sex. Her cry of shock and melted into guttural joy.

Because *yes.*

That's what she'd been waiting for—a part of him inside her. His fingers fucked her relentlessly, his palm still firm against her clit all the while and before she knew it, Karine was on the edge of coming.

Just like that.

Karine's lips trembled with every word when she said, "Y-yes ... oh, my God, *yes*, I came here for this. Please don't stop."

Who was that girl?

It didn't sound *at all* like her.

Yet, it was.

That was the best part.

"I'll never stop," Roman murmured in reply.

The words wrapping around her like a dark promise she hoped he kept. It was like the floor had disappeared under her feet, even the walls around her drifted away, while he took her over the edge. He didn't slow, the only softness he showed was the sweet kisses he dotted along the back of her neck and shaking shoulders until Karine came. It was the wet sounds his fingers made between her thighs that truly pulled her under—it was almost embarrassing how wet she was, and yet the sound still made her fly when he uttered, "Fuck, do you feel how much you're loving this, so wet, Karine."

Roman held her up through the orgasm—the floor hadn't actually disappeared. She just couldn't remain *up*, knees buckling as the pleasure raced out of her mouth in a high, aching cry of his name.

For a moment, she forgot everything. Where they were, every monster that had reared its ugly head in her life and nightmares—*everything was gone.* That was bliss for Karine. Nothing could be more perfect.

Except, apparently, the man who gave it to her.

Karine fought to catch her breath as the feeling came back to the soles of her feet, and on wobbly legs, she became a little steadier while her palms flattened to the door. Roman pulled his fingers out of tender pussy, leaving her clit throbbing, and her inner walls still shuddering.

This time, it was Karine who spun around to face him. She wrapped an arm around his head, pulling his forehead close enough to touch hers. The tips of their noses grazed—and like that, she ensured that he had nowhere to look and nothing to see, but her.

Karine had decided she liked that—*him and her*—his eyes on only her.

"I told you not to stop," she said, her throat tight and voice husky. Could he hear what he had done to her—could he see it in her eyes?

She wanted him to.

Roman flashed a smirk that made her breath catch. "That's what I want to hear."

Between them, her hands stroked him overtop his boxer-briefs before slipping under the fabric to find him heavy and thick in her palm. She loved the control she found when she tightened her hand around his base, and felt him jerk against her from the pressure. He watched her while she tugged along his length, finding the right pressure and speed to make him moan for her.

"Would you suck me clean," he asked, his words rough through chopping breaths, "after I've fucked you, Karine? Would you?"

Didn't he know?

"I'll do anything for you."

And she'd like it, too.

The semblance of control he'd maintained seemed to be lost when she stared him in the eyes and said those words without even hesitating. In another dizzy second, she found herself turned back to the door again, and her shorts ripped down her legs. He was an overwhelming presence behind her, the thick head of his cock sweeping through the wet lips of her pussy.

And then he was pushing in.

No warning.

That first thrust came harder than she expected it to, sending her up on her tiptoes from the force. He was right there to hold her in place for his next one though, and every beat of his hips that came after was faster and rougher than the last.

Roman took her hard, and Karine didn't want anything different. Throwing her head back, pressing her eyes closed as he started to pound deeper, the slap of his hips to her ass only adding to the moans spiraling from her.

His palm found her throat.

Karine was lost again.

To him.

To everything.

He didn't stop fucking her until he'd spilled every last drop of his cum inside her, and even then, his last thrusts came long and deep, only serving to smear their mingled fluids on the insides of her thighs. She'd still suck him clean.

When he asked.

She would.

His fingers unfurled from around her throat, and Karine let her head fall forward to rest against the door. Trembling, but needing to know, she asked while he was still hard and pulsing inside of her, "Should I leave now?"

Better to rip the Band-Aid right off.

"You're fine right where you are," he murmured, the reply ghosting over her skin and leaving goosebumps in their wake. Karine melted into his arms when he added quieter, "With *me*."

• • •

Karine was trying her best not to fall asleep. She didn't want to repeat her mistakes the last time they'd been in bed together, sleeping their time away when she would much rather spend it wide awake and studying the man next to her.

He was a storm of things she didn't understand—a picture placed in front of her that *should* terrify her, but he didn't.

Not much had changed.

He still felt safe.

Still smothered her in *heat*.

The thud-thud of his heart in his chest echoed through her back while his arms stayed wrapped tight around her under the sheets. From time to time, she could feel his hot breath falling on her nape, but he said nothing to let her know he was still awake. He also didn't need to.

"I spent my twenty-first birthday with you," she said, the secret slipping into the darkness.

Behind her, his reply was a low rumble mixed with his sleepiness. "Did you?"

"I didn't tell you before—it didn't seem … important."

"Karine, everything about you is important. It's a fucking shame people have made it worth their while to teach you otherwise."

"Do you still want me to tell you what I want?" she asked.

"Of course, I do."

Well …

"I just want to be okay."

Not that she knew what that was supposed to feel like. It seemed like something out of her reach, but still somehow possible. *Now*.

"You *are* okay," Roman said, his lips finding her bare shoulder. Karine closed her eyes, the smile forming easily. *So true*. She wasn't accustomed to happiness that was real, but she found a piece of it with him. "But it's fine to know you want to be better, too, babe."

Right.
Karine wouldn't forget it.

EIGHT

The scratched *ROMAN* etched into the left corner of the diner's booth made Roman smile as the memory flooded his mind of exactly how it got there, and the way his father had laughed at his eleven-year-old son's antics.

"Knew I shouldn't have let him give you that knife," Demyan had mumbled through chuckles and a bite of the food he'd been chewing.

Between them sat a whole pile of pancakes—stacked six high. In a corner booth tucked away from the rest of the diner where he had spent too many mornings to count with his father, a table full with toppings of every kind separated the two.

Roman was all about hazelnut spread, and maple syrup. His father liked blueberries and whipped cream.

Roman grinned sheepishly, but didn't bother to hide the pocketknife his newest bull had slipped him that morning saying, "Just for you, Prince."

"It's only little—no one will even see, Papa."

Demyan shrugged. "No, no one would say anything otherwise, Roman—they wouldn't dare."

Somewhere along the way, Roman forgot that the respect and place he had was because better men worked hard for it to be so. He traced the letters of his name carved into the booth with the pad of his thumb, knowing he couldn't go back to being that younger version of himself sitting across from his father ever again, but still longing for a simpler time in his life.

His father always picked the diner whenever he wanted to sit down with his son, one on one, and when he thought back now—Roman only had fond memories here. Even the black and white checkered tile floor brought back images of him racing across it to jump into *their* booth.

Roman couldn't remember the last time he'd eaten at the diner with Demyan, and that kind of bothered him. He didn't have much of an appetite lately, though. Not since he left New York—since he was *forced* to leave New York. Food seemed unimportant in the grander schemes of things going on in his life, honestly.

Since, his father seemed to think it wasn't wise to have important conversations over the phone anymore, he was supposed to meet up with the man at their old haunt for a chat. Except Demyan hadn't shown up yet, even though he was the one who called Roman's hotel room at *six* in the fucking morning, and demanded to see him.

Even if he hadn't been able to hear the agitation in his father's voice over that phone call, he knew something was up. It had to be for Demyan to leave his house before seven.

It was the nagging memory of the look Karine had given him when he ended the call that kept Roman lost to his thoughts while he waited for his father to arrive. She'd been sleeping in his arms, her face tucked against his chest, when his phone rang. The noise made her stir, but it was him reaching over to answer the call that woke her.

He wished she hadn't.

She never slept well as it was, and it didn't take long for him to notice the more she did sleep, the less Karine seemed to work on autopilot.

Either way, he couldn't ignore a call from his father whether it woke her or not. Roman had paced the room while he talked to Demyan, feeling the weight of Karine's stare leveling on him the whole time. There wasn't much in the conversation that she could decipher, but that didn't stop her from listening.

When the call had finally ended, he turned to face her only for her to immediately ask, "You're leaving, aren't you?"

Naked under the sheets and sitting up in bed, she had looked like every inch of his wettest dreams with the fabric clutched to her chest, hiding her breasts. Her hair had fallen over her face in a mess, giving her a bit of a *just fucked* look, and those plush lips of hers sat in a pout that did *wonderful,* but also terrible, things to his mind.

He'd wanted to stay right there.

With her.

In her.

Except he couldn't.

Instead, Roman had walked right up to Karine, and pushed some of that hair off her face, tucking those thick, dark strands behind her ears while she stared up at him with those big, wide eyes framed by sweeping lashes. He thought doe-eyed was as much a look someone had as it was an aura they gave off.

Every inch of Karine screamed frightened, and *fragile.*

Sometimes.

Her voice sounded cold and hollow when she had asked him that, and it killed him a little bit. His hand traveled to cup her cheeks until he could hold her face with both hands, and tilt it up so he could hold her gaze, too.

"But I'll be back. I won't be gone for long, Karine."

As fast as he'd held her, she'd pulled away to bury her face into the pillows. Just the fact that she hid her face from him said a lot—a few hours was probably an overwhelming amount of time for Karine. He was tempted to call his father back and cancel the meeting, even if it gave him a bit more time to work Karine into the idea of Roman leaving. Which was foolish, and even he knew it.

Still, Roman had considered it.

What was happening to him?

She provoked urges in Roman that he had never known existed within himself—he was *not* soft, selfless, or concerned about anything or anyone except for himself. Or he hadn't been … for a long time.

Karine was not the same.

He didn't understand why.

The truth of the matter, whether he liked it or not, was that she had turned into a liability of sorts for him. A weakness—the very last thing he needed—because he did care about her, and that simply meant someone could use it against him.

Or her.

"I'll be back," he had told her, then, still waiting for her to stop hiding herself from him, "As long as you keep asking me to do it—I'll keep coming back. *I promise.* You trust me, don't you?"

It took a few more seconds before Karine had turned her face out of the pillows so he could see the tears that had welled in her eyes. Something else to cut into a heart that he thought had been dead for years.

So much for that.

"That's the thing I'm scared of most," she had whispered before he left to meet up with his father, "I trust you too much, Roman, and I don't know if I should."

That might have been easier to swallow had he not seen the look on her face when he still needed to walk out of that bedroom.

Roman wasn't so lucky.

• • •

The longer Roman was made to wait for his father, the more he regretted leaving the hotel suite in such a hurry. It didn't help that his paranoid nature chose then to remind him the longer he hung around in a public place, the bigger of a target he became for any Yazov man who might be watching him.

If they were watching.

Roman didn't know.

ᴛʜᴇPROMISE

That's why he *was* a paranoid fucker. Not knowing drove him insane. There was far too much happening that he didn't know a thing about in Chicago to feel at all safe.

He'd already called Marky to keep watch outside the diner, and his friend had arrived at the same time as himself, along with another guy from an Avdonin brigadier's crew. At least, he could rely on his best friend being punctual.

But apparently, not his father. Not that he would *ever* make that particular comment to Demyan's face. Roman was a lot of things, but stupid wasn't one of them.

And he was being a bit of a prick, to be fair. Demyan had a lot of other shit to deal with that didn't involve Roman and his manufactured problems that stemmed from a selfish want to feed his own desire.

Karine.

His bored—but careful—gaze darted to the window. Roman's booth wasn't directly next to the glass, so they easily avoided being seen unless someone was peering inside, but it meant he couldn't keep an eye outside, either. Well, not the full scope. Only a portion wasn't enough to soothe his nerves.

Marky would do his job.

And the other man.

It was all about trust, wasn't it?

Distracted by the chaotic mess inside his mind, Roman didn't even notice when Demyan finally showed up until he slid into the other side of the booth with a quick, tight smile while his hands worked to unbutton the heavy tweed jacket he wore over his suit blazer. His father had the unique ability to make a low-key entrance when he wanted to. He was also a natural at attracting the room's attention at times. Damn near the second his father sat down, all three waitresses working the diner's floor turned their booth's way until the one closest to their position seemed to win the contest.

"Just like old times," he said while Demyan surveyed the diner with a fond softness to his stare.

Demyan was also quick to check the windows—and the fact there was nothing *to* see from their favorite booth.

93

"Well, mostly. Some things still changed, son. We certainly did."

He wasn't wrong.

Roman also didn't want to get into that subject with his father at the moment when he had more pressing matters to deal with first. Undoubtedly, Demyan wanted to discuss Maxim and what he'd found out about the Yazov bratva, or the current events in Chicago, but he needed to get *his* idea across first.

Something that was just as important—even if only to him.

"I've been giving this some thought," he said before his father could start the conversation where he wanted to while the waitress moved to pour a cup of black coffee for Demyan.

Roman said it at the right time because the presence of the waitress assured his father wouldn't discuss anything but the food and weather around an unknown female. At their silence, the waitress smiled—bubbly and sing-song—with a greeting already on the tip of her tongue.

He assumed that kindness and personable attitude worked with most other people, but Demyan didn't even met the woman's gaze when she asked, "What can I get for you guys?"

His father didn't hesitate to reply, "A stack of pancakes."

Roman nodded, adding, "Blueberries only for fruit. Do they still make the whipped cream?"

"People complain about the stuff in the can unless it's for pie, so," the short brunette replied with a shrug.

"Because it sucks—whipped cream, too."

Demyan grinned to himself before saying, "Hazelnut spread—anything else is good for toppings, too. The usual. Thank you."

Before the woman could even think she'd begun earning the likely hundred-dollar tip his father would leave on the table, she was shooed with a wave of Demyan's hand and nothing more. While he *would* discuss the weather or food, if he had to, nobody could say the man liked to.

Dismissed, the waitress headed away from their table without as much as a glance over her shoulder. Demyan worked on adding sugar and cream from the table to the famously *strong* black coffee, telling his son at the same time, "You were thinking, you said—about what?"

Right.

Now or never.

"Our property in Vermont," Roman replied, already making his father's brow dip dangerously, "… maybe that's where Karine could stay. Instead of moving from one hotel to the next in the city. I think that's part of her issue, why she can't sleep. She doesn't stay in one place long enough to get comfortable, so someone is always up at one hour or the next. If you get what I mean."

Demyan picked up his coffee and took a big gulp, holding the steaming mug against his lips long enough for Roman to think it might burn, but his father had no reaction. Pain, he had learned a long time ago, was something his father *used.* Something he had managed to control.

But other than the knot in his father's brow, Demyan offered no other response to Roman's suggestion of taking Karine to their private family property in Vermont. The place was sacred—to his grandparents, even his father. For reasons he was sure he didn't even understand, but the fact his father didn't speak for more than a few seconds had Roman's heart thundering loud in his ears.

"What's happening in Chicago—why did you call me here?" he finally asked.

Clearly, something was happening.

So, let's get straight to the point, then, Roman thought. His father glanced up at him with his jaw tight, muttering, "I spoke to Maxim last night. The fucker finally returned my calls. *Imagine.*"

"And?"

Demyan chuckled dryly, shaking his head. "Honestly? I don't know anymore than I did before he called me. I have more questions than I do answers, and a part of me thinks that might have been the point."

Picking the coffee up for another sip, his father pulled it away only to say, "He ended the call about as fast as he started it. He made some strange—well, he apologized to me, and told me to convey to Karine that he loved her."

That last bit came out quieter than the rest. Offered to Roman as if he should consider it more carefully than the rest, and he did. He didn't miss it, but it didn't impress him … considering Maxim's treatment of his daughter .

Some things couldn't be forgiven.

To him.

Sitting a bit stiffer in the booth, Roman mutter under his breath, "What fucking shit is he on, or—"

"I got word about what happened last night at the Yazov mansion," his father interrupted before Roman's anger could make itself properly known. "Presumably straight after Maxim called me."

That froze him in the chair, though.

Cold.

"There was a big fire. Everything burned down. The mansion is as good as gone, or so I was told."

"The fuck," Roman said. "Seriously?"

Demyan didn't break his stare. "Roman, they found remains. Everyone else was apparently evacuated. I'm serious, yeah?"

"Everyone *except?*"

Because his father was talking like he already knew, and if that was the case, Roman would really like him to spit it the fuck out.

"Maxim. Unofficial word is that it's confirmed. The official side could take weeks to make the rounds, and I'm comfortable going with what I've got on the unofficial side of things, frankly."

Well …

Shit.

Roman fell back in his seat with a thump, his hand cupping his chin and under his throat.

Maxim Yazov was dead.

Had the plot fallen through?

Did his warning come too late?

Roman took a second before he spoke—he wasn't sure where his feelings fell on the news of Maxim's death, and he didn't owe the man anything. There was also someone else in the equation who may feel very differently when she learned her father was gone.

"Things just changed," Roman said, drawing his father's gaze to his.

Demyan nodded once. "Yes, it has. And not in a good way for us. You can be sure that Leonid and Dima are scrambling to handle the situation in their favor—just like they intended. However, that distraction isn't going to last long, Roman, and very soon they'll come looking for that girl you're hiding in your hotel room."

Roman hoped it was a slip of the tongue—that his father didn't actually keep tabs on which room Karine spent last night in.

"You'll be dead in weeks. So will she," Demyan added after a moment. "You'll have very little time once they figure out where she is, son."

He didn't need the goddamn reminder.

Roman's foot tapped a nervous beat against the tile. "Vermont. Our lodge. Did you even hear me mention it, or—"

Demyan dragged in a hard breath, shooting Roman a look that quieted him as the waitress from earlier returned with an armful of topping options that she scattered across the table.

"Five more minutes for the pancakes, guys."

"Perfect," Roman replied with a tight smile. "Thanks."

Once she was gone again, Roman waited for his father to speak first.

"Maybe the outside will do her good," Demyan finally said.

Fuck.

Really?

Roman honestly hadn't expected Demyan to give him permission to use the property, deep within the Vermont wilderness, hundreds of acres of private, raw land only accessed by two roads. Both gated, and protected. Powered by gas and solar power generators, weekly trips to a nearby town would provide pretty much everything they needed as they might need it.

But it was precious to his family, and he knew that, too. A safe haven they had used for years when the times called for it. No one *except* family and his father's most trusted men—those that Demyan chose to protect his wife, or himself, his *kids*—had knowledge or details of the place.

"The long walks and the lake," his father said with a shrug, "always helped me."

Right then felt like the proper time to give his father the other news.

"I've found someone—a doctor for her."

"Oh?"

"Nothing a bit of bribery—or blackmail—can't make work, I guess."

Roman might be trying some attempt at being the *good guy* where Karine was concerned, but he still had to be who he was at the end of the day to make shit work. He could never be a saint.

Demyan pointed at his son. "And it'll put some distance between the two of you."

Roman hadn't considered that.

Not yet.

It wasn't that he'd assumed he would stay with Karine at the lodge in Vermont either. He just hadn't considered the minor details because the overall picture had finally started to make sense to him when he had the idea in the first place.

"Karine won't like that," Roman admitted.

Quietly.

He didn't want to say it, but he felt like he should. How would she cope alone? None of this was easy.

Demyan studied him before saying, "Something tells me you don't like the idea of being far from her, either."

Right on time once again, the waitress arrived with a beaming smile and a stack of pancakes to quiet the two men. He was grateful that his father seemed happy to let the woman serve them for a moment because it gave him a few seconds to gather his thoughts.

Roman knifed through three pancakes in the stack of six as the brunette left as fast as she came. He wasn't hungry, but his body needed sustenance, and it gave him something to do with his hands. Both good things. He didn't want to delve too deep into what exactly he felt for Karine.

He didn't need to be told to know he already felt *too much*.

"Vermont does feel like the safest option for everyone," Demyan eventually said, breaking the silence between them. "I agree there, Roman. Do you understand what I'm saying?"

He nodded, but said nothing.

Understanding he'd have to be separated from Karine for a long period of time in the process of everything worried him. *A lot*. But he'd been the one to suggest it—even if he hadn't thought it through—and his father was up for the plan, *and* ready to remind him of why it was a good idea in the first place.

"It will also give you the opportunity to go about business in Brighton Beach without her in tow. If you're being watched by Dima's men, they won't know where to look for her if she's not with you. On the other side of that same coin, it may give us a bit of time if they come here expecting her with you, and she's not. Either way, it works."

"I don't need to be convinced. It was my idea."

In a sigh, Demyan murmured, "But you don't like it."

Roman could have just as easily brushed it off, and if he were a humble man, he'd admit he didn't need to say anything because his father could already see it written on his face. For once, though, he didn't want to be any kind of man except the one his father expected him to be, so all he said was, "You're right—I don't like it."

"Is it ... a sense of responsibility? A duty for what might happen to her if not for your meddling?"

Roman said nothing because what he was really thinking about was the look of disappointment and sadness on Karine's face when he was leaving the room this morning. That had very little to do with his sense of responsibility, or duty.

What was she going to say when he told her they would have to live apart for a while—would that push her back?

For once, Demyan didn't seem to mind his son's silence when it was clear he also wanted an answer. The two men ate their pancakes in silence, and eventually gulped down the remainder of their lukewarm coffee.

Roman wasn't entirely sure how he was going to break the news of Maxim's death to Karine, either. How complex and dark was the relationship with her father that she'd somehow manifested a whole identity to kill him?

What he knew to be true about Maxim's relationship with his daughter certainly didn't lend toward his final message for her. Because *yeah*, Roman hadn't forgotten about that little detail from his father—he wanted Karine to know her father loved her.

What the fuck was he supposed to do? Wouldn't it be a better idea to shield her from it now that nothing could be changed? That seemed cruel, too, but he really did believe the past should stay where it belonged.

"Your mother could join her in Vermont," Demyan said without warning, breaking Roman from his thoughts.

He looked up, then, not quite sure he'd heard his father right. "Ma?"

"You know, she used to be a nurse. Sure, she worked mainly with kids and in the NICU, but she could help if Karine needed something."

"I thought you wanted her far away from—"

"Seems our issue with Chicago, and Karine, might be around for a while. Your mother would appreciate knowing, in that case. It'll keep her safe, too, if activity picks up in Little Odessa," Demyan added.

Placing his cutlery to the table, Demyan then pulled out his wallet and left too many bills to count in the middle. The waitress, whom he didn't even particularly like, would get a decent tip—as Roman suspected.

They stood up together, the rest of the day looming ahead of both men, but for entirely different reasons, Roman suspected.

"Son," Demyan said right before he stepped away from the table. "I give it no more than a week before Dima's men start to find their way here. That's how much time you have to settle the girl in. Go to Vermont with her, but within the week, you need to be back here if you want to come out of this thing alive. Don't draw them to her."

Demyan walked away from the table after that, leaving Roman to follow him out with his parting words ringing in his ears. As casual as he made that last remark sound, Roman had seen the look in his father's eyes.

Demyan wanted to keep his son alive. Probably even more than Roman did for himself.

NINE

Roman hadn't realized just how bad he'd be itching to return to the hotel, to see Karine and reassure her that he was back, just like he promised, until he walked into the suite. And the very second he did, it was clear that Katina had been around to say hello.

The suite was *trashed*.

Broken glass scattered dangerously across the floor. The large vase from the table had found a new home, after it apparently crashed into the flat screen television on the wall. Only a trampled mess remained of the red roses that had made for a beautiful centerpiece. The coffee table had a crack down the middle of its glass top, and the further in Roman walked, the better he could see a milky substance forming puddles on the floor. Bloody drops trailed along, too.

Fuck.

The growled curse came from under his breath, but even his anger didn't diminish the panic welling in his chest. The quiet state of the chaos and the fact there was no obvious sign of a message to him didn't leave him feeling like this had been an attack on them. He called for her—Karine, first—even though every scrap of evidence in front of him screamed *Katina.*

If she was still around, she wasn't going to respond to being called Karine, either. Not by him. Not when he knew better.

"What the fuck is going on here, man?"

The irritated question came from the man who emerged from the main bathroom of the large suite. Roman stopped his search of the room at the sight of the bull nursing a wounded hand. He'd been assigned to keep an eye on Karine and the hotel—but at a respectable distance that shouldn't have caused a problem.

Still kind of seems like it did.

Despite the man's injury and demand for answers, Roman didn't really have it in him to give a shit at the moment. "How about *you* tell me what the fuck happened here— where is she?"

Tripp—a trusted man close to one of his father's spies for the organization—gritted his teeth, his only effort to keep his simmering anger at bay. It didn't take very much to remind the man of his place, and exactly what he was supposed to be doing.

"I'm not sure," the bull muttered, shrugging one shoulder. "Her carer—that other woman—is looking after her, I guess. Or, *trying* to keep her in check. The second she cut me, I figured that's what would keep happening if I went within two feet of her again. Didn't seem like a smart choice, all things considered, you know?"

Well ...

"Karine did this to you?" Roman asked, taking a cursory glance at the man's wounded hand. He couldn't see the injury, but the white towel soaked with bright red stains said the cut had been fairly deep to bleed as much as it had.

"You bet—I had no idea she had a knife shoved down the back of her pants." Tripp was still doing his best to keep his facial expressions under control, but the sharp sarcasm couldn't be missed. Clearly, he'd never been bested by a girl before—and certainly not by one who looked like her. "It's been an interesting day."

That nearly made Roman smile, but he caught himself just in time. *Barely.* The seriousness of the situation wasn't lost on him—Katina was getting worse by way of making it even more difficult to manage her.

She was the only one he felt was a wild card. Not that he couldn't trust her, necessarily, just that she worked for the benefit of one thing, and one thing only. *Herself.*

"What did you do to provoke her?"

That was the real question.

Or the right one.

The bull shook his head, the disbelief coloring his widening gaze leveling on Roman. "Man, I swear, they went down to the restaurant for breakfast. Both of them. I stood at a distance, like I was told, didn't even say hello. Everything was fine until it seemed like they were having an argument. Shit got a little loud—well, Karine did. People at the other tables started to stare, and I stepped in to see if they would like to move the conversation elsewhere. It seemed like the best choice."

Roman hands balled into fists at his side—another fucking mess to clean. A public incident wasn't something they could afford at the moment. How many people saw—how much was this hotel damage going to cost him? His mind went through a million different issues while the bull continued speaking.

"And what the fuck is her name, anyway?" Tripp asked, arching a brow. "Because you told me Karine—*just to know*, right, not to use—but the woman kept calling her something different when they were downstairs."

He opted not to respond to that, verbally or otherwise. This guy didn't need to know about the inner workings of Karine's mind, never mind her everyday life. Not that he had the answers to the questions that would come even if he did explain the different identities, either. That was half the problem.

ᴛʜᴇPROMISE

Someone needed to explain this—to him, so he could understand, and more important, to Karine. This was *her* life. How had no one given her the tools to live it?

"You must have done something to provoke her," Roman said, without inflection. "Something that made her attack you."

The bull's nostrils flared with a dark chuckle. "Let's just say she doesn't like being touched. I was just leading them back up to the suite, trying to get her into the elevator, the second my hand touched her back—"

"You touched her."

Tripp heard the dark dip in Roman's tone, and his throat bobbed with a hard swallow in reply. "She lost her shit. Like ... *crazy*, man. I've never seen someone flip so fast. And violent, she was—"

"I get it, Tripp."

The bull quieted, then. There was a part of Roman that wanted to curl his hands around the man's throat and force him to take back his words—the vicious side of himself that knew he could painfully explain to Tripp exactly *what* he had done wrong, here. The only thing worse than the sudden urge to do violence to a man who was only doing his job—without the info to properly do it, to be fair—was the fact Roman's *emotions* drove him to feel that way in the first damn place. He wasn't prepared for the way words cut into him when he heard someone bitch about Karine, or make comments that were insensitive, even if it was from ignorance.

Tripp had also made valid points about the way he did his job—it was the only thing that saved him from the violent thoughts spinning in Roman's thoughts. That, and nothing else, though.

"Footage?" Roman asked, instead.

"I'll have to look into it. I'm sure there are cameras in the restaurant, but money talks, bullshit walks," the guy replied.

Right. Almost any mess could be cleaned for the right price. Except it was still one more thing for him to do, or make sure *was* done. New things were constantly being added to the ever-growing pile of responsibilities on Roman's plate. Not that he had the time to worry about it.

From the corner of his eye, Roman noticed Masha appear at the end of the hallway.

"I'll handle it from here," he told the bull.

Tripp grumbled his way to the door, and stepped outside.

Roman turned to Masha, and noticed the bloody towel in her hand.

"She really went for it this time, didn't she," he remarked to the trembling woman.

When Roman really thought about it, he understood her, actually.

Katina, not Masha.

He could understand why and when Katina made an appearance—it was every time Karine felt like she was losing control. She answered that removal of power with brilliant violence from a beautiful face. She was vulnerability in the flesh capable of causing the worst kind of trauma.

But just because he thought he understood a facet of Katina—well, that didn't mean he had an overall picture. He had waited for the bull to leave the suite entirely before he spoke to Masha, but she still remained silent, even though she stared back at him.

He wondered, if like him, Masha had come to accept the reality, too—that the only thing they could expect from Katina was violence.

"When did she show up?" he asked, deciding each word he posed very carefully.

For good reason.

Roman suspected a lot of things about Masha, but one of them actually worked to her favor ... even if it didn't entirely work to his. Like the fact he believed she *was* loyal to Karine—probably even loved her—but that didn't mean she cared about what happened to the rest of them.

Masha's wet stare and sniffles gave away her emotions— beyond the scared and shocked she should be, there was something else. *Sadness.* Guilt.

"Do you feel it's your responsibility to keep them under control?" he asked, then, as Masha chose to remain silent.

^{THE}PROMISE

She did answer, finally.

But only to say, "Soon after you left. She was upset you had left—abandonment is her worst fear, do you understand?"

Roman opened his mouth to respond, but Masha cut in quickly, her voice still soft and mindful, but firm all the same. "No, I don't think you do ... even if you do mean her well, I don't truly think you do understand what it is like—to be the one person who knows that if you don't *help* her, no one will—but you're getting a taste."

He eased his attitude.

But not by much.

"What happened, then?"

Masha sighed. "I'd convinced Karine we'd go down and get breakfast, but she wanted to wash her face. And then she just walked out of the bathroom."

"Katina, you mean. I'm sure you know as much as I do," Roman started, "that Karine and Katina are not the same person."

Masha remained silent at that. She had no answer, and he wasn't expecting one. He did think it might be beneficial for her to know something Katina had once told him, though. The way Masha spoke made him think that it wasn't something Katina had also shared with her. Was that because Katina trusted *him*, or because she didn't trust *her*?

Roman figured ... Masha should know what he did, if only to better care for Karine. Because he did think the woman had good intentions. "Katina pretends to be Karine—she'll manipulate that way."

She stilled. Then, slowly, Masha glanced up to meet his gaze. "I wondered, but ..."

"What?"

"She's new—I couldn't pinpoint exactly when she started coming around. It could have been before the first time I met her, but I'm the last person Katina cares to speak to. You understand?"

He didn't, but he did at the same time.

And what was done was done.

Likely.

"Are you okay?" he asked, eyeing her hand.

Masha looked down, the bloody smears on her hands not at all concerning her as she nodded quickly. "Yes, of course, I'm fine. I was just cleaning up, but I heard you arrive. That man cut his hand, and there was a lot of blood."

"He cut his hand, *or* his hand was cut?"

Even her choice of words were habitual. How long had this woman been the one saving grace in Karine's life—and why did she still feel like an unknown piece to the puzzle to him? Masha kept her head down, refusing to reply or correct her words.

Roman figured—*her choice*. None of this was her fault. "Why don't you go down to reception, and see if you can find more towels, some fresh sheets, whatever you need. If someone approaches about a noise complaint, or to ask questions, tell them to call through to the room for me."

Masha looked almost relieved when she met his eyes again. "You'll be okay here?" she asked.

It took a nod of his head for her to hurry away.

Roman hadn't bothered to ask where Katina was, but frankly, he didn't really need to.

• • •

Outside the bathroom attached to the master bedroom of the suite, Roman listened to the gentle slosh of water against the marble bathtub inside. He had a mind to leave her be, if only because he could sense she was safe, but he had a feeling that wasn't how to best work with Katina.

He did knock lightly before opening the door, his only warning to his entrance. Steam rolled through the open doorway the second he stepped inside only to blink furiously to get the misty sting out of his eyes. He moved towards the bathtub where he found a pleased Katina submerged right up to her shoulders in water hot enough to turn her skin pink.

And *God*.

She was a sight.

ᵀʰᵉPROMISE

Her especially pale skin was colored only by that heated flush, but her cheeks held an extra pinch of pink. Silky dark hair had pasted to her face and chest, making her eyes look big and watery. She stared up at him with those plump lips of hers parted slightly, like she might be ready for him to lean in and take a kiss. She would make the perfect picture of a dangerous, mythical creature emerging from a misty lake, capable of seducing and devouring her victim before they even understood what had happened.

The fact he'd noticed how tempting her mouth was proved he wasn't immune to her charm.

He knew it was Katina, not Karine. He knew it from the dip in her brows, the keenness of her gaze; how the edges of her lips curled softly in a *maybe*-smile. The chill that ran down his spine while she watched him wasn't entirely cold, but it still tingled with a thread of fear. It was in her eyes that he found it—how those orbs swept him up, and then down.

Everybody was prey.

"Oh, good, you're here," she remarked, rolling her eyes.

Katina wasn't at all bothered by her nakedness, or the fact she was entirely on display for him under the hot water.

Though he wouldn't ask, he couldn't help but wonder about last night—even that morning. He'd had Karine, felt the way she shivered with delight when he'd buried himself so deep for her to take his load, then fell asleep with her in his arms only to wake up beside her. This was not the same woman. Did Katina have those memories? Had she experienced it at all?

He couldn't be more in over his head.

"I heard about what happened earlier," he noted, raising his brow as if to offer it however she wanted to take it. "Thought you might need someone to check on you—make sure you're okay."

Katina cocked her head to one side, the little knot in her brows furrowed deeply. "Why shouldn't I be okay? I'm great."

That smile grew on her face.

Sensual, and *wicked*.

Roman stepped in her direction to get a bit closer, and only hesitated when he saw her pulling a paring knife out of the bath water. She didn't do it in a threatening way, but just held it up over the water where he could see it.

Like she intended for him to know she still had it. Apparently, nobody had been able to take the knife away from her, yet.

Roman eyed the knife, then Katina again. He wasn't afraid of the weapon, and she wasn't exactly threatening him with it, so he was fine to act like it didn't really matter.

She gripped it tightly while she made the blade dance along the surface of the water, the small pot lights overhead catching the glint of the metal, and the waves of the steaming water to dance along the tile.

"You know, none of this would have happened if you had just been here like you said you would be," she told him, her tone almost careless though every word had its own impact for Roman. Now, she wasn't looking at him, as the knife in her hand had gained all of her attention.

"No, it probably wouldn't have," he agreed. "The first mistake they made was letting you go downstairs."

Katina's smile deepened into a smirk, her enjoyment of dissecting the scene of her own violent-making clear when she replied, "Well, they couldn't have stopped me even if they wanted to. I wanted to eat at the restaurant."

She turned to him with bliss-hooded eyes, and he only urged her on.

"And what did you do next? Did you ask for a knife to cut your fruit with?"

She breathed in deeply, and he made a careful effort to keep his gaze from wandering to where her breasts rose and fell, just beneath the surface of the water.

"I do like my fruit, and I like it sliced just so," Katina said with a nod and a teasing smile while Roman shook his head.

It was the sound of his disappointment falling out in a sigh that seemed to bother Katina the most when she scowled suddenly. He didn't think she actually cared about what he thought until that moment.

"That man shouldn't have touched me," she snapped.

^{THE}PROMISE

"Maybe not, but he was also trying to keep you safe."

Katina hissed a breath past clenched teeth. "You're the one who made her feel unsafe."

He stopped at that. Katina's lips trembled as she pursed them together, almost pouting, but not quite because it was clear she just wanted to *stop* herself from talking. She had allowed that split second of weakness before the stoniness returned to her eyes again.

"You're talking about Karine?" he asked.

"Yes, you already *know*. You were supposed to make her feel safe here—you didn't. We talked, remember. In the car, *we talked*, Roman. You left. Abandoned her. Made her wonder if you'd ever—"

"Of course I was coming back," he interjected, refusing to even let her get the words out. "I know that being here isn't like being back in Chicago—but goddammit, the bubble that Maxim created around your whole world doesn't exist here. I can't be in her sight twenty-four-seven. It's just not possible. There are other problems to handle. Things I have to take care of to keep her safe."

From his vantage point, he could see the dribble of blood on the blade of the knife. Most of it had been washed away in the bath water, but some remained. The faintest trickle. He watched as Katina brought the blade closer to her face, heart thudding in his chest. She was only predictable in the way that she was unpredictable. He didn't know what she was capable of doing next.

Not that he wanted to, but he watched her for the moment because he might need to stop any act of self-harm. She didn't suggest it, but he assumed the only way to know for sure was to plan for the worst, hope for the best.

"Karine doesn't understand that," Katina continued, her words a low murmur. So soft that Roman had to lean closer to hear her. He wondered if she actually meant those words for him, or just herself.

The tip of the blade met her bottom lip as her gaze transfixed on his once more. That mouth of hers—the same one he'd kissed last night, parted with his own, tasted until she was gasping for air—was now painted with the smear of

111

red dribbling down to the tip of the knife. Katina didn't seem bothered by it, although Roman didn't know whose blood it was. She licked it without warning, making every muscle in his body grow taut.

"You'll have to kill him now," she told him.

Not once did she take her eyes off him, either. It was easy to forget who the predator was in the room when she was beautiful. Heavy and thick in his throat, he forced the lust down and focused on forming the words struggling to get out.

She bobbed gently in the water, the wavy surface lapping against silky, wet pinked skin. He knew exactly how that skin felt to the touch—how soft and perfect she was sighing softly when he tasted it.

Why was he enjoying this?

She was violence and sex wrapped in one. Dangerous to him in all the worst ways.

"The bull," she replied with a casual wave of the blade, the glint catching her eye as another fleeting, vicious smile curved her lips. "Anyone who hurts me, even if it's with one touch—well, they have to die."

Roman rocked on his heels, sucking air through his teeth while he considered that statement. His mind raced to come up with a way to combat Katina on the spot. She was glowering up at him, proudly, with her chin thrust high, expecting an instantaneous answer. The only one she felt was acceptable.

He also couldn't let her think it worked that way. She was already vicious enough without him giving her an all-out pass to cut every soul that so much as looked at her in a way she thought *hurt*. There was no doubt times when she had been justified; today was a good example of the fact it wasn't *every time*.

"But you've taken care of it already. You say he hurt you, and you hurt him back," he replied. "You can trust you've taught him a valuable lesson about how you should be treated."

Katina's breasts heaved with a breath. "That's no fun."

ᴛʜᴇ PROMISE

His grin was probably too devilish for his own good. He knelt down on the tiled floor by the bathtub, meeting her at eye level. She sniffled quick, heaving her shoulders up from the tears she held back. He'd not been expecting that.

"You don't need that, do you?" he asked, nodding to the knife.

Maybe because she was done with her game, or she truly did want to give the weapon to him, Katina handed it over. The second he had the blade stuffed down the back pocket of his pants and—presumably—out of her reach should he be quick enough, Roman asked, "Is that what you were trying to do in Chicago? Hurt the people who hurt you?"

When he looked into her eyes, he expected to find the answer, even without words. That was exactly what he got because Katina said nothing.

"Don't fuck this up—I'm trying to help."

Katina's brows furrowed. "What is that supposed to mean?"

"You're a smart girl. You'll figure it out."

Her lips trembled before she hid it by pressing them in a grim line. Roman decided, they could both have their pride.

"I want to talk to Karine, and I'm sure she would like to see me. Can I have her back now?"

He didn't know if *Katina* could control when she switched. It didn't seem like Karine could. Was it *triggered*, in some ways? On-demand in others?

Jesus.

He worried that he knew as much as she did, and it wasn't nearly enough.

Katina glared at him, and he held her gaze, calmly. If there were other things she wanted to say, she didn't plan on sharing them with him today. Her nostrils flared with a shaky gulp of air, and she swung her face away from him.

He caught the way she closed her eyes tight, her body momentarily going limp almost in the same second she regained control. Still, he lunged forward to circle her sinking body with his other arm before she fell completely into the water.

Already blinking back at him, a familiar warm gaze glimmered. For a few moments, her pupils shifted from side to side, confusion tugging at her brow, but then she saw him.

That pink in her cheeks reddened. *Visible* happiness reflected in her clear, wide eyes, and it damn near took his breath away.

"You're back," Karine whispered, smiling wide.

"Yeah, babe," Roman replied, ignoring the inner emotional war that started to rage. "Of course, I am. I promised."

TEN

Karine had never been to Vermont before, but because Roman said it's where it was best to be—well, she knew she was safe. Not that she understood why they were there in the first place. Those unanswered questions were easier to ignore when he was around, though.

She was less muddled, then, not so overwhelmed by everything and everyone. More sure of herself—her feet had finally found steady ground to stand on when he was next to her.

And that was terrifying.

Vermont was beautiful. Woodlands and small county towns had guided their arrival to the private property owned by Roman's family. Or so he explained to her when she gained the courage to ask during the drive. She couldn't remember the last time she heard birds chirping in trees, but given the leaves had changed to bright yellows, oranges, and fire-reds, she didn't think swooping swallows dancing between branches would be around for long.

Lost in the beauty of the trail surrounding a serene lake that Karine thought might be nice for a swim if it was a bit warmer, she had never been … *calmer*. Happier, even. That had a lot to do with the man walking alongside her, his hand woven with her own.

"I do miss the pool," Karine said quietly.

She felt Roman's gaze slide her way at the admission, but she continued observing the quiet state of the lake. The pool in her father's house was the one thing she sincerely missed about Chicago—probably the only thing—but she didn't mind as much at the moment.

"Well, it's a little cold to be swimming in that, but another time," Roman said, tugging on her hand as the trail cut into a fork—one path leading up to the front porch of the lakehouse while the other continued around the water's edge. "If you want to come back, maybe."

She didn't reply, but she liked the sound of it. He led her on the path heading to the looming lodge with large panel windows that formed into a high triangle where the peak of the roof reached for the cloudless, blue sky.

On the porch, Karine stood next to Roman with her hands tight around the charcoal-stained banister as she peered out at the lake. She glanced at him, taking in his strong profile with his sharp nose. His dark beard was neatly trimmed again, and his white silk shirt clung to his perfectly chiseled torso. He'd left the top two buttons of the shirt undone so she could enjoy the way his throat bobbed with every swallow.

No man had ever made her feel this way—just standing beside him was a test of her control, the goosebumps were already dancing over her skin from his proximity—and she knew what she wanted from him next.

Honesty.

"Can you tell me why we're here, Roman? What we're really doing?"

He turned away from the view of the lake to meet her gaze, and she knew it, then. He planned to give her exactly what she wanted.

ᴛʜᴇPROMISE

"I've brought you here because this is the only way I know how to keep you safe," he said, never once breaking her stare as the truth came out. "There are people who might come after you—who are probably already looking for you. They'll come after both of us, but my priority right now is you."

Karine's reply was as soft as the sound of her racing heart, "You mean Dima."

Roman nodded. "You were promised to him. We both know that means something. I can bet they're not happy you're gone, but I can't say for sure whether or not they know you're with me at the moment."

Karine sighed into the sweet, fresh air that surrounded them, willing the fears starting to swirl in her mind to disappear. What else could she do? "Okay."

She hadn't expected Roman to reach for her without warning, but she didn't even flinch when his fingers brushed against her cheek as he pushed back some of the hair that had fallen across her face. As he pulled his hand away, he grazed the very tip of her nose with the pad of his thumb, saying quietly, "It's not entirely okay, but I *am* trying to make it that way, babe."

Yeah, Karine knew.

She was calm again—just like that. All it took was the sweep of his thumb, tender and quick, to stop her racing heart.

"This is the place I can keep you safe," he added after a moment, "and where you don't have to worry about a thing while I do it."

She replied with a jerky nod before looking out at the lake again. A rowing boat bobbed in the water next to a small dock, a canoe, too. The fleeting—but still undeniable—thought of how easy it would be to take one of those boats out to the middle of the lake, and finish everything that stabbed through Karine's mind at the sight. Her next breath came out shaky at the dark truth she wished wouldn't fill her thoughts with self-hating hisses of *it's true; you're useless, a burden.*

She didn't *want* to die, but none of her thoughts were a lie, either. Things could be a lot simpler; everyone's hands would finally be washed of her.

Karine even wondered if anyone would miss her.

The man beside her quickly reminded her that someone would when he murmured her name, drawing her attention once more.

"Karine," Roman said firmly. She met his eyes, hoping he couldn't see how mean her own mind could be staring back at him in the tears that formed when she blinked. His hand found her cheek, then, and stayed when he added, "I want you to know—no matter what happens, or when it happens, if where you want to be is with me, then I'll make sure you stay there. You hear me?"

At first, she said nothing. That didn't bother Roman. His thumb stroked her cheek when she curled her fingers around his wrist.

"Do you promise?" she whispered.

She was starting to believe those.

His.

"Yes," he replied without hesitation. "I promise."

Trapped under the weight of his stare and the softness of his touch keeping her happily present, Karine reveled in the sense of being free and possessed at the same time. It was such a foreign thing to her. At never wanting him to stop making promises—even if they might be all lies—or reaching for her, reminding her why she wanted to be alive.

What was he doing to her?

"I'm not really sure how to do this," she told him, waving a hand between them. "Or even what this is, you know?"

A sheepish smile answered her back. Roman's dark, husky chuckle replaced that smile with something far more tempting when he replied, "I don't know how to be that guy that does this shit, either, but I'm trying. Half the time, I'm not even sure that I'm saying the right things, but I keep saying them anyway—hoping you understand, and trust me. That's all I've got, Karine. This is it, here we are."

She'd never seen him so unguarded. Oh, she'd had him *wild*, hard, and wicked in the dark. He'd given her shiver-worthy words buried into bedsheets, but nothing quite like what he just said. Nothing so freely.

Bliss heated up the back of her neck, coloring her cheeks a soft pink when she admitted, "You're doing a good job of being that guy, though."

That made him smile again in that humble way—it was kind of sad how seldom he smiled. Except she didn't smile very often either, unless it was like this with him. She found herself smiling all too often, then.

Karine's tongue swept nervously over her bottom lip as another question danced in the back of her mind, and since he was already being open and honest … "But keeping me safe from Dima isn't the only reason you've brought me here, is it?"

Roman lifted a single brow high. "How did you—"

"I wasn't always sleeping when you were on the phone during the drive. Even if you thought I was."

He only shook his head, but his grin didn't falter a bit. "Good to know. And yeah, I found someone who can help. *You*, I mean. They might be able to help you, or give you advice and assistance for a bit. At least, while you're here. If you're open to it—I won't make you do it, Karine."

She doubted he knew it—or, maybe he absolutely did— but Roman was the first person to actually do something to help her. He recognized she needed it when everyone else had been fine to ply her with medication and hide her away where she couldn't be seen.

It also wasn't that simple.

Karine couldn't blame everyone else without admitting some of her own faults, too. She hadn't entirely accepted that something was wrong, even if she knew it, that didn't mean she understood it, but at least she was willing to say she *had to*.

Wasn't it time?

His hands slid lower, curving along the column of her neck and further down until he was cupping her shoulders at both sides. She was still on solid ground with him—she might not be the pillar holding up in the storm, but she didn't have to be if he was there.

"It's normal to feel afraid of the unknown, huh?"

She laughed, light and airy. "That might be the only normal thing about me, then."

He hadn't been expecting that, but his answering laughter was a beautiful sight to behold all the same.

"You know what, maybe that's what people should like about you," he replied, quieting Karine's laughter just like that. "It's exactly what I like about you."

Well, then …

• • •

The petite woman sitting at the other end of the sunlit day room in a royal blue pencil skirt was cream silk blouse, was a psychotherapist who had essentially been blackmailed to be there. Karine had figured that much out already—it was all the other details that she didn't have bothering her. There was no other way to explain the doctor's sudden presence when she had a feeling that doctors like the one staring at her had referral and wait lists as long as they were tall.

Karine didn't hide the fact that she was openly assessing her as much as the woman was trying to study her, too. She'd barely let the doctor get a sentence or two out before demanding her own information.

What was she doing here? How had she made her way to the middle of Vermont?

Karine knew Roman had brought her here, but on what grounds? How much was she being paid?

Every question came out faster than the last, and by the time Karine was done asking all she had to ask, the two found themselves in an uncomfortably long staring contest.

That was fine.

Karine had time.

As it turned out—the doctor did, too.

"You don't trust easily, do you?" she asked Karine after minutes ticked by in silence.

Karine frowned. "What did you say your name was again?"

"Michelle. Michelle Yang."

Right.

THE PROMISE

Ph-fucking-D.

"I don't know you to trust you."

Michelle lifted one shoulder as if to silently say, *and?* "Would you like me to tell you things that are important to know about me?"

"You still haven't answered my questions."

The doctor nodded with a laugh, but her joy was short-lived when she replied, "My brother has a gambling problem, and he ended up owing money to the wrong people. Not that I don't understand *why* he's found himself where he has, I do, but he makes it hard to care sometimes. His children, though ... well, I do care a great deal about what happens to them. So, here I am, Karine."

From the way Michelle avoided looking at the far end of the room—where Roman sat watching the exchange without inserting himself because Karine asked him to be there—it was highly likely that the *wrong people* her brother owed money to were the Avdonins. Or someone with close enough connections to Roman's family that he had been able to pull weight.

The woman hadn't wanted Roman to be in the room with them. In fact, she'd insisted on privacy to facilitate the most effective first meeting and *session*. But that wasn't what Karine wanted; to be alone with a stranger, already twisting inside from anxiety eating her alive.

She didn't think this would be easy, but *goddammit* ... it didn't have to be hard, either. She wanted Roman with her every step of the way, if he would be there, and hadn't been able to suppress the smile when he agreed to be in the room with her.

There was something settling about knowing he was willing to face all the darkness with her, to peel back the layers and uncover everything there was to find inside her. Even the things she didn't know about herself. It felt a bit like Pandora's box, really, but some things just had to be done.

So fine.

She'd do it with him.

As comfortable and safe as she felt with Roman, Karine couldn't say the same about the woman who was there to help her. Part of it could certainly be blamed on the invisible itchiness under Karine's skin making itself known—the undeniable urge to flee from the conversation they were about to have. The rest of it was just … her nature.

Karine couldn't help it.

Everyone hurt her. Not a single soul had ever given a shit about her, and she wasn't going to start trusting that had changed just because the woman introduced herself as a specialist at the top of her field.

She peeked Roman's way, then.

Well, almost everyone.

Every time she came close to leaving the room, she turned to look at Roman, and he would nod at her. It encouraged her to stay. Just a little longer, to see if the feeling improved. Honestly, that was the *only* thing keeping here there at the moment.

"How about," Michelle said, "I ask a few simple things … just to be sure what you're dealing with? I was told a little bit, and I suspect that's really what'd you like from me, Karine. To *know*."

She dragged in a stinging, shaky breath. "Yeah, I would."

"So, can I ask?"

"Okay."

Michelle nodded with a smile, and glanced down at the black notebook in her lap. "Why don't you start by telling me if there are chunks of time in your day to day life—when you just black out? Do you have moments like that? A lot of time where you don't remember what happens or how you end up where you do."

Karine stared at the woman who was examining her, trying to focus on the shape of the spectacles resting on the bridge of her freckled nose instead of her voice.

Yes, there were times like that.

Much too often.

Michelle glanced up at Karine's silence, but she managed to tip her chin down in a half-nod that at least did its job. It was enough for the doctor to make a note of it in her book.

<small>THE</small> PROMISE

"How often in a week? Less than ten, more—"

"It depends."

"Why is that?"

The answer was not so easy.

Karine glanced over her shoulder at Roman who sat exactly where he had been a few minutes ago. His presence gave her strength, but it didn't dull the sharp, blinding shame that spiraled through her when she told the doctor, "Some weeks were worse than others—the medications didn't help when it came to having any real understanding of time, or days ... specific months, even."

Michelle met her stare, asking only, 'What medications?"

"I really don't know ... well, you see—"

"That wasn't something Karine had a choice in—it was just a method used by people around her to keep her compliant, and manageable," Roman spoke up from his side of the room. The first time he did, and she was grateful that he saw her struggle and was willing to help.

The doctor didn't even look his way, but did make a note of it in her notebook before coming back to Karine with a gentle smile. "Okay, back to the time thing. Other people know, don't they? They are aware of exactly what you did in the time you find yourself losing?"

"I mean, Masha says stuff sometimes, and other people do, too, but *I* don't know ... I never did what they say I did."

Her words came out in a rush while her hands trembled where she had folded them in her lap. She didn't like that idea at all. It nearly made her sick to think about how much time she couldn't account for—empty spaces in her memory where there was just *nothing*. She was always brought back to consciousness with a gasp, and a throbbing ache at the back of her head, and she couldn't quite say it felt like waking up.

Because it didn't.

Unable to stand the crawling sensation under her skin, or sit still a moment longer, Karine stood up from her chair with a jerk. She needed to move to do this—to give those thoughts in her mind space to breathe.

The woman's gaze stayed on her as she paced the length of the room, and so did Roman's.

"But then I have times when I see things—like I'm remembering them," Karine said as she toyed with the ends of her hair, still pacing. "But they don't feel like *mine*."

"Do you hear them?"

"Sometimes."

"Have you seen any evidence from the other identities?" Michelle asked when Karine rounded the middle of the room and headed right back for the windows in mid-stride. "Something that interests them but has nothing to do with you?"

"Drawings. Sketches left by Katee."

It pained her to say one of the names—to finally accept it for what it was—because a part of her had been avoiding doing that. Just … *saying it*. Out loud.

"Are they any good?"

Karine shrugged at that question. The truth wasn't hard to say, she just didn't care to do it because it didn't matter. No matter how hard she tried, she would never be able to recreate those sketches herself. They were made by a different person. And yeah, they were good.

What difference did it make?

"Do you hear voices that you don't recognize, or that other people can't hear—ones you can't explain, that say things you're frightened of, maybe? Or do you see things other people can't or don't see?"

"No."

Silence filled the room. The only sound was the scratching of the pen while Michelle made more notes in her book. Maybe she was waiting for Karine to continue, but she didn't know what to say. Eventually, she found her way to the tall windows where she could enjoy the view of the lake and towering trees with sprinkling leaves.

"Do you want me to explain Dissociative Identity Disorder to you? Perhaps you don't fully understand it—the *mechanics* of it, we'll say. Although, I'm not fond of that word. It's very distinctive from other disorders in certain ways, but DID itself can look very different from person to person."

Karine's reflection showed the proof of her flinch, but no one else could see it except her. The woman had already mentioned the name of the disorder in the initial course of their conversation, but she had been quick to turn the questions around on the doctor at that point.

But there it was.

Karine looked over with her heavily hooded eyes. The woman continued.

"The most common question I'm asked from patients is what makes DID different from say, a disorder like schizophrenia, or even a state of psychosis where you're hearing voices—and the answer is simple. Those are chemical, the voices they hear don't exist. Yours do. Essentially."

Still wary, Karine blinked, taking that in.

Michelle didn't miss a beat, continuing on, "Something has happened in your past, maybe several incidents. A trauma, of sorts, a memory that you have fought very hard to suppress. Those with DID often say they've collected traumas, each shattering into fragments, and with it, a new identity who takes those memories and moments on as their own. There's not always a new one with every trauma, but the bigger point there is—"

"Does it go away?"

Across the room, the woman in the perfectly pressed pencil skirt and expensive blouse took a moment to set her pen down on the notebook in her lap before she removed the black-rimmed glasses from her face. Karine was glad Michelle took her time to consider a reply before she just blurted one out, and that she regarded Karine with kindness and sympathy as she did it.

"I'm sure you remember when I said it can look different from person to person?"

"And?"

"It has disappeared in some individuals, with therapy and time."

"What about meds, or something?" Karine asked.

"It's not chemical, Karine. Medication doesn't actually work for DID—you can't medicate away identities that exist inside of you. Some people do well in therapy, and find that the fragments come back together again ... others live with their disorder and identities for the rest of their life."

Karine picked at her nails as she tried to figure out what that could man. "Will there be ... more of them?"

"Not necessarily."

"But maybe."

"Not everyone is the same," the woman reiterated.

She waited again for Karine to comment, but none was forthcoming. Karine just wanted to listen, and assimilate. Absorb it all—*make it make sense*. Or make it better. She wasn't really sure which.

Or if that was possible.

She wanted it to be, though. Wasn't that what Roman asked of her before this session? To not fight it, to approach it with an open mind, and no matter what she heard in this room—he would still want to kiss her outside of it.

So, that's what she was doing.

Trying.

"From what I understand about your case," the woman continued, throwing Roman another cursory glance. "From what I've been told, I should say, one of your identities appeared at a very young age, right?"

"Katee," Karine spoke up, braver now than she had been. "Although I don't think she's been around lately. Maybe she's gone."

The last time Katee appeared was that night in New York when she drew a sketch of Roman when he was asleep. No one had suggested to Karine that the little girl showed up since, and she couldn't bring forth any of those foreign memories to say different, either. She desperately wanted this woman to tell her that was a good sign, but she had a feeling that wouldn't actually be the case.

The psychotherapist made more notes in her book, and then looked up again with a purse of her lips. "It's possible that she's gone, but I'd be careful to say so with confidence. There have been many instances where an identity has altogether disappeared over time. Sometimes through therapy and circumstances improving, the mind shifts back together like I said, but other people have had identities just

THE PROMISE

… leave for no apparent reason. But if—again, as I understand your situation from what's been explained to me—you've only had specific identities that haven't left, then perhaps Katee isn't gone. She's just … fine where she is."

Karine released the breath she'd been holding, but she couldn't tell if it was from relief, or not. In some ways, it felt like it. For others, not so much.

Either way, she found Michelle was saying exactly the things Karine needed to hear. In between the things that scared her, or left her worried, there was hope. Not perfection, but it didn't need to be. She just wanted *something* …

The woman talked like Karine could have it. Whatever *it* was.

Her throat felt dry with nervous excitement, and she gulped it down. Michelle continued staring, her gaze turning curious in a blink, and Karine sensed another question was on the horizon.

"Maybe if Katee felt safe and secure enough to disappear … even if for a while, I wonder if that means the circumstances that caused her to appear in the first place have disappeared, too? You see," the woman murmured, folding her hands neatly into her lap, adding quieter, "Awareness of the identities often brings with it memories … be they shattered, or not your own, as you say. Some are still there. Maybe yours aren't, but I feel like I should ask. Do you remember what happened to you, Karine?"

She turned away, then, her throat was still dry, but it wasn't quite the same. The excitement she felt a moment ago had quickly turned into fear.

Why did Michelle have to ask *that*?

Why?

Things were going so well, too. Fear wouldn't let her speak, though, it never had.

"I don't want to talk about monsters today," Karine replied in a whisper.

ELEVEN

Claire arrived the day after Karine's first session with the psychiatrist. Roman didn't want to make a big deal of it, in fact, he didn't even want to introduce his mother as a nurse, and spook Karine. That wasn't why he wanted his mother there to begin with, even if it *was* a benefit.

Then, Karine's face had brightened the moment Claire walked into the lodge, and he introduced her as, "This is Claire, my mother."

He hadn't been entirely sure of just how much information was given to his mother about Karine, but didn't seem like an important thing to worry about when the two first meet. The connection was instant—Claire's natural kindness and maternal presence had always surrounded her like an aura someone could feel when they were close enough to her. Karine was sucked in like a magnet.

Roman wondered if that was because of the absence of a *real* mother-figure in her life. Even though she had a caretaker who clearly took over some aspects of a mother, he didn't quite think that was the same. Karine probably just wanted someone she could learn from—who would have nurtured her, and kept her safe the way a mother does.

He shouldn't have worried about Claire's arrival at all, honestly. Karine was staring, her eyes wide open and excited, and instantly a smile spread on her face that made Roman nervous.

The only true model of love that he had witnessed was what existed within the relationships of his family—his mother and father, grandparents. That didn't mean Roman had ever been able to grasp what it felt like, but the way Karine's smile formed so brightly, making his heart race with a nervous happiness, when he introduced her to his mother might have been the closest thing to him finally understanding it.

Love.

Or what it meant to be in love.

Roman didn't really have time to work through the realization because in the next second, he was watching his mother throw her arms around Karine in a welcoming hug.

"And you must be the beautiful Karine I've been hearing so much about," Claire said.

He was once again reminded how different Karine and Katina were when she sunk willingly—and with a wide smile—into the embrace. But then again, he couldn't say he had ever seen Karine hug Masha that way, either. So, *wholly.*

Maybe it was just his mother, and the effect she had on everyone around her.

"I'm sorry, I don't know very much about you," Karine admitted as the two pulled away, and Roman stayed a step or two back from then, "but it's nice to meet you."

Claire laughed at that, reaching for Karine's hands to clasp tightly with her own.

All Roman could do was stand back and watch them, a little on edge because he'd already witnessed new things and change could be hard on Karine. Yet, neither of the women seemed to notice his presence in the room, content to greet one another whether he was there or not.

"For some reason, my son likes to keep me a secret," Claire said with a roll of her eyes, and a teasing grin thrown Roman's way.

Karine's smile grew even wider at that, finally turning to face him. "Well, you and I have that thing in common, then."

It still astonished Roman how Karine managed to have a sense of humor in the middle of the chaos that was currently her life. That wasn't easy, but it spoke to her character more than he thought she even realized. She was stronger because of it.

What a fucking shame.

He thought she should know it.

• • •

They had lunch together that was prepared by his mother—if she was there, she had to cook—and enjoyed the meal in the sunroom where Karine and Claire managed to thoroughly make him feel like the third wheel. The entire time. Not that he really minded. Roman was just glad to taste a home cooked meal, made by his mother. He couldn't remember the last time he'd been able to eat her food. God knew there was nothing like his mother's cooking.

After lunch, the psychiatrist, Michelle, who had agreed—or rather, been *assigned*—to remain at the lodge for the duration of Karine's isolation suggested that she take Karine for a walk. He wasn't fucking keen on that idea, as it was better for him to assume the woman's intentions than just *trust* what she said. Regardless of what they might be. She was there to help Karine, blackmailed, *yes*, but she would still be paid well for her time in the end, beyond just her brother's debts.

Nonetheless, she *was* there to help. He had to keep reminding himself of that, even after Karine agreed to the private walk.

There would always be bulls keeping an eye on Karine at all times, even when she was just going for a walk on their grounds. So really, he didn't need to be paranoid, but he couldn't help himself. He had never worried about someone—*not like this*—as much as he did for Karine.

It was constant.

Festering, almost.

Roman decided to give her some time alone with Michelle, while he stayed back to help his mother with the dishes. Or rather, his mother made the suggestion but when she did so, it really didn't come off like he had a choice. Besides, he wasn't stupid. Michelle had a job to do that was imperative to Karine's well-being and recovery, and this was a part of the reason why they were there in the first place.

His foolishness was not.

Standing together in the kitchen, side by side at the sink, he dried while his mother washed—something that reminded him of his childhood. Despite the help his mother always had in the form of maids, and even a chef at times, she still liked to wash her own dishes. Especially after a meal.

Roman did, too.

They had spent a lot of time as a family at the Vermont lake property when he was growing up. Over the years, they had extended and added to the lodge itself to turn it into a massive mansion-like structure that still retained the look of a log cabin in the middle of the woods. Only a *big* one. It was supposed to be a home-away-from-home for them, and the Avdonins had achieved exactly that.

Five families could comfortably fit inside the home and live in peace with room to spare, and across the lake, a smaller lodge was owned by close friends of his grandfather.

So, the decision to bring Karine to Vermont was an easy one. While a war may rage outside, she would be safe here. Or at least, Roman hoped she would.

"You know she has every chance of getting ... I'm not sure better is the right word, but—well, it's the best I have."

His mother's off-handed comment interrupted his thoughts, making him blink to focus on her again. She gave him a soft smile of understanding. Like she knew what was on his mind—*Karine*. Her words also served to let him know she did have a bit of an idea about Karine's overall situation, and not just minor details.

Good.

His father saved him that conversation.

"Better is as good of a word as any, Ma," he returned with a shrug. "She's in a better place as it is. And yeah, I'm hopeful even if nothing says I should be. Michelle Yang is one of the top in her field. If she can't help Karine, then I don't know who can."

"You understand, though, that it depends very strongly on whether the patient wants to do their part in recovery and healing. It doesn't matter how much money you throw into care, or what kind of doctor you have on hand, *they* have to want it, too. Do you feel like she does?"

"I think she does, most of the time it seems like she does. It's not … it's not a clear path, not every day is the same, you know?"

Claire smiled at him warmly, and with just that look alone, the kindness of his mother dragged him in like a magnet, too. Undoubtedly the best soul being he knew to be genuine, and loving. Unlike his father, and most men in their life, his mother was always willing to give people a chance. She found the good in the bad, actively creating silver linings of her own making whenever she needed to do it. There was no better suited and qualified person to keep an eye on Karine when he did have to finally leave … he took solace in that.

It helped.

A little.

"DID manifests itself in a variety of ways, which is why it is so difficult to treat. As it is with most mental health issues, the disorder can be unique from person to person, but especially so with this disorder. So, recovery techniques and timelines all depend on the person's individual situation— some people never lose their alters while others—"

"Michelle explained a bit of that," he said. At his mother's questioning stare, he added, "Karine asked me to sit in on her first session."

Not that he would have given anyone a choice. Maybe the *illusion* of one while he stood directly outside the open door. Karine was his top priority. No excuse.

^{THE}PROMISE

"Ah," his mother murmured in a low hum, and he recognized that tone. It was the same one she was careful to use whenever she would be delivering bad news, and didn't want to cause alarm. Like the time she told him his dog had died. "Well, I wonder if her situation is trickier. Considering what her life must have been like hidden away, untreated with no real care or help … the circumstances that caused the disorder." Claire sighed, shaking her head but still managing a smile. "Well, those are all things she has time to deal with now, right?"

Karine's first session with Doctor Yang had certainly left him feeling inspired about their situation. He found himself more reassured as his mother spoke that he was doing the right thing here. Even if he was in over his head.

"I don't know what to expect from here, really, and I'm sure I've taken on more than I can handle," he admitted, though it was the hardest thing he'd had to do. Mostly because it was more than just Karine's DID—that was only one part of the equation of unknowns around her.

And him.

Them.

Was there even a *them* to begin with?

There it was—yet another unknown to leave him feeling unsure of himself, or everything else. Either way, Roman felt fucked. He didn't show the mess of his feelings to his mother. She didn't need to know, but he'd be a damn liar if he said she didn't already just by staring at him.

She was his mother, after all.

Claire nodded.

"I'm not sure if you want to hear it, but for the record, I do think you have given her the best chance by bringing her here … the doctor, too. All of it, Roman. I'm sure any of it is better than what she had."

Claire turned the faucet off, then, and dried her hands on the towel he'd been using for wet dishes, before turning to her son. The pride he found staring back from her surprised him, but left him confused, too. He couldn't understand what his mother had to be proud of where he was concerned.

"She's also here because I fucked up again," he told Claire.

Because even if she didn't know those details—she hadn't said one way or another—he did, and that was enough.

"I don't think you're giving yourself enough credit, baby," his mother replied with a soft pat of her palm against his cheek.

He couldn't remember the last time she'd called him that, and his chuckle hid the choked edge to his words when he said, "Been a long time since I was a baby, Ma."

Claire didn't miss a beat. "You're always *my* baby."

Right.

Moms were moms.

"Yes," she added after a moment, giving him a nod, "you've taken on more than you can chew, or rather, more than you're used to, but it's one bite at a time, Roman. That's how you eat an elephant. A single bite at a time."

If only that analogy applied.

"Except I'm not dealing with the same kind of shit I'm used to here."

"If there's anyone who can bring that girl out of her dark place—it's you. I've seen the way she looks at you. She trusts you. God, she looks for you even when you're in the same room. That is huge for someone with a complex sense of self like she must have. To find someone they can trust completely, think about it."

Roman did.

He didn't *want* to, though. Self-doubt was a real thing, and he'd been battling it more often than not lately. He wasn't proud of that.

Their gazes drifted to the kitchen window over the sink as Karine and Michelle came into view. The two women walked the trail that weaved throughout the dense trees at the rear of the property. He couldn't see her face clearly, but the way she walked with her shoulders loose and her hands gesturing at the leaves above, he knew she was okay.

Christ.

He wished that helped his heart, or the worry still drumming deep. Here he was worrying about Karine's reaction when he left, but how was he supposed to deal with it if this was how he felt when she was just outside?

"Your father was right," his mother said, breaking through his thoughts again. "She's just ... she seems so fragile."

He said nothing to that, he knew better. Karine was much stronger than she appeared, even if she was breakable, too. He'd learned that on his own, and he honestly believed it was better for others to do the same. They'd have a better respect for Karine, fragile or not.

"Thank you for doing this, Ma," he said instead. "For being here."

Claire gently brushed her fingers on her son's cheek, and he pulled her in for a hug. He'd stolen a quick one earlier, but this was different. *Longer.* Tighter, with her hand sweeping his back like she'd done so many times before. Fuck, he'd missed his ma. So much.

She laid her head on his shoulder, and he kissed the top of his mother's head.

While she drummed her fingers affectionately on his chest, she told him, "You know I would do anything for you, Roman. You're mine. I love you. That's what people who love us do."

• • •

His mother left him in the kitchen, saying she wanted to have a bath and call Demyan. He'd rolled his eyes at that— remarking at how they were going to spend hours talking on the phone just because they would be apart for a while.

"I'm sure you're starting to understand it yourself. As they say, distance makes the heart grow fonder," Claire had replied, giving her son a happy wink as she left.

And that, in a nutshell, was his mother.

Roman cracked open a can of beer from the fridge and made his way to the front porch, knowing good and damn well he'd opened up too much to his mother maybe. It wasn't like he screamed *share the feelings*, but then again, she could read him like a book. He didn't really regret what he told her, not when he needed someone to listen.

The front veranda was his favorite part of the house. It overlooked a hill on one side, and the lake waiting at the very bottom.

He had spent hours here, drinking with his grandfather, toughening his liver, Anton once told him, when he was a teenager. Just the thought of Anton made him want to speak to the man. His grandfather would have all the answers, or at the very least, he'd say what Roman needed to hear.

He made a mental note to call him soon, just as Karine and Michelle appeared at the bottom of the hill. They'd taken the trail down and around fast.

He noticed, then, so fucking aware of how his heart always seemed to quicken every time Karine came into view. Michelle was already walking away, headed towards the other end of the large lodge where she was being housed. He'd given her the option of using the smaller property across the lake, but she opted to be in-house with Karine to get as much time in with her as possible.

Karine looked to be in a better mood now—she smiled with a wave at him from the bottom of the hill. He considered going down the path and meeting her halfway, but he wanted to watch her walking towards him. Wanted to focus on the way her hips swayed sensually in that flowy yellow dress she was wearing. Even the way the gray shawl she'd taken outside draped the delicate line of her shoulders. Or how her hair blew in soft waves behind her from the cool breeze.

He could get used to this.

Watching Karine.

From the corner of his eye, he saw one of the bulls at the front of the house, tucked off to the side near a bush. The guy had been on the phone, but now he was putting it away and walking towards Roman, too.

"For fuck's sake," he grumbled under his breath.

What next?

Just when he was settling in to enjoying this scene with Karine, someone had to interrupt it.

ᵀᴴᴱPROMISE

Peter hurried to Roman, but Karine was still only halfway up the hill. He waved at her to make sure she knew he wasn't trying to blow her off.

"What the fuck is it now?" Roman asked, not trying to hide his contempt at all.

The bull was unaffected. That should have been bad sign number one.

"You have to hurry up here," the man replied.

"What are you talking about?"

"I've just spoken to Marky. He's been trying to get in touch with you directly, but your phone's been turned off since you got here, basically. They need you back at Brighton Beach pronto. You're going to have to leave as soon as possible."

The fuck?

"Says who?" Roman asked, narrowing his eyes at the man. He was also aware of Karine edging closer. This was not a conversation he wanted to have in front of her.

"The FBI," the guy replied. "Apparently."

Roman threw a nervous glance in Karine's direction, just to check how close she was, but thankfully, she was still out of earshot. "What do you mean the *FBI*?"

"They've been sniffing around—asking people questions about the shit that went down in Chicago," Peter replied, shrugging, "A couple of agents trying to get a sit-down with the boss, or someone else. Maybe you. Who knows?"

"And if the FBI has somehow made a connection between me and the Yazovs, then Leonid and Dima can't be far behind," Roman muttered to himself. "That's just fucking perfect."

Not.

Peter didn't offer Roman any other option when he said, "The order came down from your father—he wants you to head back to New York *fast*. Get the hell out of here before they find you here, and start watching your every move."

Roman clenched his teeth so hard his jaw actually clicked.

"You're leaving me here?"

Oh, Christ.

He'd become so absorbed in what Peter had to say that he hadn't noticed her walk up behind him in no time at all. He thought he had a few more seconds with her out of earshot, but no. Not that it would have helped because he hadn't even heard her steps approach. Karine was good at that—floating.

Roman whipped around to face her, and immediately saw the heartbroken expression on Karine's beautiful face. Whatever hope and happiness she had built in the past hour evaporated into thin air. Her smile was gone, and it cut him deep.

Behind him, he could hear the bull shuffling away with a quiet, "Shit, sorry, man."

He didn't give the guy any more attention, instead focusing on Karine to say, "I have to go, but I'll be back, just like I did last time. It's no different—you can trust me."

She moved closer to him, searching his eyes frantically for a lie. He wasn't sure how much longer he could keep looking at her because this wasn't going to end well. He could already tell—she was panicking.

"So, you're just going for a meeting somewhere? Is it for a few hours, or—"

It was like a dagger was being thrust deep inside him and twisted into his heart before being ripped back out again. Emotional pain was just as real as physical, he was learning.

"No, not for a few hours. I have to go back home for a while. I'll leave tomorrow, so we'll have tonight together before I head out. At least."

He offered that lamely.

She didn't miss it.

Karine squinted, her brows dipping dangerously as her eyes flashed like lightning. Through tight lips, she asked, "For how long?"

"I don't know," he had to admit.

Not that he wanted to.

He wouldn't lie, though.

Not to her.

ᵗʰᵉPROMISE

She shook her head, and before he could reach for or stop her, Karine had twisted away from him and was running back in the direction of the lake.

He considered letting her go—but not for long.

Roman headed down the pathway after her, but not with quite as much speed. She was too close to the lake, and he'd seen that look in her eyes before when she first saw it—like she'd already decided that if things ever got worse, that's where she'd be headed. Deep under those calm, dark waters. He didn't trust her to not hurt herself, not when she felt like he was betraying her. Even if that wasn't true. That didn't mean her feelings weren't quite real to her.

He reached her just at the bottom of the hill, some distance from the lake, thankfully. Catching her from behind, he pinned her to his chest. Her breaths came out hard, and he could feel her quivering, her shoulders heaving. She didn't fight—too hard.

"Karine, stop, please, you need to talk to me," he murmured in her ear, dragging in her floral scent with his next inhale. She always smelled like a wild meadow, fresh and free.

She relaxed quickly, sooner than he expected, really, her muscles lightening in his hold. She liked being held by him as much as he liked holding her. If only that was the case now. He loosened his grip on her, but that was a mistake. She slipped away from him.

"Karine, stop!" Roman grabbed her wrists that time, refusing to let her go even if she did flinch from his tight hold. "You're not going to do this right now."

His words didn't help.

"You don't have to worry, Roman," Karine hissed, her eyes filled with tears. "I don't want to jump in the lake, I just want to get away from *you*."

Fuck.

Those were the words to kill him.

That was all he needed to see.

Karine crying was his kryptonite. He released his grip, and she stepped away from him, but then she stopped. With eyes already reddened from the tears flowing freely down her cheeks, she glared. If only she'd just *listen* … let him talk, then maybe he could explain—

"So, when were you going to tell me that you've brought me here just to leave me as soon as you could, huh?"

Her lips quivered, and he could tell it was hard for her to get the words out. But she believed them, too. Every single one of them. That's what made this harder.

If only she would just let him hold her then he would try and make this better, but he couldn't. She didn't want him to. He held his hands up where she could see them, clear as day.

He was not a threat.

Not to her.

"I didn't know when to bring it up," he replied honestly, "Or when it would've been appropriate. I wanted to give you a chance to settle in here, first."

"No. You were just going to disappear. That's what your plan is. To avoid any *conflict*. I'm not stupid, Roman."

He wished she didn't move so quickly to wipe away the tears and then work so hard to hide the next round. The sight of her visibly struggling to hold back her hurt made him *angry*. Her weakness was not a vulnerability to him in the way she thought it was. It wasn't something he was going to use, abuse, or otherwise.

"I wouldn't do that to you, Karine. Just abandon you, *fucking never*. I would have told you I was going to have to leave, but I wasn't expecting it to be this soon. Circumstances have changed. That's life, okay?"

She looked away from him, and for a moment, it felt like she was trying to pretend he didn't exist. That hurt even worse; a million little slices over already-deep and bleeding cuts.

Roman stepped in her direction and was relieved that she didn't step away. He hadn't even told her about her father. She had no clue Maxim was dead. How was she going to react to that information? He wanted her to give him a chance to explain, but she still wouldn't even look at him.

"Karine …" he tried to say, urging her to look at him again.

THE PROMISE

She did.

When she glared at him, and then strode right past.

Karine headed up the hill again, and he didn't need to be told to understand she didn't want him following her. She still told him, anyway.

"Just leave me the fuck alone," she called back, the words carrying to him in the wind.

Another thousand, invisible littles cuts were left in their wake. Roman stood there helpless to feel every single one of them while he watched her walk away.

TWELVE

The FBI agents had been on Demyan's radar long before he was on theirs thanks to a contact he had with the bureau—or rather, a woman in the bed of a man from the bureau. It paid to know the right people.

As he sat behind the desk in his home office, waiting for the arrival of the two agents he expected to meet shortly, Demyan already knew more about them than they ever would about him. In fact, he spent his time flipping through a file on both of them while he watched the camera footage of his front gates where their black, nondescript sedan would soon appear. It was one of three security cameras he'd recently had installed on the property, in very carefully chosen locations for reasons like tonight.

He'd dealt with a few officials in the past—cops, more times than he could count, but a handful of agents from the FBI had crossed his path before, too. The two whose file had come attached with pictures were not familiar faces.

Fucking perfect.

ᴛʜᴇPROMISE

More pests to watch.

He was sure they were fully aware of who he was—nature of the business, considering the FBI had been created for the very purpose of catching criminals like Demyan. His contact simply allowed him the very valuable time to do his research on them, too.

Maybe the bastards thought they were going to surprise him by turning up at his house in the middle of the day, but he had unfortunate news for them. This was exactly where Demyan wanted them. On his turf, on his terms. There wasn't much he could do to avoid a confrontation with the FBI when their investigation related to the recent Yazov activity probably connected his son to it.

He could control how that confrontation happened, though.

At least, he'd acted fast enough to send Claire away. He didn't want these fucks breathing anywhere in his wife's vicinity.

He had two of his men in the room with him—one, a brigadier he considered a friend, and the man's bull, just because. He could have chosen other men, higher ranking men in his bratva, but what mattered the most was that he had *anyone* there. Vor or vory who would be trusted enough to ensure his activity with the FBI didn't break their code of conduct. He'd have gotten his father there, but the agents decided to speed up their visit by a day, and left Demyan with no choice but to call on who he had closest.

Demyan didn't mind witnesses.

Both stood behind his chair. One—his friend—shifted his weight from one foot to the other. It was his cue. Demyan looked up at the screen to see a black car drive up to the gates. A bull stationed there went through the instructions to ask a few general questions before letting them through, despite the badge they flashed in his man's face. As if that made a fucking difference.

Demyan shuffled the pages back into the file in front of him, unhurried and already over the meeting before it could properly begin, and handed it back to one of the men behind him.

He didn't like doing this. Beyond the fact that it was a fucking waste of his time to sit down with agents he had no intention of actually engaging, it meant putting their operation at risk. But it had to be done.

Especially if he was going to protect Roman, and the girl. *Christ.*

Couldn't forget Karine.

Claire had been all too happy to let him know just how much she already liked her. He was entirely unsurprised because he didn't expect anything different from his wife after he'd let it slip that he was positive Roman was more than just interested in the young woman.

It was more than that for him, though. Maxim was dead, and while he didn't feel like he owed the man anything, someone had to keep his daughter safe. If it was Vera, Demyan's daughter, he would expect *someone* to do the same.

The empty glass in front of Demyan was finally noticed by one of the men behind him, and then filled with vodka without a word. He picked it up, and took a sip, and then another as he waited for the inevitable arrival of his guests.

He considered downing the glass.

It would be his third.

Nah.

No more, he told himself as he put the glass back where it belonged, still half-full so his man didn't go for another refill when it didn't need it.

Demyan needed to think straight—like fuck would an official trip him up in his own home. That just wouldn't happen.

The fifteen minutes it took before there was finally a knock on his door went by in silence. The Avdonin family estate was big, the home a maze. It took them time to arrive at his office, but Demyan was as ready as he would ever be.

The bull rounded the desk and headed for the door, opening it and stepping out for just long enough to allow the agents access to the office. He retook his post without introducing himself, or even meeting their guests' stares after they had entered the space, badges in hand.

‡PROMISE

Two men in dark suits. Dark sunglasses hanging off their front pockets. Hair in buzzcuts. Practically clones of one another if the man to the left wasn't an inch shorter than the other. Unimpressive, basically.

"Mr. Avdonin, we're sorry to bother you today and just show up like this to your home, but we were in the state and had some questions. I'm agent Packard and this is agent—"

"Mahon," Demyan said, bored. "I know who you both are."

The men had strode right in and stood at a respectable distance while Demyan remained seated at his desk. The two behind him didn't make a move or speak, either.

If the agents were surprised or taken aback by his demeanor, or the number of men in the house alongside the boss, then they were careful not to show it.

Demyan's lips curled in a smile. They had no idea that they weren't in control.

"How can I help you, gentlemen?" Demyan asked, gesturing to the two chairs that had been set up across from the desk.

The men glanced at each other, nodding in silent conversation before they took their seats. He'd considered not offering seats at all and making the assholes stand, but people tended to trust a kind hand before a mean one.

"We were hoping to speak to you in private, Mr. Avdonin," Agent Packard said, tipping his gaze in the direction of the men behind Demyan.

He only shrugged, and rested deeper in his chair. "I will not be asking my men to leave the room. If you've come all the way here to speak with me, I'm sure you wouldn't want to leave without actually doing so, yes? Which you will—go on, ask me to speak to you alone one more time."

Agent Mahon shifted in his seat while Packard offered an anxious smile.

"Of course, Mr Avdonin," the shorter, Packard, said, "whatever you're comfortable with. Either way, this is just an informal chat."

Informal.

Right.

Demyan wouldn't even bother to entertain that nonsense, but his gaze pierced between the two men, taking in every nervous jump of a knee or the way Mahon wiped away the sweat on his upper lip with the back of his hand. It didn't feel good to slowly realize a situation was not going as one planned.

Except his.

Demyan was just fine.

"What are we chatting about today, gentlemen?" he asked, gesturing for one of the two agents to continue. "Cut the bullshit, if you will, and get straight to the point. None of us have a lot of time to spend here, do we?"

That made the two sit straighter.

Good.

Thankfully, the agents got the hint.

"Your good friend—Maxim Yazov. We're sure you've heard of his passing," Packard said while Mahon simply stared at Demyan.

"I wouldn't say we were good friends, but yes, word has made its way through the circles about his death."

"We are just trying to interview people connected with him to see if they have any insight on what took place in Chicago when his estate was burned—"

"I'm sorry?" Demyan asked, cocking one eyebrow high.

"The fire. Come on, Mr. Avdonin, you know about the fire. If you know of his death, then you know of the fire," Packard replied, tossing his partner a smirk.

Nice try.

"I'm sorry," Demyan repeated, "that you thought you should come all this way to ask me about a fire that happened while I was in New York. *Yes,* I did hear about the fire, too. Terrible thing. The Yazov family has my condolences."

The agents stared at him, hoping he'd offer them something more, let a little extra slip, but he didn't think so. A few seconds passed before the agents decided to throw another question Demyan's way.

"Yes, terrible business. They're still investigating the incident," Packard continued.

"The scene, you mean?" Demyan asked, weaving his fingers together on his desk. "The estate—there's a reason to be there this long? Mustn't have been an accident, then."

Mahon shifted in his chair again, while Packard's jaw twitched with his irritation at using the wrong word—letting Demyan flip the script. The agent certainly wouldn't want to come out of the meeting needing to admit that he said more than he should have.

He didn't. Demyan knew exactly what he was saying. He'd planned every word.

"Do you have reason to believe a crime has been committed, Mr. Avdonin?" Mahon asked, leaning forward a bit in the chair with his hands clasped over his knees as he regarded Demyan. "I'm sure you know the reason we're here in the first place is only because your son was recently in Chicago, and affiliated to work with the Yazov organization. See, we thought the fact he disappeared shortly before the fire might have been … related. Do you have some information you can share with us?"

Demyan hoped that the fact he smiled coldly back at the man, entirely unconcerned and unbothered, told the agent nothing he said was surprising. That he knew exactly why the two were there, and they would leave with much the same information they came with—*none*. He had to smile. Whatever else he felt about them, his disdain mostly born from the fact they were the law and he was lawless, they didn't appear to be idiots. Did they really think he would just tell them what he knew?

Because they *asked?*

"I'm sure you don't need me to tell you how many miles separates New York and Chicago," Demyan returned. "How could I know anything that happened there?"

"You were connected to the man. We have the intel to prove it, Demyan, and the fact your son was doing business in the Yazov territory confirms it. Try again."

"What, you want me to say that I met Maxim Yazov a few times over the years? Fine, what difference does a friendship make?"

"And you were never in business together?"

This time, the question came from Mahon.

"Never," Demyan said, never breaking eye contact with the man. "We don't share the same ideals on business, to be frank. And no, I don't need you to confirm the fire was intentionally set to know it. The little that I did understand about Maxim Yazov was enough for me to know he would never set fire to his own house, just to kill himself in the process. A king doesn't just burn his castle."

Not one like Maxim.

The staring contest between the men stretched on, as did the resounding silence. Demyan simply followed the agents with his gaze when the two stood up from their chairs after passing one another a quick glance. He no longer bothered to hide the contempt in his stare, either.

"If you have ever been in business with Mr. Yazov, now would be the time to tell us all about it," Packard said. "Otherwise, if we find something, we might have to come chat again. It might not be like this, then, Demyan. Think about it."

Demyan was unmoving. "Are you threatening me?"

"Warning you," the taller agent replied.

"Consider it unheard."

The men gave a respectful goodbye and thanked him for his time before they quickly took their leave, and showed out by the bull in much the same way he'd shown them in. Only this time, he didn't come back because he would be walking them to their car. Demyan hoped he'd given them exactly what they needed to shut them up for a while, and keep them off his case.

Once the door closed, and he was alone after the only other man in the room took his leave, Demyan sipped on the vodka again, and turned to the screen on his computer. The glass was nearly empty by the time the agents' sedan rolled up to the gate once more. The vehicle stopped while they waited to be let through. The passenger window had been rolled down, and there, he saw Packard look up straight at the camera.

Demyan mashed his teeth to hold back the rage when the man waved, and the car pulled beyond the opening iron. For now, they were gone, but it wouldn't be the last time he saw them.

That much was clear.

THIRTEEN

Karine woke up the next day with Roman's name already on her lips. As if she'd been dreaming of him all night. God. Maybe she did. She still couldn't remember her dreams. It didn't matter that he wasn't in the room with her—because she'd demanded he stay away from her—and yet, *impossibly*, it felt like he'd been touching her all night. That he had his arms around her up until the very minute when she opened her eyes.

Eyes that brimmed with tears she couldn't blink away while she struggled to focus on the sloped, log ceiling of the bedroom overhead. Already, she was remembering that Roman would be leaving today.

Barely awake, and it hurt.

Karine wasn't ready for how it would feel when he was actually gone.

Refusing to let her mind obsess over something she couldn't control, Karine climbed out of bed and headed for the bathroom that was attached to the room. Her steps on the cold, hardwood floors hesitated when the sight of Masha asleep on the floor reminded her that she wasn't actually alone.

Masha had made a bed for herself at the door like she'd been doing for a while. Every time Karine asked why she was choosing to sleep on the floor, like a guard at her door when she'd been given her own room, Masha's answer was always the same.

She just wanted to make sure that Karine felt safe.

How could she argue with that, all things considered? Especially now that Roman was leaving. It was one thing to be in Vermont with him, but it was an entirely different thing when he hadn't intended to *stay*.

Karine's favorite room in the lodge was the bathroom attached to her private bedroom. The moment the door opened, gone was the wood-designed focus, and instead, the space opened up to white tile and marble. Everything from the plush towels rolled into fluffy tubes inside the rows of shelves to the tub in the middle, hanging like a stretched hammock, it was all white.

Luxurious.

Calming, in a way.

It was essentially a spa in the middle of nowhere with a spot to sit and enjoy tea or breakfast at a window nook, a freestanding shower with a view of the trees outside, and even a masseuse table.

There was no denying that Roman was going to leave her in the lap of luxury, even though he *was* still leaving her. Karine just wasn't interested in any of that—she didn't care how big the house was or the enviable amenities the place had to offer. None of it would make a difference when he wasn't there.

She splashed icy cold water on her face at the sink, and took a moment to stare at herself in the mirror. Soon, in only a few hours, Roman would be gone and then she'd be alone. She couldn't escape the thoughts, the creeping fears slithering around her spine, or even the deep sense of impending abandonment that wouldn't leave her fast-beating heart. No matter how many times someone tried to assure

Karine those feelings weren't real, another fight she'd been battling for most of her life, she didn't listen.

How could she?

She *felt* it.

Rational or not.

It was still there.

Sure, she'd have Masha, Michelle, Claire and even the handful of bodyguards who were supposed to keep her safe—none of them would make her feel the way he did, though. That was thing, and she didn't know how to explain it.

Would it even matter if she did?

Had she been wrong in trusting Roman, in getting so wrapped up in the way he made her feel that she forgot he was still just a man? And every other man in her life, well … they had all taught her the same in one way or another. In the end, the lesson never really changed—but goddamn, it *always* hurt.

She pressed her eyes closed, and searched her mind for those conflicting voices that sometimes warred within her. The voice of Katee, soft and mellow, telling her she just needed to forget. The commanding, older, more authoritative Katina who would say she should fight. *Hurt people only hurt people, Karine.* That was the only way for her to survive.

Yet, as much as she searched for those voices, she couldn't hear them. Even the fractured fragments of her mind, a mess of her own making, didn't seem to want to help Karine today.

Just my luck.

The only thing she found when she opened her eyes again was the face staring back at her in the mirror. Her own.

Sadly.

If even the identities meant to protect her from pain wouldn't save her, Karine wasn't quite sure what could. All she wanted, more than anything, was to make her way back to bed, hide beneath the blankets, and stay there for the rest of the day.

Or forever.

^{THE}PROMISE

Either worked.

What did it matter?

"Karine, dear?" In her distraction, Karine hadn't noticed Masha coming to stand in the open bathroom door. She met Masha's eyes in the mirror, already shaking her head when she asked, "Sweetheart, are you okay?"

No.

Not at all.

"I don't want him to go," she said softly.

Her lips quivered.

Even her hands shook.

Karine just felt ... *pitiful.* All over, from top to toe. She didn't even want to be stared at by her long-time friend, and caregiver.

Masha inched forward, opening her arms to offer comfort. Not that Karine took it. In fact, she slipped around the woman when she came too close, and darted for the door where she could see the safety of the bed willing to greet her, and take it all away.

She still heard Masha behind her, though, and what she said.

"I know you don't want him to go, Karine, but he has to. We don't always get to do just what *we* want, and it's okay if you don't understand it, but it won't change what happens. Pretending doesn't make it go away."

But it did.

It had.

For a while.

● ● ●

Karine refused to leave her room all morning, dreading that first step out to face the day more and more with every passing second. The day that would end with Roman gone.

She'd somehow convinced herself that if she stayed in the bedroom, then she could just keep pretending he never left. That he was working—doing something important in another part of the home or property.

Reality had never been a very fun place for Karine to be. Masha knew her too well, and even though she called Karine out earlier in the bathroom, it still wasn't enough to stop her from doing what she had always done when things were just *too much*.

Masha had left the room to go take care of the laundry—only after Karine insisted she would be fine by herself.

When a knock rattled against the bedroom door, she didn't know who was waiting on the other side. Masha would have walked right in. She stayed quiet when a part of her dared to hope it was Roman.

Because at the very same time, she hoped it wasn't.

When Karine didn't respond to the knock, the door opened slowly with a quiet, "I *do* know you're in here. Masha told me so."

At the sound of Claire's voice, Karine sat up in the bed, still surrounded by the sheets and pillows from the night before. She hadn't even let Masha turn over the sheets and make the bed pretty and inviting again. At the sight of Roman's mother standing in the open doorway, a vicious relief pulsed in her heart.

It wasn't Roman.

Even though she had desperately wanted it to be, and it hurt that it wasn't—that was *fine*. It meant one thing, and that was most important. She didn't have to say goodbye.

Yet.

The whisper in her heart was cruel.

But not wrong.

"Can I come in—you don't mind, do you?" Claire asked, not actually waiting for a response, and entering the room anyway. "I wondered where you were when you didn't come down for breakfast."

"I didn't mean to worry you."

Claire smiled. "No worries here, but I still wanted to check on you."

"Sorry," Karine replied, fingering the sleeve of the long-sleeved, oversized shirt she had worn to bed and not bothered to change since waking up. The fraying, black fabric took up her attention instead of the watchful, caring gaze in the doorway. She found herself trying to find the words that would serve as good enough excuses, but she couldn't. She had no explanation for how she was feeling. Especially since this woman was the mother of the man she was falling in love with, and Claire couldn't possibly know it. "I felt like being in bed today, I just ..."

Claire came to sit on the edge of Karine's bed, then, quieting the lies slipping out of her mouth. Or rather, the lie she was about to tell to placate the woman in to thinking she *was* okay. It was second nature for Karine, another way to protect herself by keeping people away. But the warm smile lingering on Claire's face put her at ease, and she dropped that wall. It was so easy to do with her, she radiated a sense of security and tenderness.

She felt like a mother.

"You know," Claire said, lifting the shoulder of her too-large wool sweater as she regarded Karine once more, "you really don't owe me anything, and I hope you don't think you have to tell me how you're feeling just because of who I am. And it's okay because I understand. It's shattering every time I have to be away from Roman's father, and I hate to say it, but it's not something that gets better with time. You just learn how to deal with it. When you ... well, when you rely on someone and trust them like no one else in your life, and when they're not around you when you feel like you need them, it's normal to be a little bit lost."

Claire could read a room, apparently.

Too well.

Karine let out a sigh, and raked shaking fingers through her hair to untangle the strands. It also distracted her from the uncomfortable fact that she didn't know how to reply. Even if Claire was speaking the truth.

Not that woman seemed to mind.

"Especially when you still don't know what any of this means," Claire added softer. "And it's new. That's scary, too."

The swift urge to fall into this woman's arms, to maybe try and discover what it would feel like to have a mother's support, welled in Karine. She couldn't imagine what that would be like, but she felt closest to it sitting next to Claire.

She looked away, embarrassed by her own thoughts. *Ashamed* at the things she would like to have, but didn't know where to begin to ask for—no one thought to teach her how. Affection came with strings. Karine was tied up enough.

"I just want to be in here for a while," Karine said instead. "If that's okay."

"Of course, you can." Claire kept that same, supportive smile as she reached over to squeeze Karine's knee—tender and quick—before pulling back and adding, "You're free to do whatever you like. Coping may be only a mechanism, Karine, but sometimes it's the one thing we have. At least you're doing something."

It had to be some kind of terrible irony that Karine found it was too overwhelming for her—having people around her who actually gave a shit, spending days being told everything was on her terms.

The shift happened fast.

She was still spinning from the result.

"I just don't want you to do something you'll regret tomorrow."

Karine snapped her head up to look at Claire, furrowing her brows. "What?"

"If you let him leave without seeing you, without saying your goodbyes—you might regret it. Tomorrow or a few days from now, whenever. This could be your one chance in a long time before you're together again, Karine, we really don't know what the coming days and weeks look like. Think about it."

She did.

Not that she wanted to.

Claire clasped her hands in her lap, her smile faded though the kindness still remained in her eyes. Karine swallowed back the lump forming in her throat, but it didn't help to form the words trying to get out.

Instead, all she managed to ask was, "Did he send you—"

ᴛʜᴇPROMISE

"No," Claire interjected before Karine could even finish. "You don't have to worry, Roman hasn't sent me here. In fact, he's protective enough of you that if he finds out I came to speak to you about this, after he told everyone to leave you be, well ... I'll hear about it, trust me. He'll be nice about it—I'm his *mother*—but he'll still do it."

She gave Karine a playful roll of her eyes, and a wave of one hand. "Oh, well. I just thought I should say something—we weren't exactly spying on the two of you, but everyone couldn't help but see what happened when you weren't very private about it, either. I won't pretend my son is perfect."

The lopsided grin on Claire's face made Karine relax further, but her sweet laughter, drenched in the love she felt for her son, blanketed the room in invisible warmth.

"He's *not* perfect," Claire repeated, "but there's a very good chance he wants to be perfect for you. And trust me when I say when it comes to them, that makes all the difference."

"Them?" Karine asked.

"Avdonin men. They're all the same. Every single one."

"I know he's only trying to help, and I'm grateful but ..."

"Who asked you to be grateful—to thank him, or *us*? I'm not saying this because any of us expect anything from you, Karine. I'm saying it so you'll see what I mean. Everything Roman does, he's doing for your sake. Even if you don't like it. Nobody said you had to."

Well.

Claire didn't offer the truth harshly, but there it was. All the same. The former lump in Karine's throat had now settled heavily in the pit of her stomach. Despite how much she hated the reality of the day, it still stared at her right in the face. There was no looking away.

"I don't want to regret this tomorrow," she murmured.

"Then go speak to him today," Claire added. "If there's one thing I've learned over all these years ... well, they will make mistakes. Even if they are perfect for us, they're still human, too. And they'll crawl through glass if they have to— to come back to us, they will. If they have to."

Karine knotted her fingers together, glancing at the open door. Claire hadn't closed it, and she couldn't help but wonder if that was by design. "I'm not too late, am I?"

"You're not. He wouldn't leave without seeing you," Claire replied.

FOURTEEN

By the time Karine stood in front of Roman's bedroom door
on the third floor, she had a moment where she wanted to
turn away. Not knowing if he was actually inside, not
wanting to be *wrong* ... she almost didn't knock.

Claire claimed he wouldn't leave without seeing her, but
Karine couldn't say for sure. Still, she shoved down the fear,
knocked on the door, and waited. Before she could consider
turning away a second time, the door pulled open and she
faced a very tired Roman.

"Karine," he said, eyes heavy-lidded like he hadn't slept a
wink. "I was starting to think you weren't going to let me say
goodbye, babe."

Yeah.

Her, too.

She stepped past him into the room, heart thundering the
whole way, and he shut the door behind her. Just the sound
of the latch closing them in sent a delicious thrill down her
spine.

They were alone.

The world was gone.

Everything was perfect again.

She kept her back to him, refusing to look at him while she said the words she had come to say. It just made it easier.

"I shouldn't have shut you out. I'm sorry if I made you feel like you're doing something wrong," she said.

She kept a steady voice, but *barely*. She had to be strong, get the words out, and go from there. That's what she kept telling herself, even if it was terrifying.

Roman let out a heavy sigh, and she heard his palm rub against his beard. "I wish I could explain everything to you, Karine, but I don't have the time or all the answers except to say I don't really have a choice at the moment. You're going to have to trust me that I'm doing this to keep you safe, and we can figure out the rest later."

She spun around to face him. "I know you didn't ask for this responsibility—of being responsible for *me*."

Roman stepped towards her, but kept his twitching hand at his side. She wondered if it did that because he had to keep from reaching out and touching her. *God.* She wished he would—that made everything better.

"I'm sorry that you're going through all this because of me," Karine added, twisting the end of her index finger to make the bone crack because the pain steadied her resolve even more. "I know you and your family wouldn't be in this position if it wasn't for me."

"Karine, stop it."

She didn't, twisting another fingertip, cracking it again when she muttered, "And I do understand that you can't tell me *everything*, but I don't like knowing nothing, either, okay? I always know nothing. It doesn't *help*."

"Karine—"

"And, well—"

"*Karine.*" Before she could twist and crack another bone, that sharp ache getting her from one sentence to the next even though the anxiety had swelled in her throat beyond the point of comfort, he was there. Unfurling her hands, twining her fingers with his to stop the self-harm offering her relief. "Stop it, I said."

She just stared up at him, unmoving. Roman remained still, too, staring right back.

"And not just *this*," he told her, his fingers tightening around her own, "but blaming yourself, too. Stop all of it. *I'm* not blaming you for any of this. It's not your fault. They know it, too."

The breath she hadn't realized she'd been holding came out in a rush, right alongside her words. "I just ... I can't help that you're the only one who makes me feel *okay*, but I won't when you're gone, Roman. I won't be okay at all."

"Don't you see what you're worth to me?"

The question was simple. Her perception was the problem. Knowing so and fixing it was two different things, however. Karine was still working on that.

"I want to," she admitted. "I want to see it, but it's hard when I've never been worth much to anyone before."

Did he realize that?

She knew it was hard to understand.

He pulled her to himself, flush against him, and in that second, she melted. Every last hint of doubt she ever had regarding his intentions, about what he wanted from her— was gone. Just like that.

When he held her, nothing mattered.

She was right about him all along.

"I'm not a complete idiot, I know this isn't easy, Karine," Roman said, his words muffled into the top of her head while his arms tightened around her. "The reason I'm here— fuck, why I want to be here with you—is because I found something when I found you. And that alone makes you worth all of it. I just need you to believe it, too. I swear it's true."

Nothing was simple.

Not for Karine.

It couldn't be.

For him, she tried, though. Just that once to take what he said exactly as he said it, and see it as truth. She had nothing left to lose. She *was* worth something to him, he said so—what else mattered?

Karine raised up on her toes, peering up before kissing the underside of his chin. When she did, his arms fell around her waist, pinning them in place. She couldn't quite reach his kiss without help, but he seemed to know exactly what she wanted. Her mouth on his; his tongue teasing, *taking*, licking even the breath from her lips.

She missed his kiss.

The *way* he kissed.

The second his mouth met hers, he whispered, "I don't want to go, either."

Reminding her exactly who she belonged to all at once while his kiss pounded the final notes of a new song home. The bass came from the beats of her heart; his words made it all ring. And she was trapped by the melody with every flick of his tongue and graze of his lips.

He kissed her bruisingly hard, a hand tight to her waist and another under her jaw keeping her *right there*. But yes, she wanted it. Making her whine with the need for breath while the blood rushed wildly in her ears. Even in chaos, he was soothing, she only fell into it.

Into him.

Into *more*.

"I dreamed of you last night," she gasped as his mouth kissed a hot path over her trembling chin.

His lips paused in their tantalizing trek. "Oh?"

"I can't remember it."

"*But?*"

"I woke up warm."

His wicked grin formed against jawline. "And?"

"And what?"

"Tells me enough," he muttered, planting another kiss against her lips, "to say dreaming me didn't leave you *wet*."

Karine's nerves sang, her hands already working to unbutton his shirt while he simultaneously pulled down the tiny shorts she had pulled on under the oversized long-sleeved shirt. She nibbled on his bottom lip, enjoying his

^{THE}PROMISE

dark hum, before replying, "Didn't matter—I wanted the real you anyway."

"You've fucking got me, babe."

Good.

She was still in the clothes she'd gone to sleep in the previous night. Her shorts fell to the floor around her ankles; the long-sleeved shirt quickly followed, finding the pile of discarded clothes along with his when he let her drag the shirt down his strong arms.

He stopped her for reaching for the button on his pants when he said, "I don't have long—you made me wait damn near to the last minute, Karine. I've got to be downstairs in twenty."

She pouted, then.

Roman growled at the sight, kissing her harder before mumbling against her quivering lips, "*Thirty*, then. Fuck it, they'll have to deal."

Even that wasn't enough.

She'd make do.

"You have a bad habit of not wearing panties," he noted, gaze raking over her naked body when he put just a few inches of distance between them. "Or a bra."

"Only when I sleep."

"Doesn't matter. I like it."

Hell.

She'd sleep naked, curled in his lap every night if he wanted her to.

Karine didn't get to reach for his pants again, because in the next second, his hand was between her thighs, fingers seeking the sweet, warm heat he'd find waiting there. The pleased, low hum he released when his fingers slid between her folds to find her wet, and her clit already sensitive to his touch made her shiver.

"I'm gonna make you come," he told her. "Fast, and hard. And then you can take what you want from me, Karine. Whatever you want, yeah?"

An airless *yes* answered him back, but she'd said it, and it was enough. The strokes of his fingers were fast, and relentless. Precise, tight circles that make her knees weak and coaxed the moans from her one after another.

She'd wanted a taste of him—loved his cock in her mouth, the way he lost control when she sucked him, and how he looked above her when she was on her knees, but she couldn't tell him that. Couldn't look away from his eyes when he watched her lips part as the orgasm crawled closer, and he said, "Almost, babe."

Nearly there.

"But I want to taste it when you do," he added.

Roman's hand stopped then, and he dropped to his knees all at once with wet fingers slipping into her sex as his mouth took the place overtop her clit. He sucked hard, then rolled the swollen nub with his tongue with rapid, firm flicks as she rocked against him.

It was the sudden finger against her ass, pressing and circling the tight hole before slipping in knuckle-deep that really threw her off the edge.

She hadn't been expecting that—it was new, and *different.* Good, yes, but shocking all the same. The intensity of the sharp pleasure that accompanied it was unlike anything she'd felt before.

Already, she was addicted.

The relief of the orgasm crashing down was instant, but she lost everything else for seconds. Her ability to think, to *breathe.* It was all gone while her fingers scraped along his scalp, and she fell beneath the waves crashing through her body.

Karine had barely had time to come down from the high before Roman was standing, his hand still caressing the tender, slick flesh between her thighs when he leaned in for a kiss. She took it, tasting herself on his lips—a tart, heady flavor.

He made her breath catch when he grinned, lips hovering over hers. "You liked that."

She knew exactly what he meant.

"Make sure you do it again."

Roman liked it best when she surprised him—coming out of left field with a reply he wasn't ever ready for. Now wasn't

The PROMISE

the exception to the rule, and before she knew what happened, he'd thrown her over his shoulder and was carrying her to his bed. She clung to him, wrapping her limbs around him, so she could feel the strength of his every sinew.

Those wide shoulders; his steel pecs. How the bands of muscles in his back flexed under her fingertips dancing down his spine.

His hand cracked against her ass, earning him a high pitch squeal that melted in a moan when he squeezed the same spot to massage away the sting. His murmured, dark promises into her skin where he kissed as he walked, tickling and teasing her all at the same time.

She was still trying to figure out how or why *this* man would want her. What had she done to deserve him?

Roman sat down on the edge, sliding her down his body until she had settled in his lap. She threw herself into him, into his fierce kiss, and his wandering hands. Her hair fell like a curtain around his face while he molded her to himself. His cock was already thick, and underneath her, the length straining against the fabric of his slacks. Unashamed, she grinded her hips into him, not at all caring that her own wetness might leave a mark behind on his pants.

Good.

Something to remember her by.

"God, *Karine*," he uttered, her name a prayer on his lips.

She lifted from his lap under his urging, but only for him to undo his pants and shift them down enough to free his erection from the confines of his boxer-briefs. He stole another quick kiss, pulling her down—closer and closer, straight on to him. His cock dove deep into her with one quick stroke.

She was already wet.

Already *hungry*.

That desire pooling in her belly was aided by the orgasm she'd already had, and Karine couldn't get enough. The feeling of his thickness stretching her full, burying *deep* ... those clenching, inner muscles of her pussy shuddered with racing bliss.

She couldn't contain it.

Karine cried out with pleasure. He could make her come just like that. Her clit was on fire, throbbing to be touched, and she reached down to do just that while her other hand steadied on his shoulder. She felt exactly how slick and hot she was for him, every brush of her fingertips making her hips jerk into his cock.

If he would let go of her then, she knew she would've fallen. She held on to him, his shoulder, but it felt like air. Complete surrender *was* possible. She found it when he was inside of her.

"Ride me," he demanded, all husky and hoarse. "Come on, Karine. *Take it.*"

She did, rocking in his lap, her fingers working wild circles into her clit while his mouth lavished attention to her body. Across her chest, over her breasts—his tongue lapping at her peaking nipples before he dragged them between his teeth. The pleasure was sharp, but beautiful. The deeper she took him, the faster she worked her body against his, climbing higher again, the more he urged her on.

Just like that. And, *fuck, you're so beautiful. Fuck me, Karine, fuck me how you want, baby. Take it the way you need.*

The soft kisses he dotted along her collarbones was a complete contrast to how hard his fingers dug into her sides. She fucked him harder, and he touched her *slower.* Karine dragged her nails against the back of his neck with desperation, almost there but not quite.

And yet, no matter how hard she fought to get to her orgasm, she couldn't help but watch him, too. That struggle to keep himself in control while she rode him to bliss. How his lower lip quivered when he let out pants of air that mingled with her own heavy breaths.

They shouldn't fuck like this, and she knew it. *Raw*, every single time. That choice was going to catch up to them eventually, but dammit if she cared now ... because she didn't. She liked the way he felt inside her when he was bare. How that thick vein on the underside of his length pulsed when she clenched around him; how they *mixed* after they came. She even liked his stickiness between her thighs, and cleaning it away later, touching herself under hot bath water and *remembering* while she did it.

Roman grunted a low *fuck* under his breath, and she knew that sound. He was struggling, just like she was, to keep it together because nothing felt like this. Nothing was better than them together this way.

She couldn't quite remember how she found herself on her knees all of the sudden ass pulled high on the edge of the bed, but it didn't really matter. In the next moment, Roman was pounding deep into her from behind and Karine was already flying.

Screaming her orgasm into sheets she balled against her face. He fucked her hard like that, enough to ache, so deep she'd feel him for days.

And then he came with hot spurts to her backside, and along her lower back while she watched him over her shoulder through half-closed lashes while he jerked himself to a finish.

White, thick, and *warm*.

Marking her, in a way, as his thumb smeared the cum against her skin where her back melted into the roundness of her ass.

"I'm never going to forget the way you look when you're like this," he said, still breathless and touching himself on her.

He couldn't know it.

Didn't.

But that was exactly what she wanted to hear.

• • •

He gave her those thirty minutes he promised, letting her climb on top of him naked in the bed, and curl up into his waiting embrace. At first, she'd counted the minutes just in case. All the while thinking, *you told me thirty; I want each one.*

But he didn't move an inch.

Not unless it was to touch her.

Their limbs were tangled with the sheets. Karine could feel the dampness on his skin, his strong masculine scent mixed with the undeniable whiff of sex still lingering in the air. *Their* sex. She tried to commit that to memory, too.

"No matter what happens," she started to say, so quiet that she couldn't even be sure he had heard her. "I want you to know you did the right thing—taking me with you was the right thing, Roman. I found where I wanted to be."

In a way.

A very important way.

"And thank you for doing what you've done for me," she added. "What you're still doing."

"Hey, it's not a *no matter* kind of thing." He hooked a finger under her chin, tipping her face upwards to him. "I will always come back to you, Karine. Even if I'm in pieces."

He kissed her nose, her lips, then her chin. She drew in a deep, anxious breath, the exhale shaky even in her chest.

"What did I tell you, huh?" he asked. "As long as you want me, I'm here."

"I don't want to think of you in pieces—what does that even mean?"

"It means you have nothing to worry about."

She rested her chin on her folded hands right in the middle of his chest, enjoying the way he watched her. The longer their gazes locked, the more her need for him started to grow all over again. To have him inside her; his words were always easier to hear when he was fucking her. It was the only way she could satiate her insecurities. If he was close to her, they wouldn't taunt her.

Instead of feeding into the selfishness, she told him, "But you won't be here, and you can't blame me for wondering if you'll be able to come back."

Or if he'd be alive to, rather.

"Karine," he said her name firmly, making her gulp when that hand of his came to lay against her cheek. "I'm going to ask you again—do you trust me?"

Honestly?

"More than anyone, Roman."

Or anything.

"Good, because that's really the only fucking thing I have. There's not much else that's good about me, babe, but that I can give you. My loyalty to *you*. If I say something, I'll do it. For you. Do you hear me?"

She nodded once.

"I've never trusted anyone before," she whispered.

It felt like it shouldn't even need to be said, but she did it, anyway.

"I know."

He kissed the curve of her shoulder, and then slowly started to ease her off his chest. She wanted to grip him hard, with both hands. She'd do anything—even something drastic right then—to make him stay.

But she couldn't.

Or ... Karine knew she shouldn't.

So, she let him go.

Roman stood at the foot of the bed as he dressed himself. Those thirty minutes were up, and Karine could feel the tears coming.

No. She wouldn't do that to him. Not now when he had to leave. She didn't want the sight of tears streaming down her face to be the last thing he saw before he walked out of that bedroom, so she stifled the hitching in her throat and the sting in her eyes.

Just a little bit longer.

When he was gone, she would cry.

Only then.

"I'll see you soon, right?" she asked, sinking back into his sheets.

His bed.

It smelled like him, and now her. *Them.* She had no intention of leaving his room anytime soon. Or ever. Fuck anyone who tried to make her do anything different.

"You know it," he told her.

So sure.

He'd finished dressing fast, and before he carried his bag to the door, he came around the bed to her side again. She didn't really need to ask the question echoing in the back of her mind, because she knew what his answer would be, but it still felt right ... so, Karine asked, "You promise?"

He took her fingers, pressing the tips to his mouth, the kiss featherlight. "I do."

"Be safe, Roman."

This man.

He winked.

All sinful, and gorgeous.

And now, very possibly, *hers.*

"Be *good,*" he told her.

Well.

Karine would try, but …

"No promises."

FIFTEEN

One week crawled into two, and Roman felt every fucking
second of those days tick by. From the moment he left
Vermont, he became painfully aware of the time passing,
because for once in his life, he was doing everything but
what he wanted to do.

It took so little effort to be selfish.

And *so much* not to be.

In the back seat of his friend's newest car, Roman killed
time watching the streets of a familiar city as Marky
navigated the road. They were trying to kill time. Marky had
a habit of changing vehicles far too often for Roman to keep
track of which one the guy was driving on any given week;
his access to fleets of stolen vehicles did not go unused.
Which, in a way, helped them with their current situation
considering he had to stay on the move. Roman was doing
his best to avoid a run-in with the FBI like Demyan had
experienced.

At least, his father had managed to keep the bastards off his shoulders so far, but Roman wasn't sure how much longer that would last. His constant paranoia about bumping into the FBI was only aided by the fact he was still waiting for someone from Chicago to turn up out of the blue, too.

A proverbial target had been placed on his back in more ways than one—a dangerous way to feel for a man like him. Repeatedly checking over his shoulder, eyes darting everywhere when he entered any public space, the never-ending movement because a still target was far too easy to hit.

When Leonid or Dima did eventually hit, he wanted to see it coming. Really, it was the only thing he *could* do.

Work was entirely out of the question, even if Roman thought it might serve as a good distraction to the fact he fought every day not to return to Vermont. But no, a decent, worthwhile scheme wouldn't serve the purpose of staying out of sight and on the move. He hadn't been involved in any of the chop shop business since he left Chicago with Karine in tow.

That shit was trash, too.

Nothing was in Roman's favor. Life was having a good laugh at his goddamn expense.

He had an itch he couldn't scratch—an ever-present desire to return to some semblance of normal, or what his normal *used* to be.

That just wasn't possible, and really … he wouldn't take any of it back, if he could. It meant no Karine, after all, and the idea of that bothered him more than even the fact he couldn't be with her *now*.

Roman figured that said something.

He just wasn't ready to say it, too.

Eyeing Marky in the rearview mirror only to find his friend was focused on the bumper to bumper traffic, Roman pulled out his phone and dialed Karine's number. He'd gotten a bull at the lodge to arrange a phone for her the very same day he left. Shit, he had to figure out something, didn't he?

THE PROMISE

From what he'd been told, the phone at least eased the impact after he was gone. Karine answered the call at the start of the second ring, like she'd been waiting for it.

"I missed your voice," were her first words.

Roman grinned. "Oh?"

"It's kind of stupid."

"Or cute."

Even he raised a brow at the choice of word he used—*cute*—not at all something he would usually say. Marky didn't hide the fact he shot a glance at Roman in the rearview mirror, either.

His reply was a look—it said everything. *Fuck off.*

"Are you having a good day?" Roman asked, going back to what mattered.

His phone call.

Karine.

Sprawling deeper into the backseat, he tipped his head back to stare at the roof of the car. Like that, he could picture Karine's face. How those pretty, perfect bow-shaped lips would form a smile when she spoke. He just wanted to see her. Every inch of her.

Fuck, yeah.

That's what he was—*fucked.*

He missed her, too.

"I think so," Karine said after a pause.

"You *think* it was a good day?"

"Well, we did a lot of walking."

Roman held back the snort at how her tone dipped. He'd come to learn over the course of their many phone conversations that while Karine *loved* the lodge, the property full of dense wilderness, and the safe space it allowed her, she also liked to just … *be*. Sitting under a tree with a blanket, curled in bed watching the fire crackle in the fireplace. But she wasn't the *active* type.

A stroll was great, long walks … not so much.

"Anyway," Karine said, drawing him from his thoughts. "Michelle and I, we went for a walk around the lake right after breakfast, then we kept talking and talking, and lost track of time."

He did chuckle at that. "So, did you really mind all the walking if you lost track of time?"

"*Listen.*"

His next laugh came out full force, and Karine quickly joined in. It made Roman happy to hear that dance in her voice, a chirpy sweetness he hoped meant that she was still taking the distance between them better than he'd expected. If he was honest, though, he got a strong impression that her sessions with the psychiatrist were making a huge difference in the ways Karine approached different things.

"What did you talk about today?" he asked, making her scoff playfully in response.

"You know I'm not gonna talk about that. Nice try."

"Ugh, straight to the heart, Karine," he said. Then, just as fast, Roman added, "Just kidding."

Fact was, he *didn't* push her to discuss the things she talked about with Michelle. Karine had made it clear shortly after he'd left Vermont that the woman suggested she didn't unless she was truly ready to, and he didn't think she was.

That was fine.

Mostly.

Roman wasn't a liar.

Or he was trying real hard not to be.

Karine only laughed at his joke, but that was because she hadn't heard the slight dip in his tone. *Thankfully.* Just because he was letting her call the shots didn't mean he was comfortable with every choice she made. He *did* wish she would tell him what was on her mind all the time—every single secret Michelle had managed to pull from the depths of her mind. Only so he could try and figure her out, *understand* Karine better, maybe.

But they weren't his secrets to know.

And he already had enough of his own.

As Karine chatted on, telling him about the things they'd found on a new trail, his thoughts wandered to the fact that he was hiding something crucial from her, as well. He hadn't told Karine about the fire. No official statement of Maxim's death had been made—sure—but that didn't change what they believed. Her father was most likely dead.

THEPROMISE

Most *definitely* dead.

That would be a loaded statement, the very second it came out of his mouth, because he knew what would come next. It was inevitable. She would eventually ask him who had done it, and Roman would have to lie to her again.

He *hated* that.

"Anyway, then Jimmy, you know, the—"

"Mmhmm, the bull," Roman interjected, refusing to delve into his thoughts more than he already had. *Fuck it.* He should just enjoy his chance to talk to Karine, and not issues that he couldn't currently handle.

Karine continued, "Yeah, him. He was like a kid, I swear it. Running up to us with two shotguns, looking like a madman with a smile on. You should have seen Michelle's face, Roman. I *died.* She was ready to bolt—I don't think she's come that close to a gun before."

It was her soft giggle that made his grin grow wide in an instant. He loved that sound. Every time he doubted himself, or felt like he didn't know what he was doing—that he was risking everything for the sake of a woman he couldn't even have at the moment—he reminded himself of these conversations. How she laughed, the way she could be bubbly and sweet, despite everything.

If that wasn't strength, what was?

"Why did he have two shotguns?" he asked, clearing his throat.

"He was going to teach me how to shoot skeets."

She didn't contain the excitement in her voice, and that alone was *wonderful,* but Roman felt a surge of petty jealousy. All the same, there it was.

He did *not* wear that monster well.

A part of him believed his parents were to blame—that from the second he was born, despite having an older sister, he might as well have been an only child. They spoiled him. Gave him things, told him they were *his,* and never once expected Roman to share.

So, he didn't.

Ever.

Well, apparently that shit had translated into his romantic life as well because the jealousy was *real*. He wasn't given much of a choice but to share Karine's time and attention when he couldn't be there to fill up every second of her damn days.

Roman knew Jimmy—the guy was decent. He trusted the man to get the job done and keep Karine safe, but he'd never discussed socializing with her. In fact, he'd told all the bulls to leave her alone unless she made the first step to close the bridge. The rationale behind that was she *was* free to do whatever she wanted, as long as she wanted to do it. If Jimmy and she were becoming friends, and she was comfortable with a particular bull, then Roman had no say in it.

And it wasn't a bad thing, his father had pointed out to him when he dared to bring it up to the man. If she felt more comfortable with a particular bull, it could make things better for her in many ways.

Demyan wasn't wrong.

Roman just didn't *like* it.

There was that monster—again.

Besides, the more she engaged in these things, the more distracted she was going to be from his absence. However, the alternative reality where she enjoyed shooting skeets and laughing with one of the bulls—he practically buzzed with envy.

Not that he let it show.

"And how'd it go?" Roman asked.

"The lesson?"

"Yeah, babe."

"Not too bad," she replied, a smile coloring up her words brightly. He couldn't see it, but he swore he could hear it. "I hit a couple. Jimmy said I was a natural, but I think he was just being nice."

"Jimmy is a lot of things but nice for the sake of being nice is not of them. And I'm not surprised. You have the potential of being good at everything—you only have to *try*."

<small>THE</small> PROMISE

Nothing he said was untrue, but it still stung a little to say it. He should have been in Vermont teaching Karine to shoot skeets over the lake.

"How are you?" she asked, then, not giving him the chance to respond before she added, "I feel like whenever we talk, I just end up monopolizing the conversation. It's always all about me."

Right.

"Because you're what matters, Karine."

She gave a little sigh. "You haven't told me anything about how things are going there."

He preferred to keep their conversations light because he had enough on his mind already. Not that he expected her to understand.

"I don't want to talk about things that aren't important," he settled on saying. "I want to talk about you. Besides, there are some things I just ... can't discuss. You understand, don't you?"

Karine was quiet for longer than he liked before finally saying, "I do understand."

"But it's not easy, right?"

"You said it, not me."

Roman laughed darkly, and scrubbed a hand down his neatly trimmed beard. "So you know though, just because I'm not giving you all the details of my day-to-day life right now, doesn't mean I've forgotten about you."

"No, I know that, too. I just ... everything sounds scary and complicated. I figured I should at least ask, you know?"

It was complicated, but he wasn't sure what she was talking about.

"Why do you feel that way—has something happened there, Karine?"

It took her a second to respond.

A second too long.

"I've just overheard some things. That's all. Mostly the guys talking amongst themselves around here. I heard one say Leonid was acting as the boss in Chicago. I don't understand what that means. What about ... *my father?* What's happening?"

177

Fuck.

Roman quieted—he didn't know what to say. Well, shit, he would be having a word with the bulls to make sure they were careful about what they said to each other. Especially when they thought no one was listening.

Clearly, someone was.

He didn't want Karine overhearing anything else. Every piece of news she learned would come from his mouth alone. This was fucking bad enough.

"Things sound dangerous, Roman," Karine told him, her tone turning shy when she added, "I just want everything to be over ... so you can be here with me again."

"Me, too, but I can't make the world move faster, Karine."

"Funny."

Roman arched a brow. "What is?"

"It definitely feels like you make *my* world go faster."

Maybe so.

It just wasn't the same thing.

Unfortunately.

• • •

Marky dropped him back off nearing midnight at the Astoria Hotel where he'd been staying the last two nights, and they had spent most of the day driving around doing fucking nothing. Roman was imprisoned in his own city. A place he had once felt was his kingdom had become a constant reminder that he wasn't free to do as he wished.

The cloud of the FBI and the Chicago bratva hung over him after he'd said goodbye to his friend and headed for the hotel's entrance, but Karine wasn't too far from his thoughts, either. A few more nights and he was going to move to a different, random location. That was the plan so far.

Roman intended on heading to the bar first before he went up to his suite. He wasn't doing much drinking in public, but he planned to bypass the wait staff bringing him up a bottle. Why not get it himself?

ᴛʜᴇPROMISE

Drinking himself to oblivion seemed like a good way to get his mind off things. Even if it was just another way to deflect his own feelings. Roman had come to learn he didn't really deal well with his own pain. No matter the reason for him feeling it, he just wanted to *bury* it.

However, his plan came to a screeching halt when he walked into the lobby and found his father waiting there. Demyan stood with two men whom Roman knew as lawyers the family had on retainer. Affiliated men who knew the cost, and benefits, of defending criminals. If his father had lawyered up, it could only mean one thing.

The law was somehow involved.

"Say as little as you can," Demyan opened the conversation when Roman walked up.

Trouble had arrived.

He nodded at the stoic, sharp-dressed lawyers literally on standby next to them. "What's going on?"

"There are two FBI agents waiting in your suite."

"And you just let them go up there?"

"I gave them the key for the room, actually," Demyan replied.

He started walking in the direction of the opening elevator, followed on his heels by the lawyers. So, Roman had no choice but to follow them, too, getting more pissed off with every step he took after his father.

"Do you want to tell me what the fuck this means?" he called, barely below a shout, at his father's back.

Roman was done being keeping calm.

"It means that you're going to have to meet with the two bastards, but it doesn't mean you'll be talking to them."

Ah.

That said a lot.

Clearly, the agents hadn't given his father a choice in the matter.

"I thought you had it under control," he said, stepping in beside a scowling Demyan on the elevator.

"I did have it under control. For over two weeks. It's time you met with them, and shut them up for at least another few. I don't like it, but it was going to happen eventually."

Roman brushed a hand through his hair in frustration while the others packed into the elevator together. The lawyers stepped in before one of his father's bulls followed them in, too.

"My other man went up with them to the room," Demyan explained.

"Say nothing, or very little. They have nothing to *make* you talk, anyway. If they had any proof, they wouldn't be demanding an informal chat."

The lawyer who offered that nice piece of information while the elevator climbed floors earned himself a glare from Roman. He knew how to handle officials; he'd been doing this shit—or watching other men do it—for his entire goddamn life.

"I didn't intend on speaking to them at all, actually," he snapped back, "and one might think the fee we pay to keep you on retainer would keep any *informal* meetings off the table in the first fucking place, huh?"

He could have delivered that insult in a softer manner, but he didn't have the patience or care, really.

"Well, it's happening now, so you should be prepared," Demyan interjected.

The elevator doors slid open, and they all stepped out to the corridor in pairs of two, except for the bull who exited first to check the hall.

"What do they want to fucking know?" Roman asked.

Wasn't that what mattered here? He waited for an answer while he and his father led the way to the suite at the end.

"About what you'd expect. If you have any connection with the Yazovs. What you know about the fire. What business we have with them."

"And what have you told them?"

"Nothing," Demyan replied.

The two of them exchanged a quick look before Roman swiped his card through the lock and pushed the door open. Everyone else followed him inside.

The two agents were already seated around the coffee table in the sitting room that greeted the guests upon entrance.

™PROMISE

Neither man stood up to greet Roman, or the men behind him.

"Roman Avdonin," the man on the left said, his badge already in his palm and facing out. "Special Agent Packard."

Neither man extended their hands and Roman stood back, pushing his hands into the pockets of his pants. There was no need for a *nice to meet you* here. No doubt, these agents had seen his face plastered on their cork boards for years.

"What do you want?" he asked.

Why waste time?

The faster they were gone, the better. Even though nobody made a move he could sense the shiftiness and disapproval in the movement and murmurs of lawyers behind him. If only Roman gave a single shit.

"We just wanted to talk," the other agent said, shrugging lightly. "Like we did with your father some time ago. Maybe clarify a few things."

"Like what?"

"Chicago."

"Apparently, it's very windy up there," Roman replied dully.

Neither agent seemed very impressed by his dry humor.

"Specifically, we would like to discuss your recent trip to Chicago," Packard explained, not even taking the bait.

Roman shrugged. "I had a friend to visit, so I went up there for a few weeks. What's the big fucking deal?"

"I hear it was more than a couple months, right? And what is this friend's name?"

Well, if that was how they wanted to play …

Roman could go straight to the point. "Are you charging me with something?"

The man chose to ignore that question.

"Did you associate with the Yazov family while you were in Chicago? Specifically, the boss of the organization, Maxim Yazov?"

"What do you mean by that—*associate*?" Roman returned just as fast, even rocking on his heels. "I'm not sure if you're aware, but the way I associate myself with people may mean a different thing to me compared to you."

"Did you meet his men, or him? Talk to any of them? Bump into each other? Conduct any business?"

Packard's impatience showed itself, no longer interested in the game he had started, so Roman decided to use that to his advantage. If he was getting on the man's nerves, *good*. Twitchy and on edge was exactly the way he wanted the agent to be. It made him more susceptible to making mistakes because the truth was simple.

The Avdonins needed information, too. They were still working blind when it came to Chicago. He would take anything he could get from these assholes, even if he had to play a few games to do it.

He shook his head, telling the agent, "Nope. Didn't send them any greeting cards, either."

The two agents glanced at each other briefly, and with that one look Roman knew they had nothing. No proof, and probably no leads on whatever trail they were trying to chase, either. But there was something else that didn't sit quite right with him.

"Why are you so interested in the contacts of a dead man?" Roman asked.

"For the record, the remains from the estate have still not been positively identified," Packard said, crossing his arms over his chest.

Another sign of frustration.

Roman decided to poke it. "You may not be sure of it, but if Leonid is running the show, he must have said something. Made an official statement through the proper channels. Speaking as a man in the life, *I* would."

How else did a boss make his new position clear?

People needed to *know*.

"We'll ask him when we see him," the other agent said, finally finding his voice again.

Actually, he hadn't even introduced himself during their conversation. Strange, that.

It was the threatening look his partner threw him that seemed to gain Roman's father's attention.

"So you haven't spoken to Leonid?" Demyan asked suddenly. "Nobody from the organization?"

"Seems like he's even harder to get a hold of than you," Packard replied.

That made Roman smile.

Just a little.

He wasn't sure how long the FBI would be sniffing around Avdonin business, but to him, it seemed like these fucks were going nowhere. Their frustration was palpable, and if anything, the official side of their issues might soon be gone.

Something to hope for, anyway.

However, that joy was short lived. Roman didn't miss the fact that the agent gave him exactly what he was looking for.

Information.

Nobody knew where Leonid was.

What about Dima?

Were they hiding from the FBI, or looking for Karine?

"We're done here," one of the lawyers spoke up.

The agents didn't look like they were going to agree to that. If only that would make a different, but ... *no.*

Roman turned away from the conversation, then, headed for the bar in the corner of the room while the lawyers did their thing. He needed a drink, and poured himself three fingers of dark rum.

"We have other questions," Packard said.

"Our apologies, but this is as much time as Mr. Avdonin has today. He can't help you with anything else. For further questions, have them delivered in writing to my office so we can take the appropriate time to discuss them, and his answers, with our client."

While Roman gulped the rum down his throat, he watched the two FBI agents stand up. They didn't hide the fact that they weren't happy about being made to leave, but that was the game they agreed to play when they questioned him.

One of the lawyers walked the agents to the door of the hotel suite, while the rest of the people in the room remained exactly where they were.

The agents were gone moments later, making Demyan turn to his son.

"So, Leonid is missing, then. If he's underground, it's safe to say Dima has probably done the same."

"Something tells me they're not just hiding out doing nothing in the middle of nowhere," Roman replied, already annoyed.

Demyan shook his head, saying only, "You need to watch your back, son."

"Perfect, so nothing much has changed."

SIXTEEN

Michelle had encouraged Karine to meditate—something she hadn't tried before, and didn't know very much about until the doctor brought it up. It wasn't the easiest thing to do, requiring more concentration and focus than she was used to when the purpose was to *relax*. Even though she'd been suspicious of the idea at first, not believing it would help her in any way to get that deep inside her own mind, she decided to follow Roman's advice.

She kept an open mind with regards to Michelle and the journey she was taking Karine on.

Two weeks of practising day after day, and it finally felt like it was making a difference. Clearing her mind one measured breath at a time, weightless limbs releasing any tension, and everything was … *quiet*.

Soft, even.

Her favorite time to meditate was in the morning—like now—so it was the first thing she started her day with, sitting cross-legged on her bedroom floor, facing the open window where the fresh scent of the lake and woods flowed in with a light, chill breeze. Her lungs filled with crisp air. The now-usual echo of voices in her head were all but gone, having faded farther away with every passing minute and each breath she took.

When Karine finally did open her eyes again, her mind was empty. Not in the way it used to be before—when she was always muddled and confused by medication. It was a new clarity she hadn't known existed.

Karine bounced up off the floor with a smile and changed into a fresh set of clothes, satisfied that she had properly started her day. The rest of it always went better like that.

Masha and Claire's voices floated from the direction of the kitchen as Karine made her way downstairs, following the mouthwatering scent of breakfast wafting through the halls.

Her appetite had improved, too.

More than she expected.

Michelle correlated her newfound interest in food to the fact her senses were no longer numb—eating wasn't just mechanical for Karine. Not something she *had* to do just to sustain her life. She actually enjoyed the textures, even the way food looked, and especially the smell and taste.

She even wanted to learn to cook.

More than anything, Karine wanted to tell Roman. He called her every day, ready and willing to hear each second of her days repeated to him without complaint, and every time she found that she missed him a little more. It didn't even matter that whenever she wanted to hear his voice, all she needed to do was text him, and he called her back. It was never enough to leave her satisfied—the invisible hole in her heart grew larger still.

And even if he couldn't call her back straight away, he eventually did. Never left her hanging. Those promises he kept meant the world to Karine. Especially the small ones.

"You're looking … *happy*," Claire declared, pouring steaming black coffee into mugs as Karine took a seat at the table. Masha chanced a glance over her shoulder from where she cooked at the stove, seemingly relieved to see her.

"You do," Masha agreed.

THE PROMISE

But she offered nothing more, and quickly went back to the food on the stove. They weren't in the Yazov mansion anymore, but Masha still couldn't view herself as Karine's equal even if she wished that wasn't the case.

Shaking the wisps of sadness off, Karine turned her attention on Roman's mother. "Thank you, Claire. Meditating is helping. And good food, too."

Claire joined her at the table with a laugh. "Good food helps with *everything*. As long as it's not Russian food—just don't tell any of the men that. They might feel some kind of way about it."

Karine shared her smile.

And made a mental note.

Masha continued to cook breakfast, standing with her back turned to them and barely even making an effort to stay in the conversation. Not that Claire would mind if she *did* join in, but it was what it was.

"Michelle certainly seems to know what she's doing, doesn't she?" Claire asked, reaching for the sugar and milk dishes between them to pull them closer to her steaming mug of coffee. "As long as it's working for you, that's what counts."

"I tried getting Masha to do it with me, but she didn't want to."

Masha threw an embarrassed smile and short laugh over her shoulder, murmuring in reply, "I have work to do, laundry and cooking and—"

"Don't worry, Masha, I get it. I didn't really want to do it, either."

"Sounded a bit out there?" Claire asking, arching a brow.

Karine shrugged. "I mean, at first? Yeah."

"It requires a lot of skill and discipline, more than people realize, and it's definitely not for everyone. *But*, that also makes it quite an achievement that you've been able to pick it up, and you enjoy doing it," Claire added.

Compliments were a strange thing to Karine, but she had heard more praise in these two weeks than ever before in her entire life. Self-confidence wasn't as odd of a concept to her, but it was just as unknown and out of reach.

Until now.

She was learning.

"Thank you," Karine replied, blushing into the sugar Claire handed over for her to add to the coffee in front of her.

Masha brought over a plate of scrambled eggs with mushroom and spinach, sliding it in front of Karine as she smiled and said, "Just how you like it."

"The way *you* make them," Karine corrected the woman. "I just like the way you make them, Masha."

For a split second, the two women couldn't break their stare. Claire remained silent across the table, not drawing an eye to her, but Karine felt her curious stare all the same.

"I know," Masha eventually said, her voice still soft. "Just the same, Karine. Eat up."

As fast as Masha was to leave the table, Karine didn't have time to consider the exchange for long before Roman's mother said, "Yes, eat—you'll need the energy."

Well, that had all of her attention.

"Why?"

Claire winked, and pointed a manicured nail Karine's way. "I was thinking we could do something together today. I spoke to Roman about it, and he agreed it might be a good idea. Maybe we could go to the local farmer's market in the village."

Karine couldn't believe what she had heard.

Back in Chicago, her father would never have suggested something like that—*so public*. He never encouraged her interest in the world outside of the one he curated for her, and a part of her maybe understood why. Not that she liked it. Someone else had always shopped for her, or he had personal shoppers visit the mansion so Karine could choose what she wanted on the rare event she was allowed to for a special occasion.

As curious and hopeful as she felt, the buzz brought on by Claire's own excitement at having a day away from the lodge, Karine was still hesitant.

"I've never been to a farmer's market before," she admitted.

ᴛʜᴇPROMISE

"*Oh*, you'll love it," Claire said with a wave of her hand before sipping on her coffee. Setting it back down to the table, she added, "You'll find something different at every vendor's table. Lots of handmade treasures—art, certainly. Lots of lovely things to sample and buy, *and* interesting people to talk to. But only if you want. We could make a day of it, if you're interested, of course."

Was she?

Too much.

Karine bit down on her lip, another problem poking at the back of her mind. "Masha doesn't enjoy places like that."

Masha had returned to the stove, cooking more eggs and still had her back turned to them. Not that her lack of attention mattered. She didn't need to see her expression for Karine to sense she didn't approve.

"It'll just be the two of us for today," Claire said. "And a bull. Maybe Masha can take the morning off, I'm sure she could use some time to herself."

"I don't need any time to myself," Masha protested.

Not once turning away from the stove.

So she *was* listening.

Karine's heart raced.

This was a small thing, sure. Just a short trip for the day with Claire—it really wasn't a big deal in the grand scheme. Except to Karine, it would be a brand new experience. A taste of freedom. A look into what her future might be like.

She hadn't ever known that feeling, never mind that kind of life, with the constant disapproving shadow of her father looming over her. A cloud that was now out of reach. She couldn't help that Masha was uncomfortable.

It was something else Karine learned.

Growth *hurt.*

"I love it—let's do it," Karine said suddenly.

Masha did turn away from the stove, then, her cheeks ruddy with frustration. They were never separated, especially not when Karine went out anywhere. It was clear her caretaker didn't trust her, even though she was slowly starting to do that for herself.

Claire caught her looking in Masha's direction.

"Don't worry, it'll be fine, Karine. I'll be right there with you, if you need anything. *No matter what.*"

Karine wet her lips. "Or who?"

Because that was a possibility, too. With Karine, the who was sometimes more concerning than the what.

That made Claire smile.

Just a bit.

"Or who," the woman agreed. "And like I said, Roman *did* think you'd really enjoy it."

Well ...

"I already said yes, but if Roman thinks I should, then I really can't say no," Karine said. "When are we leaving?"

• • •

Despite Claire stating a bull would go with them to the market, he drove in his own vehicle, but still followed their every movement once they arrived. Karine was starkly aware of his presence close by, even though he wasn't always visible to them. It made her feel safer when she realized how many people were there.

Thrilled at the sight of the primitive, homemade sign for the farmer's market, Karine ignored the unease that snaked inside her belly. The village was rural with a small population, and it seemed like the whole community had set up stalls to sell one thing or another.

Claire had been right.

There was ... *everything.*

Crafts, homemade food and baked goods. Handcrafted clothes and accessories, jewelry, old books, trinkets and more. Every vendor they passed had something new, and unique, to look at.

Shiny.

Pretty.

Old.

Or interesting.

Karine was overwhelmed by it all, and if it hadn't been for Claire who didn't leave her side every time she became distracted by yet another thing, she might have gotten lost in

the maze of tables and tents. It was harder than she expected
to contain her excitement and the nervousness that
constantly bubbled through her between the *things*, the
people, and everything else.

Each time she felt claustrophobic, she turned to Claire
who gave her a reassuring smile. At the very least, it
reminded her that she wasn't alone.

They slowly made their way around the stalls, even though
they took care not to speak to anyone unless absolutely
necessary. The idea of conversations with strangers was
enough to make Karine want to run the trip back to the
lodge. Claire was as careful as Roman would have wanted
her to be—never inviting questions from any of the people
at the market, but not drawing attention by being rude,
either.

"How are you feeling?"

Karine peered over at Claire, smiling around the sticky mess
of maple syrup twisted around a popsicle stick. A treat they
had picked up at a vendor near the entrance giving them
away for free. "Honestly?"

"I expect nothing less."

"Thank you for this, Claire. I've never ... done something
like this. Just gone out, and—"

"Been normal?"

"*Felt* normal, maybe."

Claire nodded, and then weaved an arm around hers with a
bright smile. "I was looking forward to us spending some
time together, away from the lodge and all. It didn't hurt that
a change of scene is nice for us both, although Masha didn't
seem very happy with this arrangement, did she?"

Karine sighed. "She's not used to us being apart, I think.
But if you ask me, we've probably spent too much time
together. In very close quarters, for a *very* long time."

Walking side by side, arm in arm, with her, Claire cleared
her throat, asking only, "Do you think she'll be with you
forever, Karine—or better yet, do you want her to stay?"

Not that she wanted to admit it, but Karine had found
herself considering that very question more often than not
recently. It just wasn't ... an *easy* conversation, considering

the life she'd had and how big of a role Masha played. She was glad to be able to discuss it with someone else, even if it wasn't comfortable to do so.

"I'm not sure," Karine admitted. "There's a big part of me that hopes she'd want to have her own life. One away from me. She's spent so much time looking after me. Doesn't she deserve to make a life for herself, too?"

"She may not look at it that way," Claire responded in a murmur.

"Maybe not, but I would like her to. I don't want to need her forever."

"But what if what she wants is *you*?"

Karine hadn't considered that.

What would it even mean?

Claire squeezed her hand encouragingly. "And you won't always need her, sweetheart. Sometimes, it's more about what we want, you know?"

She did, but she didn't at the same time. All she wanted then was something—*someone*—that she couldn't have. Karine couldn't help but miss Roman. She wished she'd experienced the market with him. Hell, she would have been too distracted by his presence to even notice her own nerves. He just had that way about him.

As much as she wanted to ask him to come back to be with her again, she never did. The words always danced on the tip of her tongue when they spoke—threatening to blurt out every time their conversations started to come to an end, and she would have to hang up the phone.

But ...

She made a promise to herself that she wouldn't say a thing. She didn't want to put Roman in a situation where he felt torn between her, and what he needed to do to keep them safe. Besides, he asked for trust, and she was trying to do that. She would savour the moment she saw him again, instead.

Because she knew she *would*.

He wouldn't let her down.

ᴛʜᴇ PROMISE

"That would look gorgeous on you," Claire said, breaking Karine from her throughs when she came up to her from behind.

Not only had Karine seemed to wander a few feet away in her distraction, but she didn't even realize she had clasped on to the buttery material of a dress hanging from the eave of a vendor's tent. Feeling the soft fabric between her fingers, she peered up at the item that must have subconsciously caught her eye.

The bright red made her blush.

It certainly *stood out.*

Not at all like her.

Claire pulled it down to hold it by the hanger for them to see the dress better. The color wasn't the only daring thing about it. With a deep, sweeping back that wouldn't leave anything to the imagination once worn, the front plunged pretty deep, too. A dress that would only suit someone who was comfortable with their breasts free of a bra because nothing would hide the straps or hooks. The bottom flared like a skirt, but it was actually a jumpsuit, Karine discovered when she widened the bottoms.

"I've never worn anything like this before," she whispered, unable to hide the shyness in her gaze. Everything about the jumper was designed to draw attention, and that had never been a priority for her.

In fact, she actively tried to do the opposite.

Her father wouldn't have approved, and neither would Dima. Oddly, that only made her want it more.

"Well, then you have to get it. And if you need a better reason, red is Roman's favorite color."

Karine met the woman's gaze. "Really?"

"From the time he was two, actually."

"Well—"

"I'm going to take that as a yes."

Claire had already handed the red jumper over to the vendor who quickly packed it up. The butterflies beating inside her stomach decided to make themselves known again at the idea of Roman's eyes lighting up when he saw her in it. But the nervous sensation was quickly stamped out by the heat that followed, a thrill chasing the desire straight through her bloodstream in no time at all.

Would he like it?

How much?

She wanted to find out.

Claire paid the vendor, dangling the paper bag from the crook of her elbow when she turned to Karine again.

"Thank you," Karine said. "You really shouldn't have."

"Well, we couldn't come all the way here and buy nothing," Claire said with a smile and a nod at the bag, "and *this* deserves a good home. It'll look great on you, just you wait and see."

"I'm not sure it's the kind of thing I should just ... wear whenever."

"Actually, it is. If it fits, you like it, and it's comfortable, then why shouldn't you wear it whenever you want? You don't need an occasion to feel good about yourself, Karine. And sometimes that starts with liking the way you look."

Huh.

She'd never thought of it that way.

Claire winked. "Besides, I'm sure you'll have a reason to want to wear it soon."

What did that mean?

"I know you don't want me to thank you for bringing me here again, but—"

"You're right, I don't. It's like we're all suffering from cabin fever back there," Claire added. "I needed this as much as you did."

That was fair.

Karine grinned. "It's not just that, but I guess what I'm really trying to say is that inviting me along made me feel like ... you actually want to be around me. Most people don't, or they're afraid of me. *Confused* by me. It's not their fault. I'm not an easy person to understand. I know that."

Claire sucked in a deep breath. "You don't scare me. You don't scare any of us, Karine. Is that strange to you?"

"Yes, it is."

"I'm sorry."

"It's okay. I'm just not used to people who care."

⁔ᴇPROMISE

"A shame, that," Claire muttered. "I'm sure it's a big change, but I guess … at least it's a change for the better. Even if it does feel strange."

Yeah.

She told herself that a lot, too.

Karine opened her mouth to say something more, but it was then that someone bumped into her. It was nothing more than a quick brush of the shoulder against her back as they passed by a crowded stall close to another.

A simple mistake.

Even she knew it.

Still, Karine gasped, the swell of panic tumbling her forward, but Claire grabbed her with both hands. Once more, her racing heart was back slamming against her rib cage with every hard beat that made breathing impossible.

"You're okay, Karine. It was just someone walking past. It's nothing to worry about." Claire searched her wild gaze, peering straight into Karine's soul and trying to keep her attention with every carefully chosen assurance. Her next gulp of air was still caught painfully in her throat, refusing to push through the tight column of muscles choking her silent.

"Should we just go back to the lodge? There's nothing more to see here anyway."

Karine nodded frantically. "Yeah, please, if you wouldn't mind. Let's go back."

Truthfully, she had lasted way longer at the farmer's market than she actually expected to. That was a win in her book, even if it ended like it did. Not every step forward had to be a leap.

Right?

SEVENTEEN

When Roman arrived at the lodge, he couldn't find Karine anywhere. His gut reaction was to panic—despite the fact that he knew someone would have informed him if anything had happened to her, there was no ignoring the cold trickle of fear starting to seep through his bloodstream.

No matter how irrational, it was there.

Roman had been waiting for this moment, for the second when he could lay his eyes on her again, and she'd take his breath away. Like she did the first time he saw her in the pool at the Yazov mansion. Most nights, he still went to sleep rewatching that scene in his mind.

"Roman!"

His mother's startled exclamation greeted him instead of Karine. She'd found him standing silently in the middle of the lodge's kitchen. He didn't realize he'd been staring blankly out through the kitchen window until he was forced to turn away from it.

ᴛʜᴇPROMISE

Since he left, Roman had come to realize how easy it was to lose himself in thoughts about how far they'd come together already—Karine and him.

It felt like a lifetime.

He knew that meant something.

It *had* to.

"Hey, Ma."

Claire rushed his way, throwing her arms out so he could pull her in for a tight hug. "What are you doing here—does your father know you came?"

Roman didn't want to answer that, but silence was also an answer, and it didn't feel right, either. "I'm here because I had to see her, Ma. Where is she?"

Without warning, the pad of his mother's thumb came up to press at the knot forming in between Roman's brow. An almost constant wrinkle that accompanied his unhappiness lately. Only one thing had caused the discontent.

Being without Karine.

"What's that for?" Claire asked, pulling her hand away only once the knot was worked away. "All that worry for nothing, Roman. She's perfectly fine, out on one of her walks with Michelle."

Roman's teeth clicked, his jaw tightening to mask how he breathed a sigh of relief. And still, he balanced on an edge, not quite content yet. He wouldn't be okay until he actually saw her again. His heart had already made that quite clear.

"She sounds good—*calm*—on the phone when I call, but how has she really been?" he asked his mother.

"There's progression in her everyday. It's like she wakes up a little bit better each morning. Better with *something*— someone, even. She's just ... much more confident in herself these days. Clear and levelheaded, less intimidated, too." His mother patted his cheek with her warm palm, smiling softly. "Your mind wasn't playing tricks on you when you called. She's been okay."

Roman couldn't express the words to explain the relief he felt hearing that news, but he'd never really done well with managing his feelings before all this. He doubted that was going to change anytime soon.

All he'd wanted was for this to actually work for Karine.

This gave him hope. Most times, hope was nothing more than a useless lie, but he found himself leaning on it more often than not when it came to Karine. It's all he ever did for her, now.

Hope that Karine had a future where she would be at peace—so she could be herself, content and happy. He was sure the lack of ever-present medications helped with her clarity, too.

"And what about ... have there been any episodes?"

He didn't have to spell out what he meant. His mother knew exactly what he was talking about. Had Katina made an appearance—Katee, maybe?

Claire only shook her head, and that was all he needed to know.

The very fact that Katina hadn't shown up in the time he was away felt like major progress, considering she certainly seemed to be the dominant alter with a penchant for protecting Karine from *anything* she deemed a threat.

Claire squeezed his hand, then, drawing his gaze back to hers. "I know everything is a bit of a mess right now, and you're worried about her, but ..."

"What?"

"I don't think I've seen you like this before ... not about someone."

Well ...

He cocked an eyebrow at his mother, unwilling to feed into her need to pry all the secrets from his mind that she possibly could. Claire laughed a playful chirp back, but didn't once move her stare from Roman's all the same.

She probably didn't need him to spill his secrets, anyway. Didn't a mother always know?

Still, she said to him, "Just go ahead and say it. At the very least, you can say it, can't you?"

Could he?

Or better yet, did he want to?

Roman headed for the kitchen entryway the second he was able to slip from his mother's hold, tempted to just bolt. This wasn't a conversation he'd had before—not with anybody;

not even with himself, really. He knew exactly what his mother implied, and he wasn't ready to say the words.

Roman already had one foot out the door, and it would have been so easy to keep going, but he paused long enough to glance over his shoulder. Claire smiled at him indulgently, shaking her head like she knew what he was running from.

"It's just me, Roman. If you can't even tell me—your mother—how are you ever going to tell her?"

She had a point.

"I bet that's what scares you the most, too," his mom added. "Just saying it. *Telling her.*"

"Ma—"

Claire shrugged, not even giving him the chance to speak. "Remember when you were a boy, Rome, and I'd say *night, my baby, I love you.*" He blinked, still able to hear the soft call of his mother echoing through the crack in his bedroom door, the sliver of light illuminating Claire's hand wrapped around the edge of the door to close it. But she waited—she always waited for him to say it, too—and the only sleepless nights he'd had as a kid were the ones that didn't end like that. "It was easy back then ... I lived for those little *I love you, too*s. The sad thing is, being a mother means I can also still remember when it started to change."

"It's not exactly the same, is it?"

"Maybe not, but it should be just as easy. And that was my point. To say it ... *to mean it.* It's one thing you shouldn't fear. Saying it really is the easy part. It's everything else that makes it hard."

His next breath still came out staggered. It ached. Surprisingly, though, the words came out easy when he said, "I am in love with her, Ma."

Claire's smile bloomed, her palm coming to lay flat against her chest, but she said nothing. He didn't really need her to.

• • •

Roman was waiting for Karine at the bottom of the steps to the front porch when she walked up the hill with Michelle in tow. It took her a moment to notice him, just a second when she had to look twice and those already-round eyes of hers widened even more, and then she darted for him.

All at once.

She was a breathtaking sight against the backdrop of the lake. Karine's wavy, dark hair flew widely all around her, her lithe petite frame coming his way faster than he'd expected, and *Christ* ... that long, flowy yellow dress she wore did very little to hide the shape of her small breasts.

He couldn't seem to look away from his dream-come-true. One he hadn't even known he wanted until he had her.

Roman couldn't help himself, he grinned.

Like a *fool.*

"Hey, babe."

"*Roman.*"

That was all she got out before she collided with him. He had her up off the ground and spinning around in a blink. His name passed her lips breathlessly, over and over again.

Their mouths met in a slow, burning kiss that swept Roman away to another kind of paradise. This *was* paradise. He never wanted to leave her again, even though he knew he would have to.

Many times.

Nothing about this life was easy. If she agreed to build one with him—and he didn't know that she would; something else that terrified him—then that was an unfortunate lesson she was going to have to learn. *Fast.*

But if she could trust him in loving her enough to know they would always find their way back together, then nothing else mattered.

He just had to tell her.

Ask her ...

"I missed you," she whispered when they parted. The kiss could have lasted a lifetime, and it wouldn't be enough.

Karine's lips trembled from the kiss, and his own throbbed from where she'd bitten him at the very last second before pulling away. She bit him hard—and he liked it—drawing blood that she watched him lick away with a smirk to prove to herself that he belonged to her.

THE PROMISE

It was that moment when he knew—he didn't even need her to say it.

She loved him, too.

Then, Karine lowered her lashes, her gaze skipping away from his when she asked, "Did you miss me?"

God.

Didn't she know?

"You're my first and last thought every day, Karine," he admitted. "How could I not?"

• • •

Claire cooked dinner for everyone at the lodge. She wanted to celebrate Roman returning, but honestly, he could tell she was trying to keep herself distracted from the fact that her husband wasn't there with them.

He would have asked his father to join him on the last-minute trip to Vermont, but he knew he had to slip away from New York the first chance he got. There wasn't time for anything else, considering. If he'd tried to have a conversation with Demyan about it, no doubt, he would have tried to stop Roman from leaving.

With good reason.

Technically, it still wasn't completely safe for him to be there. He couldn't be certain he wasn't being followed; that Dima and Leonid weren't keeping an eye on him and trying to track Karine down. He'd known it, and still took the calculated risk for the sake of his own sanity. Just to see Karine again.

He didn't know where to properly begin *that* conversation with Karine, but he would have to talk to her about it. Karine had to be aware of the fact that Dima would still do everything in his power to take back his bride-to-be. She wouldn't like it, but knowledge was power at the end of the day.

She needed all she could get.

They all did.

Then, there was the other little detail he hadn't told her yet—something else that chased him across miles of freeway that separated them until he arrived in Vermont. Her father was likely dead. Hell, he was as good as dead. It was highly likely that the Yazov bratva, as they knew it, was finished.

Leonid and Dima had already taken over.

Who else could deliver the news? Roman was going to hate every second of it, but he would still do it ... *soon.*

At dinner, Masha helped Claire to lay out the food buffet-style across the massive dinner table. Michelle, the appointed men on the property, Karine, and Roman all made their way around the table, finding easy conversation about everything *except* whatever reason had sent him there. He was grateful for it. Claire even arranged for vodka, and Masha baked apple pie that was gone before it could completely cool for dessert.

Karine and Roman stuck together, side by side where he could keep his attention where he wanted it the most. He didn't want to let go of his hold on her waist. She kept glancing his way with silent questions in her eyes, but they hadn't gotten a single moment to themselves.

Dinner was loud.

Unsurprisingly.

The food was great and the liquor flowed until even he started to feel a bit lighter on his feet. Not that Roman showed it—he'd been taught a long time ago to hide any sign of intoxication in the presence of others, no matter who those people were. It was a hard habit to break. That didn't stop him from enjoying the show of everyone else getting drunk .

Even Michelle appeared to be having fun, and couldn't stop eyeing up one of the bulls who gave her all the attention she could barely handle. His grandfather liked to say there was something about a good-looking Russian man with a glass of vodka in his hand that no woman could ignore, and Anton's sentiment was proving right again.

Masha went so far as to laugh with Claire as they heaped what remained on the platters to the couple in the middle for whoever wanted them. Leftovers were just as much a treat as the main course in his mother's home—no matter where she was currently calling home.

THE PROMISE

Karine, in her long yellow dress, teasing him with thin spaghetti straps that showed off the delicate line of her shoulders and dipped deliciously in the front to give a peek at her breasts, enjoyed herself, too. Roman was sure he'd never seen her as happy and carefree, engaging in conversations and jokes with the others, as she was during the dinner. As much as it killed him not to constantly have her attention on him, he liked to watch her just as much.

He toyed with a strand of the dark hair resting prettily over her shoulders while she sipped on a drink one of the guys had made her with soda to make the liquor more palatable to her tastes. She passed him one of those demure smiles that always set his cock off, throbbing in his slacks with little effort.

How could she be shy?

With him?

In the two weeks that she'd spent at the lodge, safe away from the influences that certainly hadn't aided in her situation, another side of her apparently emerged. A side he had figured was lurking somewhere under the surface, if only because she had dared to show him the occasional peek.

She had made friends, too.

Another bonus.

It wasn't just Masha and her, anymore. By the way she made easy conversation with nearly everyone at the table, Karine had formed a bond with the others as well. Even her doctor. Michelle, in particular, treated her like a younger sister whose well-being she genuinely cared about if the secret, playful smiles the two women shared was any indication.

Despite the fact that she had been forced there, he hoped the doctor didn't look at their circumstance as *only* that, but as an engaging challenge. With the bonus of Karine, whose magnetic soul seemed to keep dragging people in closer and closer.

It wasn't only Michelle and his mother who'd developed a deep fondness for Karine, but the bulls, too. The handful of men had clearly become friends with her as well. He didn't miss the friendly affection Jimmy, in particular, offered

Karine when only one sweet was left on the table, and the two reached for the pastry at the same time. He let her take it with a shrug and a chuckle.

If it were other men—or maybe a different woman sitting beside him—then Roman might have felt jealous seeing the woman he was in love with getting attention from others, and reveling in it. It wasn't like that with Karine; her ability to draw out someone's softer, *fonder* side was her nature.

And the fact she beamed under the attention of everyone around her ... *shit*, it hurt to know she'd probably been craving moments like this her entire life.

What business did something petty like jealousy have messing with that?

Roman honesty hadn't expected to see the progress he found in just two weeks, but he couldn't deny the relief, either.

And there was something ...

Something about knowing she fit here—found herself a spot at a table that, before now, hadn't even existed. With these people. *His mother.*

In his life.

He was also relieved that his mother had seen a different side of her. One that she'd only revealed to him before. Now, it was evident to everyone why he felt the way he did about Karine. What drew her to him. Underneath that hazy exterior she used to sport—the one that was muddled, confused and suspicious of the outside world—lay a young woman who was funny, charming, perilously sweet, and maybe needed just a little bit of help with her confidence every now and then.

He wasn't surprised that she shined in front of others—beautiful things always did, though. Karine was certainly that. There was no doubt about it.

While Roman's thoughts whirled in his mind, keeping him silent and unwilling to draw Karine's attention away from the rest of the people at the table, she and Michelle were in the middle of a new conversation. Apparently, the two had found a secret trail in the woods and wanted to show him. Claire interrupted everyone's chatter by turning on music in the room, the sound filtering out from built in speakers overhead and all around.

"Now, nobody said anything about dancing, Claire," one of the bulls joked, making Roman's mother reply with a laugh.

He knew the truth.

"She's playing this music because she misses my father," Roman said softly to Karine when she turned, and pouted those pretty lips of hers at him. "It's their favorite thing to do at night—he listens to music, and she reads beside him."

Karine's pout bloomed instantly into a smile. "That's … sweet. You should have brought him."

Maybe.

Some shit couldn't be helped.

"He was busy," Roman replied.

He wound an arm around her waist, and pulled her closer to him until she was practically on the edge of her chair. The rest of the room drifted away, even his mother's attempts to get a shy Masha to sway to the beat with her, faded with Karine so close to him. Michelle chose that moment to head away from the table, and he was silently grateful.

"You seem happy," Karine said in a whisper, the tips of her fingers raising to trace the smile playing on his lips.

"I am. Are you?"

She nodded. "Very. I don't think I've ever had this much fun before."

"A shame, that."

"Doesn't matter."

Roman lifted a brow. "Oh?"

Karine shrugged. "It's just better with you."

The way she said it so unabashedly was music to his ears. Roman kissed her, then, leaning between them to close what distance remained, and he didn't care who watched. From the way the room silenced, but for the music, of course, he didn't doubt that everyone's eyes were on them. Karine must have sensed it too, because she broke away from the kiss, blushing.

The *prettiest* pink.

All the way down her throat, too.

Goddamn.

They needed to be alone.

Soon.

"It's too bad if you want more of that apple pie because I'm going to take you away now," he told her, unable to tear his gaze away from the sensual curve of her mouth.

She bit down on her lip. "I've been waiting to hear you say that all night."

"Really? I thought you were enjoying yourself."

"I was."

Roman smirked. "But you're not even going to make me feel bad about taking you upstairs for the rest of the night, are you?"

Karine didn't hesitate. "Not at all."

He weaved their fingers together, pulling her toward the doorway hand-in-hand, and not bothering to check over his shoulder as he went.

Roman had some important things to say to Karine, but first, he needed to take that dress off her.

• • •

He was kissing her before they even made it through the door of his bedroom because he just couldn't help himself. The door flung open under his chaotic, searching hand once it finally found the knob to twist, and they tumbled through the threshold in one other's arms. Both out of breath, tangled in each other, nothing separated the two from what they wanted the most.

Roman loved the taste of Karine on his lips. All hot, and *sweet.* Like warm honey. She coated him, every inch of him. He weaved his fingers tightly through her hair, angling her face exactly the way he wanted to keep her still, so he could kiss her deeper.

She stared at him with heavy lidded eyes when they finally parted, their fingers knotting together. With the bedroom door still open, they could faintly hear the music filtering up the stairwell from downstairs. He couldn't be sure if his mother had turned it up, but certainly sounded a little louder.

ᴛʜᴇPROMISE

"You know, I might have liked to dance," Karine whispered through a smile.

"Okay, so *dance*."

Roman lifted her arm up and twirled her around, making Karine giggle before she fell on him again, pressing herself to his chest. He certainly wasn't the type to dance, but he would for her. Hell, he'd do anything if she smiled at him like that again.

Kept smiling at him.

For the rest of her life.

Pressed tight to his chest, Karine's one hand still weaved with his while his arm held her around the waist, they swayed on the spot to the slow melody that just barely reached their spot. But it was perfect, too.

Just him and her.

He'd *missed* that.

When he kissed her the next time, she stilled, wanting his mouth more than she wanted his feet to keep moving. He pulled the straps of the yellow dress down her arms to slip them off, marveling in the way his hands covered her delicate shoulders.

"I like this dress," he said.

"I got a red one, too, but I couldn't say no to this one on the way out. I really loved the market."

His stare slammed into hers.

Karine lifted one bare shoulder, adding, "I heard you liked red."

He did, yeah.

"I can't wait to see that one, too."

Karine's quick grin had him ending the conversation so he could tug the dress lower until her perky, bare breasts came into view. He sunk down, enjoying the tickle of her blunt nails scratching over his scalp when he took her breasts in his hands. His lips lined dotted kisses down her chest, over her cleavage.

The softest sigh echoed over his head when he sucked on her nipples, one by one. Rosy and peaked, he used his teeth. All that breathiness of hers came out in a moan next.

Deep, and loud.

His cock throbbed hard in his pants, a selfish urge to get those moans of hers vibrating around his dick while fucked her mouth, but he shoved it down. Roman wanted to make her come first, and he wanted a taste of her while she did. Lifting her dress up, he got down on his knees in front of her while his fingers spread wide and flexed over her thighs.

"Roman …" she hissed when her muscles twitched under his touch, his name coming out sultry on her lips. Like she knew exactly what he was going to do next. He gave her a hint by pulling her panties down.

"I just want a little taste, babe."

"Only a *little*?"

Well …

He pushed her back on the bed, making her body bounce on the springy mattress. Karine's wriggling legs came to a still when Roman grabbed her knees and yanked her forward in the position he wanted her, spreading her thighs wide apart.

"We'll see what I can do," he returned.

Her pussy was right there for the taking—pink and already damp, ready for him. Her swollen clit peeked out from under the hood.

Roman kept his eyes on her, holding her stare as he covered her clit with his mouth. Karine raised higher on her elbows, watching him with fast pants of breath passing between her parted lips. The harder he flicked against the throbbing bud, the quicker her breaths came, melting in moans and rolling hips.

Karine dropped back to the mattress, her back arching high as her eyes slammed shut. He was relentless, but *fuck*, he had to be. Roman wanted that taste of her, hot and heady. Needed it. He wouldn't stop until she came for him.

When his cock jerked painfully in his pants, angrier because the pressure between his weight and the mattress did nothing to offer relief for him, he rammed two fingers into her without warning. He found that fleshy, wet wall of her pussy that had Karine whining in a way he hadn't heard before.

But damn, he wanted to hear it again.

ᴛʜᴇPROMISE

His mouth remained on her clit, licking slower in contrast to how hard he fucked her with his fingers. She was begging him to let her come in less than a minute like that, her high pitch keen unmistakable with every airless, *"Oh, my God ... please."*

He felt her shudder when she finally found the edge of whatever cliff she'd been balancing on. His fingers slowed only enough to massage her now swollen G-spot while she gushed enough fluid to wet his hand and the sheets. All the while, he sucked her clit in between his teeth while she rode that wave, watching her orgasm take over.

His cock protested hard in his pants. She wouldn't even care—he knew it. Lost in the intensity, he could have her bent over and be fucking her hard enough to take her breath away until he came himself, but not yet.

Roman beat down that urge, too.

Barely.

Her wetness stained his lips by the time she was done. Karine was flat on her back on the bed, her breasts heaving steadily as she tried catching her breath, a single hand reaching down between her thighs to press tightly against her clit. Sensitive, he knew. Roman had a feeling she'd *never* come like that before.

He gave her pussy one last lick before he straightened up, his hands finding her trembling thighs to squeeze again.

"I've missed that, too. But that was ..."

"A lot," he replied with a husky chuckle.

"A lot," Karine agreed.

Her laugh floated through the room, and what he heard made him smile all over again. There was confidence in the sound now, he noticed. There were so many positive changes in her to celebrate, and he was more than ready to do just that.

"But if you missed that, then you're going to love this," he said roughly.

Before she could react, he'd crawled over her, covering her completely with his body.

Karine watched him with a sly grin when he straightened her arms up, curling her fingers around the ornate wooden bars at the head of the bed. Stretched out underneath him, *spread open* for him, she was perfect.

He sat up on his knees, tugged her dress down her waist and then the rest of the way, shoving it to the floor before he started pulling off his belt and undoing his shirt.

Karine didn't take her eyes off him, watching him like she was in some kind of daze.

Naked and waiting, her eyes roamed over the tattoos on his chest, then lower to his abs, and his stomach. Finally, her stare landed on his rock-hard cock between his muscular thighs when his pants came down, too, once he'd stood up from the bed.

"I'm definitely going to love this," she murmured.

Roman leaned over the bed between her thighs, keeping one hand to the mattress and using his other to give her pussy a wet swipe with the pad of his thumb. "Will you let me use you—will you come if I use you, Karine?"

She shivered.

Her sigh echoed.

He needed to hear her say it, so he waited even as his hands came to rest on her bent knees and he fitted himself between her widened thighs. She regarded him under lowered lashes, wetting the seam of her lips with a pink tongue. And then she whispered, "Of course. Please use me."

He sunk into her, his thumb guiding the head of his cock between the swollen, wet lips of her pussy. It's where he found heaven—the best kind of oblivion as he fucked them both to bliss.

What could be better?

• • •

"Are you happy here, Karine? And I don't just mean tonight with the dinner, or my mother's little party."

They were still in bed, side by side. He'd made his way to his back while she had rolled over to her stomach, using her arms as a pillow while she'd angled her face his way to watch him. There wasn't a single woman from his past that had managed to keep him in a bed with her after the deed was done, but he couldn't seem to move whenever Karine was in one with him.

Would it always feel like this?

Like she was home?

There was no smile playing on her lips as she replied, "I think I am. I didn't expect to be, you know? I was worried about not seeing you for a while, and … everything I didn't know. But I trust you. So, yeah. I think I am."

Someday, he wanted her to say it without the maybe qualifier—he didn't want her to think about it at all, just *know*. For now, though, he'd take what he could get.

She drew circles on his bare arm with her fingertips, and it sent teasing, dancing shocks racing down his spine. Roman hooked a finger under her chin.

"I'll always come back to you. You didn't ask me to say it, but I will anyway. As many times as you need to hear it, and maybe someday you can tell me to stop because you won't need to hear it anymore. You'll just believe it."

He wound some strands of her hair around his fingers, enjoying Karine's sweet murmurings in his ears when she said, "Funny—your mom said the same thing about Avdonin men always coming back. Sharing similar traits."

Roman laughed darkly, urging on Karine's softer giggles. "More than I care to admit."

He could get used to this. Lying naked in bed with her, legs tangled with hers, and nowhere to go, nowhere to be. A lingering scent of sex in the air, soft skin close enough to taste, and sleep creeping in.

Could they have that?

In the future, maybe—could they could spend all day and even longer nights together like this? When he wouldn't have to worry about the shadows chasing them? Would she want that, too?

All he wanted was to protect her with his body, keep her in that bedroom forever, locked away from the world. But it could all change in a minute, too.

Roman didn't know what Leonid and Dima's plan was, but he wasn't naive enough to assume they'd forgotten about her. Or the fact that she'd been stolen from them—how long until they knew it was him who did it?

Or did they already?

It instantly reminded him of all the things he hadn't told her yet. About her father, the fire where she had spent all her life, or even how Dima and Leonid were still nowhere to be found.

All bad news.

Roman couldn't do it, though. He just couldn't bring himself to change the topic of conversation to what would inevitably ruin a good night for them. One of the only they might have for a while.

So, he told her something that was even more important. The thing he wanted her to know the very most.

"I'm in love with you, Karine. I love you."

She blinked at him, long lashes fluttering fast like she had to take in the sudden words she clearly hadn't been expecting to hear. The seconds ticked by. One after another, matching the beats of his crazy heart.

But then she sighed, and shrugged those delicate, creamy shoulders almost casually. "Good, because it would be strange for me to love you and get nothing in return, but I wasn't sure how I should say it."

Yeah, him either.

Until he did.

Roman rolled her way, pulling her in for another kiss so he could breathe against her smiling lips, "Babe, you just *say it*."

Because that was the easy part.

Even if it had terrified him.

He didn't see this coming.

EIGHTEEN

For the two weeks that they'd been apart and Karine was without Roman, every morning when she woke up, she felt … *okay*. Stronger when she meditated. *Better*. Clear-headed; willing to face the world.

Just *good*.

Today was no different, except that she had woken up in Roman's arms and there was nothing quite like the contentment burrowed deep in her chest when she found he was still asleep as she blinked her eyes open. Strong sunlight filtered in through the thin silk curtains that barely shielded the window, haloing the hard lines of his profile that relaxed just enough in his sleep to make him appear *boyish*. She stared at him sleeping, watching the slow rising and falling of his chest, his steady breaths assuring that he was nowhere near ready to leave his dreams.

Even if she might want him to.

How could she not, though?

The ache between her thighs, a pleasant reminder that she didn't mind, was a damn good reason for her to wake him up. Still, she didn't.

Instead, her mind drifted to the night before, and the words he'd spoken into existence. He made it real.

I love you.

There was no way to stop the smile creeping over her lips as that memory took center stage in her mind. If she were honest, Karine might say she had been in love with Roman—infatuated, really—from almost the moment they met. Every single moment, word, or touch between the two since had simply dragged her deeper into what she thought could only be a fantasy.

Until he made it reality.

Before last night, she didn't have anyone to confess her feelings about Roman to. No matter how innocent, or confusing, they might have been, there was no one to help her make sense of it all. Masha wouldn't have approved— Karine knew it without even broaching the subject with her. She was here only for Karine because she would do anything for her. Not because she actually wanted to be here, or even because she trusted Roman or the rest of his family.

That was the one thing Masha had made abundantly clear through her reserved comments on and off. Sometimes, she forgot that Karine wasn't as checked out as she used to be without a steady supply of medication. It was easy for Masha to think Karine wasn't always listening.

She listened too much, now. It wasn't like she had a choice. Regardless, the truth was out there.

Real.

Karine had to keep telling herself that—keep reminding herself that had really happened.

He said he loved her. She told him the same.

But what does that mean?

It was the one thought that wouldn't leave her mind the longer she stared at the sleeping man next to her. For them—for the future, when all of this was gone, if it even was—what did it mean? It was a question she didn't have an answer for. One of many, and that was just something new for Karine to obsess over.

Unanswered questions were the worst kind.

The *most* dangerous for her.

He'd be leaving soon. *Again.* What was going on that kept Roman away? He might not have specifically mentioned it—when he would head out again—but he still *would*. She doubted they would have very much time together.

As the minutes ticked past, she grew anxious in the sheets, restless in the silence with only her screaming thoughts to keep her company. It was only a faint echo of what it used to be before she started working with Michelle—but it was still there all the same.

They were still there.

Karine had to force herself to remain still lest she wake Roman up, because God, what then? Would he know something was wrong just by looking at her?

She didn't want that.

Not right now.

Settling on a long walk in the woods, and her morning meditations somewhere new, Karine figured she just needed a second alone. Those were the only things that helped calm her lately, but she still didn't want to leave Roman's side. Not knowing when their time together would end again only made it worse.

Every step she took away from the bed was harder, but she kept going. It was something else that she had to keep reminding herself—she trusted him. *She did.* He wouldn't do anything to hurt her.

She believed those things to be true.

Absolutely.

But how long was she supposed to trust him *blindly*?

All their lives?

Just because he told her he loved her, didn't mean they were bound to each other forever. Certainly not the way Dima had bound himself to her the first opportunity he got. Karine shuddered as she slipped out of the bed.

She needed some air.

• • •

Roman was already up and out of bed when Karine returned to his bedroom. She'd truly lost track of time, and wasn't sure how long she'd been out walking in the woods. One of the bulls had, of course, jumped to follow her at a distance that didn't feel like an invasion of her personal space.

She was never truly alone, and that was for the best. Even she wouldn't trust herself if she was actually alone. Not when Katina's voice had started to become a bit vindictive whenever she made herself known to Karine. Even the smallest things—like Karine being hesitant to take a new trail in the woods—would have her alter hissing taunts and threats of *doing it myself*.

Karine never thought she would admit it, but she did feel safer to know someone was nearby. Even if it was just a bull.

The bed was empty when she walked through the door. The sound of the running shower echoed from the bathroom.

By the looks of the bag by the door, which was left exactly where Roman dropped it yesterday—only now, it was left open with dirty clothes haphazardly tossed inside—she got the feeling it was time. Their little tryst was coming to an end. Even though she trusted it was only temporary, it still stirred all those feelings of unease in her again. The loud ring of abandonment clanged inside her heart with every beat.

Nearly impossible to ignore …

Karine *tried*.

She sat on the bed, at the very edge, waiting for him to emerge from his shower. Roman eventually stepped out of the bathroom with damp hair and a towel wrapped around his waist. His perfectly chiseled body, streaked with the remaining drops of water that had fallen from his hair, at least gave her something to admire.

Karine would have given anything to pull him back into bed—to be underneath him while she felt the heavy pressure of him above her. Surrounding her. Keeping her warm and safe. *Alive*.

⁴PROMISE

She didn't say anything. Not about those pesky worries and questions, or the fact that his open bag at the door said he was leaving. He was going to go, that was that, and she wouldn't beg him to stay.

That would hurt him, too.

She didn't think he *wanted* to say no.

He still would.

A sexy smirk lingered on his handsome face when he found her there. Silently, he picked up the fresh clothes where he'd left them on a dresser, and started pulling the items on.

"I heard you went for a walk," he finally said.

"You hear everything."

"I make it one of my priorities to know you're safe, that's all."

Karine played with the edges of the sheets absentmindedly, keeping her gaze downturned because she didn't want him to see the sadness staring back.

It was happening again.

That bleakness she'd been trying so hard to fight all morning came back with a vengeance, and right after they had such a good night together, too. What was wrong with her—what more could she want?

"Karine."

At first, she didn't act like she'd heard him. She did, though. She heard him *too* well, and the concern lingering there.

Roman cleared his throat, saying only, "Is something on your mind you want to talk about?"

In a blink, she tipped her head up and smiled at him, forcing the happiness on her face. Nothing about the way she felt right now made her *want* to smile, but learned habits were hard to break.

"No, it's not that. I'm fine, really."

Roman didn't look like he believed her. "I have to leave. I shouldn't even really be here—we're supposed to stay apart for a reason, Karine. It makes you harder to find."

She nodded because she understood. Not because she agreed, though. Those were two very different things.

"Is that what's bothering you?" The question came as he did up his belt, moving a step and then two towards her. "Or is it something else? You've got that ... sad, faraway look. Is it something else?"

Karine looked up at him sharply. "Like what?"

"I just ... shit, Karine. I'm not good at this. Talking, you know? Well, you don't tell me a lot of things, I guess. About your past, but I wonder if you think about it more than you let on. Like the things that must have happened to make you—"

"*Crazy?*"

The sharpness in her tone didn't even make him hesitate before interjecting, "You know I wouldn't say that. You're not crazy. *Nobody* thinks you're crazy, babe. Come on, now."

Yeah, she did know.

Still ...

It was the only way to keep him—and everyone else—away from that topic of conversation. It wasn't one she was ready to have, by any means.

Karine sighed, willing the heat to take the edge off her voice as she told him, "As long as the past stays where it belongs, it's better if we don't talk about it."

"I don't want you to feel like you should be hiding something from me." Finally close enough to touch her, he did just that, spreading his palms around her face, making her look up at him. While he searched her eyes, she tried her best to hide whatever truth he was trying to find in her eyes. "Anything, Karine."

"I'm not hiding anything from you, I just don't want to talk about it. What good is going back—there's nothing I want there, Roman."

Nothing good happened there.

"And that is exactly what I'm trying to do—for you and me both."

Right.

It was just her insecurities that said different.

He kissed the top of her head, lips lingering for a second or two, and tenderly stroked her cheeks with his thumbs. For a second, she was able to close her eyes and pretend like the rest didn't exist. And well, even if it did … none of it mattered.

Not like this.

Not with him.

Of course, it couldn't last long.

"I should go say goodbye to Ma before I leave. I'll see you outside in a bit?"

She nodded, pulling his hand up to her mouth so she could kiss his fingertips. It was the way he watched her hold on to his hand for a pause too long, unwilling to let go at first, but his patience to wait helped her to do it in the end.

Then, Roman walked to the door, and stepped out into the hallway after snatching up his bag.

All the while, Karine ignored the clawing urge in her chest to spill every secret she had locked up tight—if only to make him stay.

She wished she could tell Roman everything, but it just wasn't that easy. She couldn't. *Wouldn't.*

Karine couldn't actualize her past when parts of her still hadn't come to terms with it in the first place. How was she supposed to expose him to it when she really hadn't faced it herself?

She expected to hear Roman walking down the hall. Instead, she heard Masha's voice, intercepting him in the hallway. Their conversation was muffled only slightly, but not enough to hide exactly what was being said between them.

Then, Masha's tone raised.

"You can't keep her here forever. This is not the life she deserves to have."

"What, like the one she had was *better?* At least, I'm trying to do what's best for her. I'm going to keep doing exactly that, too. Whatever it takes to keep her safe; whatever she needs."

"Keep her safe from *what?* What are you doing to protect her?"

It wasn't at all like Masha to speak the way she did to Roman. Whatever had been bothering the woman must have finally pushed her to the edge if she was willing to take liberties now that she'd never allowed herself in the past.

Karine stood from the bed, and moved towards the door. She considered stepping outside the room to end the conversation, but Roman's next words stopped her from doing so.

"I'm not in a position to discuss the details with you or her right now."

"Sure," Masha said dryly. "Do you realize you're doing exactly what they did to her? What you're pretending to rescue her from is no different than what she's doing here— the prison and the guards simply have a new look, Mr. Avdonin."

"They were keeping her captive. I'm protecting her here."

Masha didn't sound affected by the harshness of Roman's reply when she said back, "*Hiding* her. The reason might be different, but the result is still the same, no?"

He must have pushed past her after this because then there was sudden silence and the beat of footsteps against the hardwood floor. Karine's heart quickened in her chest, and she struggled to find something to say or think—even if only to settle her feelings—but nothing quite worked.

Not even when Masha eventually stepped into the room. Karine still stood near the door, feeling foolish and looking the same, she imagined. Not that Masha said anything about it.

"I was looking for you everywhere," Masha said, her tone far more subdued than it had been with Roman in the hall. "I swear, whenever he's here … I should already *know* where to find you, I suppose."

When Karine didn't reply, Masha's stare hardened as she searched her eyes. It didn't take her long to figure out that Karine had heard everything.

Masha's nostrils flared, her neck turning a splotchy red in embarrassment, words cracking when she implored, "They tell us nothing, Karine. We know *nothing*. Don't you want to know what's going on?"

Karine shook her head. "It doesn't matter. I've spent my whole life not being told anything. I'm used to this—so are you, remember? It never bothered you before."

Because that was the thing.

Masha seemed to forget it.

• • •

The bottom step of the porch became Karine's perch as she watched Roman load the trunk of his car with his bag and a few other things. Claire wanted him to take some of the leftovers from last night back to Demyan, but that had been a while ago when she ran back into the lodge to prep the food.

She found it harder to ignore the sinking sensation in her heart while he readied to leave.

The illusion of them being alone was created well—she still wasn't foolish enough to think they weren't being watched. A bull keeping an eye on things, or Masha sneaking a peek through the curtains. Maybe even Claire, too.

Not that anyone interrupted.

Roman left the car door open, and returned to where she sat. Karine did her best to hold back the tears threatening to fall when he rested beside her on the step.

"It's scary."

"What is?" he asked.

"This … thing with us. *Love.* I was so happy yesterday when you came back, and now I'm so sad I can barely feel anything at all. I'm just numb. Way deep down, Roman. *Numb.* That's exhausting, isn't it?"

She certainly thought so.

"But it won't always be, babe."

While she stared ahead, Roman kept his eyes on her— examining her for cracks, Karine was sure. She dared to peek over at him, then, and he offered her a shrug that earned him a small smile in return.

"I'm sorry that we're in a tricky situation, and I don't want to leave you, Karine."

"But you will leave."

"And I *will* be back. That's how it works."

Right.

That's how this works.

"It's hard to think about what will come in the future when I'm still figuring out how to live in the present," she admitted.

"I know."

She turned to him and he took that opportunity to lean in to kiss her. Their mouths met, lips closed, soft and lingering. Every beat of her heart ached when he pulled away. He gave her chin a quick, loving squeeze and stood up.

"Take care of yourself, beautiful."

"Call me?"

Roman winked. "As soon as I can, you know it."

Karine didn't stand up to watch him leave, but she did wave when he gave her one last look at the end of the path. Roman got in his car, and she was stuck staring at fading tail lights until they could no longer be seen. Karine still hadn't moved. Not even when she heard Masha's footsteps coming to a halt a few steps above her.

"What happens when he finds you? You know he's looking for you," she said.

If she'd been stabbed and her lungs punctured, it would have felt the same as Masha's words. Karine quickly lost her air at the mention of Dima, not that Masha had been clear *who* she meant. She also didn't need to.

Karine *knew.*

All too well.

"I don't want to think about any of that right now," she murmured. "Besides, Roman will keep me safe. I believe him."

Masha walked down the steps until she stood across from Karine down below, forcing her to stare at the woman's face.

"You made a promise," Masha continued, but the sternness she tried to keep didn't hide the quivering of her bottom lip as she fought to maintain her composure. "You accepted his proposal. That kind of pact lasts a lifetime. I know you've been afforded a level of ignorance, Karine, but that's not going to fly anymore. You have to start thinking about the consequences of certain actions here. Haven't you thought about it at all?"

What?

Karine met Masha's stare, saying slowly, "It's not like I had a choice. I couldn't exactly refuse his proposal. It was forced on me. You know this, Masha. You were there. You think I *wanted* to marry him?"

She didn't understand why Masha chose now to talk about Dima, and the marriage. Today of all days, when her heart had already taken a hit, and she still had tears in her eyes. It felt a little cruel.

Unnecessary, even.

"It doesn't matter whether it was your free choice or not. The promise was made, and that means Dima is going to come after what he's owed. He's been raised in a world that's told him it's his *right*, Karine."

Shaking her head, she refused to listen to anything else Masha said. Dima was a topic best left under lock and key— *no one* would force Karine to even think about that man if she didn't want to.

"Are you even listening—do you *understand?*"

That condescension in Masha's tone was where Karine drew the line.

"What is your problem?" she snapped at Masha.

"I feel like someone needs to remind you of reality. You won't be able to lock yourself away in a room to play house with another man forever, Karine."

"Stop it. That's enough."

Masha sighed, slapping her hands to her jean-clad thighs when Karine stood, turned, and rushed up the steps back into the lodge. Today would be another one of those days— one where she did nothing but lie in bed for the rest of the day—and she wasn't going to feel guilty about it, either.

But before she could slip through the front door, Claire came running out with a phone pressed to her ear.

"Has he left? Has Roman left already?" she asked.

The panic in her voice froze Karine to the porch. Her throat went dry because she could see it in Claire's eyes, too. That *fear.*

"What's going on? What's wrong?"

Claire was too busy trying to pay attention to whatever was being said on the phone to see that her panic had triggered something in Karine that she couldn't control. The rational side of her didn't even have a chance.

"Maybe I can get one of the bulls to follow him?" Claire asked.

For the first time, Karine was viscerally cognizant of an alter coming to awareness. She felt the way Katina slipped into her skin, blinked and suddenly looked through different eyes. It was so fast, but still, she heard *herself* ask, "Is Roman in trouble? Is he going to be okay?"

It took more effort than Karine could stand to fight back Katina from speaking—*being.* She knew what it was that triggered it—the heady, taunting taste of anger and fear.

Katina's favorite.

Claire held up a finger, and Karine choked at the sudden, loud ringing in her ears. She could already see the trail of destruction Katina was capable of—*wanted to*—leave as the metallic tang of blood swept over her tongue.

She'd bitten it.

Hard enough to bleed.

She even tried to bargain with Katina—*just let me know he's okay first. I need to know.* The repeated mantra did little but distract Karine from Claire's fast words to the man on the other end of the phone call.

"Yeah it's better if he—no, he doesn't have his phone. He said he left it in New York on purpose," Claire said, rubbing her forehead with the back of her hand, and pressing her eyes closed. "But, Demyan—"

The darkness came to Karine *fast.* Just before everything went pitch-black, she felt Masha's hand on her arm and heard Claire calling her name.

After that, there was nothing.

Nothing but Katina.

Her voice, a sweeping echo.

You shouldn't have trusted him, Karine. You shouldn't have trusted anybody.

NINETEEN

Roman rolled through the four-way, driving with an arm hanging out of the window in the dark, a lit cigarette dangling from the corner of his mouth. He squinted his eyes when the smoke rose up in front of his face, a split second when his attention wasn't one hundred percent on the road.

Or his gaze, anyway.

His mind was another matter.

Instead of Karine, who always took up all his headspace, but especially when the world was quiet, the person he currently thought of, was Masha.

Rather, the words she said to him earlier. Words she said partly in fear, he knew, and because of the unknown. He didn't doubt they were still words of truth, though.

He might have been angrier with her stupid need to take a stand, if he didn't think Masha was right. She wasn't entirely wrong in saying that Karine was in a different kind of prison now. Just because she liked her new prison and was happy there—well, that didn't really change what it *was*.

It wasn't like Roman wanted to hide her away in Vermont forever. She deserved normalcy in her life.

He wondered what pushed Masha to the edge when she—knowing her place, risking punishment—chose to speak out of turn. Roman wasn't the kind of monster who would punish her for the behavior, but *she* didn't know that.

That's why he worried.

Did she know something?

Hear something?

Roman wasn't really paying attention to the road while he drove—the vast freeway bare but for a few sparse cars with headlights they didn't even bother to dim behind him, or speeding on by. *Assholes.* Shit, he was already doing twenty over the limit.

At least, he had his new apartment to look forward to.

Finally, a friend of his, connected to another captain in the bratva had procured an apartment Roman could safely hide away in. For a few months, anyway. He was exhausted moving to a different hotel every few days.

He was back to that … *no bed of my fucking own.*

Marky was supposed to meet him for a drink when he finally rolled into the city, but he needed to pop over to the apartment first and grab his phone. Not to mention, the damn time.

He didn't take the phone with him to Vermont because he wanted to disconnect from everything. There were a lot of ways he could be traced, he opted to eliminate as many as he could. It was selfish enough for him to go there in the first place. The very least he could do was lessen the trouble it might bring.

It wasn't like he was totally disconnected from what was happening outside the bubble he'd created for Karine. The bulls were there—they all had access to phones. His mother always had a direct line to his father.

Not that he expected Demyan to be impressed by his trip, either way. Some shit never changed, right?

So far, his quick jaunt to Vermont had passed smoothly, and he was glad he got to see Karine—even if it was just for a night. What harm had he done, really, even if it was only inspired by his selfish need for him to have her hear the words that had been festering inside him.

But what good would loving her do when she also learned he *still* hadn't told her the truth about her father. Maybe next time he would, so for now she could remain blissfully unaware. He, on the other hand, let the guilt gnaw away at the ice in his chest.

That shit had been melting for a while.

Apparently, he had a heart.

Perfect.

At least, it was for her.

Roman reminded himself of that as he tightened his grip on the steering wheel after chucking the cigarette out of the window. He was about to turn up the volume on the stereo touchscreen when he felt his hands lose their grip on the wheel.

All at once.

Time had never slowed for Roman—except for the moment he saw Karine in that pool—but it did right then. It didn't feel entirely the same, but the sense of impact was still very much real.

A split-second later, his body crashed to the side, and then forward. Straight into the airbag that had already blown. His car spun out of control, metal scraping pavement as glass instantly cracked and shattered all in one go.

It had flipped.

His car rolled.

Roman was already confused.

Somewhere behind the rushing of blood in his splitting ears, a horn blared continuously,

He'd been hit.

Surreal couldn't quite explain it, but then he lost consciousness, and it didn't even matter.

• • •

Fuck.

When Roman regained any sense of awareness, the first thing he saw were his hands dragging through the glass of his blown-out windows. There was a brief moment when he actually thought he was dead, but the rapid welling of pain made sure he knew that absolutely wasn't the case.

The high pitched ringing in his ears made him want to throw up, until he realized … *nope*. That was still just his horn blaring. He could scream just from the noise alone, and the pain it caused in his left ear.

No doubt, some damage had been done there.

He hadn't been moved, still half in, half out the wreckage that had become his driver's door. He wasn't sure he *could* move. It was nothing more than mere luck that he was even alive.

He couldn't feel the bleeding slice on the side of his face, but the blood dripping down his chin to make a pool of red on the cracked pavement made him aware it was there. His own blood was the one warm thing he felt when it smeared his chin, but he couldn't get his hand up to touch his face. He couldn't even seem to sit up straight.

The piercing throb at the back of his head, threatening to split his skull open, made him think the whiplash must have given him a concussion. The echo of his childhood doctor telling his father *he's going to turn his brain to mush, Demyan, get him out of impact sports* suddenly filled his mind.

He knew that pain well.

Roman blinked furiously, trying to see beyond his hands in the glass. As the seconds ticked passed, he realized the large white spot he'd been staring into was really a bright headlight shining straight at his face from only feet away.

He couldn't keep his head steady, the wobbling of his neck and his heavy eyelids promised darkness was coming soon. Again.

That couldn't be good.

Then, two figures appeared, cutting through the light. At first, he could just see silhouettes against the brightness while he focused on counting steady breaths. He knew he couldn't sleep, especially if he *wanted* to. It was only when one of the men stepped closer that he discerned Dima's face.

Well.

Shit.

^{THE}PROMISE

"I hope you're taking a good look, motherfucker." Dima's words came out cold, and calm. In a way Roman hadn't heard him speak before. It only added to the surrealness of his situation, making him wonder if this was all a dream, but no. He couldn't be *that* lucky. "Just thought you should know—we're in New York, and we need to speak to your boss. It appears you've taken something that belongs to me, and I want it back."

Roman let out what he hoped was a steady breath, but his chest still rattled against the metal and pavement. There was no question in Dima's demand—he wasn't here on belief.

So, Roman didn't bother to lie. Not that he had the strength.

"I haven't taken anything of *yours*. She doesn't belong to you," he replied, barely keeping back the groan forming. His ribs were in bad shape, too. Every breath made it more apparent.

"I want my fiancée back," Dima said, the last word cutting from his mouth like spit. "Consider this your only warning— you're lucky you even survived this one. Let's be honest here."

Dima stepped back, and the headlights that had been lighting up Roman's whole line of vision were suddenly turned off. Roman peered into the darkness, but he couldn't see where Dima went, or who the other man was that had stood silently beside him.

Just as suddenly as they'd appeared, they disappeared, too. Only the crunch of rubber told him they were pulling away, and he wasn't quite sure what happened next.

Everything faded black again.

• • •

Dima probably didn't expect Roman to be found quickly, but that wasn't the case. He learned later, while the doctor paid off by his family opted to glue the cut shut on his cheek, that Demyan was expecting an attack on him after getting last minute information on Dima's whereabouts.

Too close to home.

229

The bull staying at the lodge, sent by his father—through direction of his mother—came up on the accident mere minutes after it happened, and the Chicago pricks had already fucked off.

Roman might have been able to stave off the attack, or the worst of it, had he been plugged in even enough to get a phone call ahead of time. But his hubris wasn't as kind as it could be.

Roman had been taken directly to the private clinic of one of the doctors on the Avdonin payroll. Demyan and Marky were waiting there for him, along with a handful of other men that had been nearby when the call came in.

His father was concerned, Roman could see it in his eyes—but Demyan did a good job of keeping it under the surface.

"Just listen to the doctor—stop being a shit. You need to let them finish cleaning the rest or you'll get a goddamn infection," Demyan said.

Roman shot his father a painful sneer as he was helped into a wheelchair. The cut on his cheek hadn't quite stopped bleeding, so the doctor went for that first. But only to keep from making a worse mess.

Three nurses waited in the large room where Roman was taken despite his protests. This was nothing vodka, sleep, and some painkillers wouldn't fix. He could clean out his wounds in a hot shower and dose them with alcohol. The screaming ring in his ears had yet to stop, and the pain in his head was at an all-time high.

Roman in pain was Roman *angry*.

Simple as that.

He barely contained his snappiness and frustration as the doctor fired off commands to two of the nurses before turning his questions on Roman. There wasn't much to say.

The man wanted to know what hurt?

Shit, *look at him*.

It all hurt.

Demyan, Marky, and the one bull that had pulled Roman from the wreckage scattered around the room, keeping a close eye on the doctor's proceedings. The attack had changed everything, just like that, and now nobody could be trusted. The bratva was on high alert which meant the city would feel the impact, too.

More attention.

Great.

There was too much silence in the room. The only sound was made by the doctor while he carried out his examination once he figured out Roman really wasn't in the mood to carry any kind of decent conversation. The nurses tended to his wounds and cuts. He had to endure more stitches, and creams. Bandages, too. A lot of hands *touching* him. He hated the feeling of being poked and prodded, even if it was to his benefit.

Seeing his son's growing irritation, Demyan uttered from the other side of the room, "*Behave.*"

Christ.

It felt like he was ten again when he'd popped his shoulder out of socket after a fall from his dirt bike and wouldn't stop fidgeting long enough for the doctor to get a good grip. His father's low bark of that order was just what was needed to still Roman long enough for the doctor to do the deed.

Painfully, of course.

That was the thing.

Roman really liked to avoid pain. Just because he could handle it, didn't mean he could stand it. Not always.

After the doctor was done with his examination, he was given a list of instructions on how to handle the concussion. Roman nodded his head along with whatever the man said, resisting his nature to be an asshole, instead trying his best to speed up the process.

"And most importantly, you need to rest," the doctor said to him sternly, and then looked over his shoulder at Demyan

Who, *surprise, surprise,* nodded in agreement.

As if that bullshit was going to happen. Things needed to be done now. That much was clear. Karine had to be protected first. They were already running out of time if the two things Dima knew for certain was Roman's location, and the fact he had Karine.

Roman could rest when Dima was eliminated.

The doctor and nurses shuffled out of the room eventually, prompting Roman to stand from the wheelchair immediately. At least he was able to do that now, and he'd all but refused to get into the bed.

"You heard the doctor, son, you need to rest," Demyan said, stepping forward.

Roman reached for the jacket his father held out to him. The one thing that had managed to make it out of the wreckage of his car other than him.

"I'm sure we can find somewhere for you to rest for the night if—"

Roman had been too focused on struggling through the pain of shrugging on his jacket, but those words from his father stopped him up. "Are you fucking kidding me?"

"Rome—"

The affectionate nickname only pissed Roman off more, and he shook his head. "No. Dima is here. *For* Karine. We need to get her out of the lodge—hell, out of Vermont. I don't trust her being this far away from us."

"From you, you mean."

God.

What did it matter?

Roman's rage spilled through his heart, red and hot. "I'm not going to find a place to sleep tonight and hope he's not already one mile closer to her."

That didn't seem to interest his father, maybe that should have been Roman's first clue something else was more important, and he just hadn't figured it out yet.

"But why did Dima come to you—practically alone?" Demyan asked, making Roman pause before he shoved his left arm into the jacket with a wince. "Who came with him? Where is Leonid? His father has taken over the Chicago bratva. If *anyone* from that organization wants to speak to me, it should be him. As far as I'm concerned, Dima is fucking nobody. Think about it, that was a bold move for him to do that here like he did. The way he did, Roman."

He was hearing his father, sure, but he didn't care to listen. That was the difference. Only one thing mattered to Roman, and it *wasn't* Dima's fucking games. It was Dima himself. That was the big problem here.

"So he's feeling bold—who fucking *cares?* It's only a matter of time before they find Karine in Vermont. We need to move her. Now."

"We only have one piece of a very confusing puzzle. Don't you think before we go making any rash decisions, we should find out more? Getting answers to some of these questions could help, Roman. Leonid could have just as easily requested to speak to me himself, and we would have at least pretended to have a civilized conversation first. It's bullshit semantics—yes, but it's how it's done."

Demyan's brows furrowed in his thoughts, and it pissed Roman off like nothing else that his father wasn't hearing *him* first.

Roman glared at the others in the room, growling under his breath, "Get out. Now. Leave us alone."

That caught Demyan's attention, making him meet his son's eye. However, he didn't protest the demand, and the two of them waited in silence until every other person in the room was gone. They were finally alone.

It took every ounce of focus and strength he had to stay balanced, and not let the pain stabbing throughout his body take control, but Roman did it. He had to. "I need you to hear what I'm saying. Karine has to be moved. Dima wasn't fucking around tonight. She isn't safe out there, with three bulls watching over the whole property. It's only a matter of time before they find her."

Demyan stared at his son, then nodded. "I hear you, and I also know she's as safe there tonight as she was today … otherwise, I doubt the first move Dima would have made was to accost you on the highway, Roman. It seems like you haven't heard me, no? Something's not right here."

"*Nothing* is fucking right here. If what he did to me was a warning, what will he do to Karine if he can get his hands on her?"

"That's exactly where my question lies," Demyan continued, before moving to grab the wheelchair as Roman started to fall backward. His father said nothing as he rested into the chair, and his swimming vision cleared. "It doesn't make sense to do what he did—not if you consider we have business between our organizations. It was just violence. Just for the girl. *Why?*"

"Because Dima is a fucking lunatic." Roman managed through clenched teeth as he massaged the pad of his thumb hard into his temple to relieve the pressure there.

"I don't think that's it. I think they're hiding something, and we need to find out what it is."

"We can work on finding out all their secrets, if you want to waste your time, but we need to keep Karine safe, first."

Demyan narrowed his eyes at his son. "Karine will never be safe. The two of you will spend the rest of your lives looking over your shoulder if we don't find out the *why* here, Roman. Why is this happening? If she just needs to be found, for everything to come to an end, then like you said, it's only a matter of time. Even we won't be able to keep her hidden from them forever."

Roman hated how sharp the clarity of his reality settled in on him in that moment. The truth was a cruel bitch in the way that he never really wanted to face it—life was just easier without the moral details involved. This wasn't quite the same.

"You may think I don't get it, but I do," Demyan said, sighing as he regarded Roman still struggling with the throbbing ache of his concussion and every other injury. "I understand why you're reacting the way you are right now. I don't blame you for wanting to protect her, but you need to hear what I'm saying. There are two ways of dealing with this situation, and—"

"All I care about is keeping Karine safe."

Even though he repeated the same words, Roman's resolve slipped. What his father said made sense. Dima's move was suspicious.

All wrong from the jump.

"Thing is, how did he even know where you were, Roman—*who* provided that info?" Then, Demyan shrugged, adding quietly, "You can try as hard as you want to keep her safe, but it won't be forever. The smarter thing to do is to

THEPROMISE

find out what is motivating them to raise hell to get this girl back. There has to be a reason for it. What *is* it—why could he find you, but not her?"

Roman closed his eyes, barely soothing the pain at the back of his head. He was trying to lie to himself—thinking he could do *anything* when he couldn't barely fucking stand straight for longer than thirty seconds without wanting to puke. He couldn't spring into action right now if necessary. Once again, Dima had made sure of it.

"All I know," Roman uttered, each word slow and measured, "is that Karine doesn't want to be with him. She made that very clear to me. He was never her choice."

"And yet, she's spoken for, which seems to be enough for him to do all of this, hmm? There's something about this situation we don't know, and maybe if we find that out, a lot of this will make sense. For now, we need to accept the fact that she *is* spoken for, and we can't just run away from an agreement like that. Not in our world."

Roman gritted his teeth until his molars ached. Just one more thing to cause him pain.

"Karine doesn't belong to him. She's already mine. In every way that fucking matters."

He didn't break his father's stare. Demyan cleared his throat, clearly getting the hint.

Roman had taken *her*—not just once but many times since they first met. She had given herself to him, freely, in every way she wanted, and nobody could take that away from them. No prior agreement would change that or what it meant.

"She's not going anywhere near him," Roman muttered after a minute.

Demyan's expression didn't waver. "Well, you won't know if you're dead, son."

Yeah.

There was that.

TWENTY

No matter how hard she tried or how long she stared into the dark shadows of her bedroom, Karine couldn't get the image of blinking awake to Claire and Masha huddled over her. They'd patted cool facecloths against her face, hushed words shared between them as she came to and their attention had again turned on her.

Claire had been asking her for the month and year. Masha, on the other hand, only wanted to know how she was feeling. Karine couldn't understand *why*—the only thing on her mind was Roman.

It was the stunned, wary gazes of the older women while they watched Karine where they had laid her on the bed, that she couldn't quite forget. Their hesitance had only swirled her nerves and fear together, making her voice shake when she had asked, "Did you see Katina?"

Because she'd fought hard.

Knew that irrational fear wasn't her own.

Karine tried.

⅃PROMISE

It was all she could do.

She *had* tried.

Hope was a terribly dangerous thing, but she dared to feel it all the same. Karine couldn't quite explain the way the exhausted joy flooded her when Claire had shaken her head, whispering only, "No."

Her happiness didn't last long.

Then, what was the problem?

No one seemed to want to answer that question. Even Jimmy had avoided Karine's gaze when he slipped into the bedroom to bring Claire more wet facecloths. It felt like Karine had won a battle—keeping Katina at bay, even if she didn't know how long it would last—only to lose another.

"Is Roman okay?" Karine had asked.

The catalyst couldn't be avoided.

She had to know.

Claire had tried to brush the concern off, saying Roman had simply gotten into some trouble with his father. He wasn't even supposed to be in Vermont in the first place, apparently. Except his mother's words felt hollow—bare of any sadness, yes, but also lacking any *realness*, too.

She just wished, for once, people would stop treating her like a frail, pathetic creature and just fucking tell her the truth. She never got those answers, instead shuffled under fluffy, soft blankets that were too cold without someone else to share them with, and that's where Karine had stayed.

Staring at the shadows for hours.

Thinking.

Her personal victory was dampened by the lingering unease she couldn't quite shake. Karine couldn't fall asleep, her mind spinning though she ignored it to drown in her own thoughts instead. Their bleak haven wasn't much better, to be honest.

At least, with the late night, the lodge had quieted outside her bedroom door. Everyone seemed to be asleep, *her* chaos had passed, but what about the rest?

Where was Roman?

Why wouldn't they tell her?

The knock on the door came so quiet that she missed it at first—until the door creaked open without the person on the other side waiting for permission.

"Masha?" she called out.

But it wasn't Masha.

Karine sprung up in bed, clutching the sheets tighter to her as a male figure sliced through the stream of light. Alec—one of the bulls who had been designated to watch her every move for the past weeks—entered the room without as much as a *hello*.

"What are you—"

He came towards her, his long, aggressive strides making Karine curl into herself until he was close enough to hold out a phone for her to take. The lit up screen was the only light between them, but it was enough for her to see the kindness in his face.

And the severe line knotting his brow, too.

Something *had* happened.

Or was happening.

Karine didn't get the chance to ask.

"Here, take it. It's Roman. You should speak to him," Alec said.

Karine's heart thudded to a stumbling stop as she plucked the phone out of Alec's hand, still expecting some cruel joke to trick her out of the comfort she had just been offered. Wasn't that the way of her world?

It sometimes felt like it.

She pressed the phone to her ear. "Hello?"

"I wasn't sure if you'd be awake, babe. Are you okay?"

Roman's unmistakable voice should have been enough to soothe Karine's frazzled nerves, but instead, the jumpiness under her skin only increased to the point she had to exit the bed and safety of the sheets. Unconcerned about Alec, or the fact that her night clothes were simply made up of *Roman's* oversized long sleeved shirt, the man simply turned his back to her. For a fleeting second, she felt bad for doubting him.

But she had more important things to consider.

Like the man on the phone.

"I'm okay—now that I know you're okay."

ᴛʜᴇPROMISE

Roman's dry chuckle crackled through the phone's speakers, but it didn't quite feel true, even when he replied, "I'm fine."

"*Fine* is moot. What happened?"

Because clearly, something did.

"Dima found me. Made it a point that I acknowledged his arrival in New York."

Karine's gaze found the window where the shades hadn't been pulled. Not that it mattered because there wasn't any light for it to block out, and she was left staring at the blank canvas through the glass that was usually the lake in the day. Her voice didn't feel like her own, though it was, when she asked, "What did he do?"

She *really* thought Roman would tell her the truth—though a part of her didn't actually want him to. It was strange to constantly feel at war with herself. Whether it was the things she wanted, or needed—even her emotions.

Nothing felt sacred.

Controlled.

Hers.

But then Roman let out a hard breath, "I want to say it doesn't matter, Karine, because it doesn't, and I'm okay. I'm hoping that's going to be a good enough answer for right now because we're running out of time here."

"For what?"

"To hide," he murmured.

That coldness creeped in slowly, starting in her spine and then spilling into her belly. It soaked through her one limb at a time until Karine was frozen in place and wishing he didn't mean what she thought he did.

"I just need to know if you trust me."

Well …

"That's the easy part," she replied. "It's always been, Roman."

"Okay."

"What do you want me to do?"

"Alec," Roman said, making Karine check over her shoulder for the bull standing at the bedroom door. He had his back turned to her, trying to make it a point that he wasn't eavesdropping on the conversation. She wondered if that was partly because he already knew what was about to be said.

"What about him?" she whispered in the phone.

"I want you to leave the lodge tonight. With him. He's going to drive you to me. Just grab the few things you have, be extra quiet as you leave."

Karine's heart began racing in her chest all over again. She considered herself to be friendly with Alec—although she felt more comfortable with Jimmy, if she were being honest. That didn't mean she wanted to be in a car alone with him for who knew how long.

When Karine remained silent on the phone, Roman added, "This is really important, Karine. It might be the only real chance I have to take you somewhere in a way no one will be able to find you except for the person *with* you. Me, I mean."

"But—"

"It's just a drive, babe. A drive to *me*. You can do that, can't you?"

She clutched the phone tighter to her ear.

"Is this because of Dima?" she asked.

"He could seriously hurt you, Karine. And if he found me when I was supposed to be off the map, then that makes me think he's only a few steps away from you."

The swell of fear that swallowed Karine in one, heavy wave damn near put her to her knees. All it took was reality coming back to say hello one more time. Masha had been right—Karine *was* silly to think Dima wouldn't be back.

Sometime.

Somehow.

He'd always been there.

Ready to hurt her.

"Karine," Roman started to say, concern etching his voice a not higher.

He didn't get to say anything more.

"He killed her," she blurted out, hot tears prickling the backs of her eyelids as the darkest secret left her mouth. A truth that she had—for years—turned into a lie inside her mind. The mantra was easier than the memories. It was the first time she learned how to dissociate from her trauma.

It wasn't real. It didn't happen.

But it did.

Oh, it had.

She could see him now—*Dima*. The memory would forever be etched in her mind, but it was just a matter of making her mind hide it. Shuttering it away to someone else, *somewhere* else she didn't have to see.

Except she couldn't hide it now, wavering between the steady breaths of the man on the phone calling her name, and the memory pulling her under.

Karine could still smell the sugared rose perfume her sixteen-old-sister had sprayed lingering in the large closet where she liked to play sometimes. She'd been extra quiet so nobody knew she was in there—Katina shrieked like a devil whenever her little sister found something new to destroy.

Shoes.

Makeup.

Her favorite silk blouse.

Really, Karine only wanted to try them herself, and she *loved* Katina. More than anyone else in the world.

From where she played in the corner, she could see clearly through the crack of the French doors into her sister's bedroom. It was the shadow that passed over the corner of Katina's bed, where she'd haphazardly thrown her rose-gold comforter into a pile, that turned Karine into a statue.

Still, she could hear Roman.

Stuck between her past, and present.

He was there.

"Karine, what the fuck are you talking about—who killed her? Who is *she*?"

Her voice was faded.

In the background somewhere.

"Dima. He killed my sister."

She was nine when it happened. Life had been *so different* before that night. Not better, just … different.

There was silence between them. Stretching on while the shadow on the blanket grew larger, and Karine couldn't hide away from the scene that had stayed buried for so long in her mind.

"I saw it happen," she said, wanting Roman to know why. Why everything was so … so very *wrong*. And why it had been that way for too long. "I was there."

When she blinked, she was transported back to the walk-in closet, sugared-rose in the air, and charcoal staining her tiny fingertips. Her big sister was in the room, scribbling something in a sketchbook—Karine had stolen Katina's other notepad to do her own drawing.

She hadn't thought Katina would stay for as long as she did, leaving Karine unable to sneak back out like she usually would without drawing attention. Instead, she sketched a picture of the old willow tree for her sister to find, but it probably wouldn't look anything like Katina's carefully crafted pieces of art. Not that the quality mattered—she pasted her creations all over her bedroom walls.

Annoying their father to death.

Not that Maxim cared much lately. He was too busy, never staying at home for long because the sight of his daughters reminded him of things he no longer had. Instead, the girls were raised by the servants and whatever nanny had been assigned to them for a time.

Karine had noticed the visitor in her sister's room first— that approaching shadow didn't catch her sister's attention until it was already too late. Katina's futile efforts to ask him to leave, his very presence enough to make her voice quake, didn't work. It was the fear she heard from her sister that made Karine stay crouched in the closet, and not make a sound.

But it was the way she remembered seeing Dima watch the girls as they played in the halls of their home that kept her silent as the rapidly spiraling conversation outside the closet went from bad to worse. Some people just felt *bad*. He was one of those, but his father's constant presence in Maxim's life meant the man was around more often than he wasn't.

Karine and Katina made every effort to stay away. Lately, even that didn't work to keep hidden from Dima's unnerving view.

⁀PROMISE

The nine-year-old hiding behind thin doors with a visible crack in the middle didn't know what to do when he'd hit Katina across the face after she'd dared to step off her bed toward him, demanding he leave. She saw the flash of her sister's bare calf when she stumbled back to the bed, almost falling to the ground.

Except Dima was there, *grabbing her.*

In one second, he apologized.

In the next, he hit her when she cried.

The memory wasn't as clear, then. Her mind couldn't really process the scene of her sister's trembling legs pinned against the side of her bed, or the sounds of muffled sobs. Despite her young age, she did comprehend pain, and she couldn't get her hands to cover her ears good enough not to hear … she couldn't squeeze her eyes shut tight enough to keep the burned images away.

Karine couldn't breathe. The same way she couldn't breathe that day inside the closet. The same way her sister couldn't breathe when Dima had used Katina's bloody tank top to strangle her when Katina wouldn't stop fighting.

Karine had needed to put her hand over her mouth to keep herself from screaming. Her sister couldn't make a sound then because none would ever escape her lips again. She'd bitten through the skin of her knuckle, the sounds of those final moments one of her biggest regrets.

Taking her hands from her ears had consequences.

Her mind kind of broke, then.

All shattered into different pieces.

Sharp fragments. Never quite fitting back together the way they once did, but cutting her until she bled all the same when they tried.

"I'm so sorry," she heard Roman say.

Karine was still staring out at the darkness that overlooked the lake. The memory had already begun to fade, but the effects remained burrowed deep in her heart, filling her chest with a heaviness that only seemed to spread.

"Nobody even knew it was him," she said in a whisper. "Her death was just another excuse for my father to avoid, and—"

"You shouldn't have had to see something like that."

Maybe not.

"But that wasn't the worst part, Roman."

"Babe—just come to me. You don't have to tell me this on the phone. Let Alec drive you to me, okay?"

It was too late.

That was the thing.

Karine had kept it secret for as long as she could ... there was no holding it back.

Maybe it was a noise that drew Dima's attention to where Karine had been hiding in the closet. Either way, he'd found her there. Wild-looking, and bloodstained. Jeans shoved down his hips, and red staining his hands.

You.

That was all she remembered him saying. Well, that's where *her* memories stopped altogether. The voice that answered the monster back when he'd thrown open those French doors was not her own.

"Pl-please don't hurt me."

The first words Katee ever spoke.

Regardless of how hard Karine tried, she couldn't remember what happened next. Katee had simply decided those memories were hers to have.

Part of Karine was grateful.

The rest was terrified.

"Karine, listen to me—can you hear me?" Roman asked, the firm words forcing Karine to blink out of the blackhole welcoming her back to the safety of her fractured mind. The only place where she *could* hide. That day taught her that lesson. Her body might suffer, but her mind would be okay.

"Yes, I hear you."

"You're never going back there."

He said it like it was true, but— "I don't want to marry a monster."

"Would you marry a man you love?"

Her brows furrowed in confusion

"I don't understand," she murmured.

"The only thing you need to do is get in the car with Alec and come to me. I'll keep you safe, Karine. Just let me."

ᴛʜᴇPROMISE

She couldn't respond, and her hands trembled as she held the phone.

"But you have to go now," Roman continued. "You need to leave right now. Remember, nobody can know. Not even Masha. You have to do this alone, Karine. We can't trust *anybody*. Do you understand me?"

"Okay, yeah, sure."

Alec.

Right.

"Why him, then?"

Roman cleared his throat, saying only, "We go back from when we were kids—and he was awake, so. Shit worked."

"Oh."

"Working with what I got, babe, but I am doing something. Okay?"

She loved that he never failed to ask. Because even if it wasn't okay at all, he made it that way. *In a way ...*

"Okay," she repeated.

"That's my good girl. I'll see you soon."

Then the call ended. Karine paced her breathing, trying to get a hold of herself even though she was slipping. The man in the room—whom she'd forgotten about—didn't allow her the time she needed, but it wasn't really his fault.

"I packed a bag quick—you didn't have much. We should go," Alec said.

She turned to face him, surprised to find he was holding the bag she'd been using up for her to take. When had he even started packing?

Alec didn't mention a thing about what he'd heard on the phone call, and his gaze was still just as kind as it had been. No pity stared back when he asked, "Are you ready?"

She nodded, although it wasn't true.

Karine didn't know where she was going, or what would happen next. She'd spent her whole life devoid of answers, and she wanted that to change. So, she would start by going to Roman and asking him all the questions she had for him.

Everyone else could wait.

"Yeah, I'm ready," she replied.

TWENTY-ONE

The plan Roman had for Karine to keep her close to him wasn't one that his father particularly approved of. He was aware of it, sure, but Demyan agreed to it because he knew he wouldn't be able to stop his son if he tried. It wasn't a matter of whether or not Dima was on his way to the lodge, he likely wasn't, but Karine wouldn't remain there to be found either way. *He* had been there, so she needed to move. Roman had made up his mind already, and this was the only way to do it.

Karine came first for him.

No matter what.

It also meant that the plan needed to be executed fast, and it had to be done in secret before anyone could fuck it up. If *someone* was feeding information of any kind to Dima, then they had no other option but to be careful. But if everything went smoothly, then he was going to make sure Dima would have no rights over Karine.

Not anymore—over Roman's dead body.

^{THE}PROMISE

Demyan's focus was undoubtedly better spent on the reasons for Dima and Leonid acting strangely, but Roman had other things on his mind. That needed to be handled first.

Besides, he now had a pretty good idea why Dima was shitting bricks about Karine going missing. She was carrying a secret for him—she *was* the secret.

Essentially.

That made this all the more dangerous, too. He needed to get Karine alone, all to himself where the rest of the world wasn't watching, and only then could he tell her his intentions. All that was left for him to do was wait for when she'd actually turn up.

He was waiting on the side of the freeway, somewhere between New York and Vermont, on a small dirt road that led off into an abandoned farmer's field.

Alec promised to deliver Karine to him—unharmed and without alerting anyone else at the lodge. It was still up in the air on whether that part of the plan would actually work considering it was the one thing Roman hadn't been able to think too long about before making hard choices.
Not for one second had he believed Karine would be comfortable driving for an extended time alone with a man she only barely knew—what choice did he have?

With the time crawling past four in the morning, Roman had been waiting at this spot for nearly two hours.

And only one thing dominated his every thought. Karine's revelation had about killed him on the spot—how monotonous she had delivered to him the scene of her sister's assault and murder over a phone call.

A fucking *phone* call.

It wasn't something he was sure to forget anytime soon. Not the sound of her voice, or the picture she'd painted.

There'd never been any doubt for Roman that she was keeping something from him. Something that happened to her when she was younger. Some trauma that had somehow woven into her very soul. He'd expected it to be related to Maxim, and maybe that was his bias—or ignorance— showing, because despite knowing Dima was a real piece of

247

work—Roman never once considered that horrible thing that Karine had kept hidden would be *him*.

How terrifying the last year of her life must have been as—even if only subconsciously—she'd realized that she was getting closer and closer to being delivered back into the waiting hands of her monster. What was the likelihood that Katina's sudden presence didn't somehow correlate to a stark, horrifying reality to Karine? There was something twisted about the way Dima had clearly left Karine living, *broken*, and then orchestrated her eventual return to him.

Why?

Had she just been too young for his tastes, or was his mind more warped than was comprehensible? Honestly, Roman was willing to bet it was a bit of both. And knowing all of that did nothing to quell his urge to get Karine as far away from Dima as possible.

Forever.

What was more fucked up about it all? Now, more than ever, Roman finally felt like he got her. Like he truly understood where the fragmented pieces of Karine had been born, and why.

If only, somehow, that could make it all better. As if some magical roadmap to healing her had been laid in his hands … but, no.

That's not how this worked.

Roman lit his third cigarette in a row—the only thing distracting him from all the pains and aches criss-crossing his body from head to toe. Even the way his cheek stung every time he grimaced, pulling at the tender, glued slice on his face, was forgotten as hot smoke burned the back of his throat and lungs.

Nobody could say he didn't know how to handle stress. He *did*—it just wasn't healthy.

The doctor wouldn't have been pleased to hear what Roman had gone and done when he'd specifically been told to rest.

Whatever.

It would all be worth it when he saw Karine's face.

ᴛʜᴇPROMISE

He was halfway through his cigarette when he saw the headlights of Alec's car approaching down the dirt road. Gravel crunched under slow-moving rubber. He crushed the cigarette under his shoe, and waited with his arms crossed over his chest.

The car stopped only a few feet away in front of him, and Alec got out first, moving to the rear to open the back door.

Roman hadn't realized he was holding his breath, until he finally saw Karine's slippered feet touch the ground. A smile twitched at his mouth. She hadn't even bothered to put on her shoes.

But she was here.

Everything would change now.

Wrapped up in a quilt, Roman had to wonder if she'd even bothered to change out of her nightclothes when Alec barged in on her. That had been a risk, too—a risk that Katina might show herself if not handled *just so*.

She was frail in the headlights of Alec's car—walking straight to him through the stream of bright yellow where he waited. *Small*, yes, but still beautiful. She kept her head up, her shoulders straight—Karine radiated a strength that he hadn't noticed before.

But he loved it.

Loved her.

Alec stayed back, and Roman nodded at him over Karine's shoulder.

"Thanks, man—for everything, yeah?"

"It wasn't a problem," Alec returned easily, "my pleasure."

Alec quickly slipped back inside the car and headed off, no doubt back to New York to meet with Roman's father, and receive his next set of orders. Whether that was returning to Vermont, or otherwise, he wouldn't be punished for doing what Roman had asked.

Karine came to a stop only a couple of feet away from him, staring like he had all the answers in the world. She was far away enough that he couldn't touch her, but close enough that he wanted to pull her into his arms.

And that was exactly what he did, closing those two feet with one long stride before he'd caught her in his arms. The quilt flew off her shoulders when Roman dragged her into his chest. Instantly, she had tipped her chin up, lips pursed for his kiss, demanding he give it to her before he could even offer it.

Roman didn't mind, and by the time he was finished greeting her with tender sweeps of his lips against hers, her sigh was pure pleasure. *All* happiness.

"I thought something happened to you," she whispered when he pulled away from the kiss. The pad of her index finger traced the cut below his eye. "Nope, don't like *that*. At all."

Her joking tone was still laced thick with fear, the undercurrent shaking her words just enough for him to hear it. He didn't look great, but she had better things to be worried about other than *him*. The last thing he was ever gonna do to this woman was make her worry about him.

Simple as that.

"I promise I only look like damaged goods right now," he said with a smirk.

Karine swallowed hard, but her finger didn't pull away from the one visible injury she had decided to focus on. Little did she know, there were more where that one came from. *So to speak.*

"Dima did this to you," she murmured.

"But he's never going to do it again, and he's definitely never taking you away from me. That's what's important here."

Karine licked at the seam of her lower lip, and gripped his arms tighter. "Do you have a plan?"

He couldn't stop the smile from spreading on his face.

The next part of this was easy. Like breathing, his mother might say, if it was just meant to be. He dared to believe it was, even if he wasn't that kind of guy. He wanted to be— for Karine. He *did.*

"I have something even better—that's why you're here, remember? I have the woman I'm going to marry," he replied.

The stretch of dirt road was quiet but for the woosh of passing cars every so often from the highway, hidden only by a thin patch of trees and darkness. In his arms, her head tilted back so he could see her smile.

He hadn't expected to be nervous, really. Roman had already figured out what he wanted, after all. So when that smile of hers landed on him, he realized that he'd been right not to worry.

This—*her*—was everything he wanted.

"I wasn't really sure if you meant that literally," she said, soft but sweet.

"Really?"

Did he seem like the kind of guy to just say that kind of shit? *To anybody?*

Roman released her from his hold, dropping down on one knee in front of Karine. Her giddy laughter fell into the darkness surrounding them. He tugged on her hand, making her wild gaze dart to his.

"What are you *doing?*"

"I can't believe you didn't think I meant it literally, babe."

She dragged her bottom lip under her top teeth, unable to contain her grin. "Well—"

"Well, I guess you should think about what you're going to say, because I'm asking you to—wait, what's your middle name?"

The ridiculousness of his question even had Roman laughing, but he eventually calmed them both down with another gentle pull on Karine's trembling hand still safe inside his own. Her laughs silenced with a little gasp when he had her stare locked on his once more.

"I was serious—what's your middle name?"

Karine weaved her fingers with his. There was a hitch in her breath, a soft hiccup, when she said, "Lizabeta."

"Your mother?"

She shrugged. "I think so."

"I don't have a ring, but I promise I'll get you any single one that you want. If you want to have it designed, we can do that, too. Whatever you wa—"

"What I want is you. I don't care about a ring."

So honest.

And *true.*

Her smile deepened again at his wink, and Roman decided to just go for it. The *I love you* part of this whole thing had been easy when he simply said it, no hesitating. He wanted this to be exactly the same.

Because it was easy.

Love should be.

"Well, you better think about what you wanna say because I'm asking you to marry me, Karine Lizabeta Yazov."

He thought she might take a second. Even if only to absorb him actually saying it, but her whispered *yes* fell from her trembling, pink lips the moment he finished asking.

Nothing had ever sounded so good.

Roman was up from the ground and kissing Karine before she could blink, when she did, he felt the splash of her tears from her dark eyelashes to his cheeks. He kissed every single one of those away, but that didn't hide the questions he still found staring back in her eyes.

He wondered if she would ask them.

She was getting better at that.

It was her hand sliding down his chest that had Roman pulling away with a painful hiss. A reminder for both of them that his pain meant they were still in a dire situation.

"Sorry," she was quick to say.

But Roman had her hand back in his, crushed against his aching ribs and her body tight against his own in the next breath. "It's fine."

His lips found her forehead.

He lingered there.

Karine asked, "What about Dima, and—"

"We're gonna do one thing right now, babe. And won't be worrying about him."

He said it with confidence—even if it wasn't something that he truly felt. That was Roman's problem. He'd been taught to believe he could do anything simply because he said he could. It gave him an arrogance like no other that had served him better than well over the years.

It also made his failures all the more catastrophic, even if he had spent years drowning them in money and drugs.

This wouldn't be one of those.

ᴛʜᴇPROMISE

It couldn't.

• • •

Money talked, bullshit walked.

And Roman had a lot of it.

Money, that was.

He hadn't used his wealth to its full capacity before, but now he knew exactly where to use it. *How* to make that money talk.

The money he threw at people made them willing to turn their cheek to a lot of little details. Like when he was able to acquire a chartered private jet to Las Vegas in the middle of the night. They didn't even ask him for fucking identification—the jet was already heading that way anyway to pick up the wealthy owner who had been staying in his weekend penthouse suite on the strip.

In Vegas, their first stop was at the office of a forger who was the top in the business. He'd ordered a new set of IDs for Karine that would help them move easier, and get everything else out of the way without much trouble.

Roman had already gotten rid of his phone, opting instead to pick up two burners that were only for him and Karine to call one another when he might need to leave her alone in the high-rise, luxury hotel suite for more than fifteen minutes. He *didn't* use the burner to call anyone in New York, and wouldn't unless he had absolutely no other option.

It was just him and Karine, flying solo. Along with the pile of cash he used to help their wings take flight.

He bought a new car in Vegas—a neon green with black accents Lambo—from a friend who had helped teach Roman the ropes when it came to boosting back in the day. Competition made that friendship hard after some time, but shit still worked out for the two in the end, he supposed.

As he and Karine drove through the city three days after their arrival, it made him laugh to see how much joy the lights and the life of Vegas brought to her. She marveled at all of it, mesmerized and taken with the sights and sounds of a new city. He suspected she was as much overwhelmed as

253

he was overjoyed, but that didn't stop her from reveling in the chaos. She couldn't stop staring up through the sunroof at the way the lights danced overhead.

The best part, though?

She'd finally shown him that red dress. Well, it wasn't so much a dress as a red jumpsuit that looked like one what with the way with hugged her body and billowed in the legs—and she had never been more sexy to him because she wore it well. And she *knew it*. It showed off her slender body and accentuated her perfect breasts with the low dip in the front and back. Her dark, wavy hair flew around her face in the breeze, but it was the happiness that sparkled in her eyes that killed him in the best kind of way.

"I want to come back here someday," she said, airless in the wind.

Roman smirked. "Whatever you want—maybe we'll make a tradition of it."

"We better."

She flashed a teasing smile and he wished he could frame that moment when she looked so carefree beside him— flying high, because for only a second, it felt like nothing and no one was chasing them. When nothing was holding her back.

Because that was when he knew.

This was the woman he would always love.

• • •

They drove up to the little white chapel with an *actual* white picket fence. That made Roman squint a bit. At the end of the driveway stood a man and a woman. They would officiate and witness the wedding, making their marriage legal and binding, and overlook a few details to make it happen because of the extra cash Roman had paid to the couple.

But it was practically done. Roman had taken care of the details in advance, and all they needed to do was turn up, do the ceremony, and sign the papers. Once the woman filed it with her husband's signature, there was no going back.

_{THE}PROMISE

Now they were here.

He knew it was a bit cringe. A chapel in Vegas. Cheap looking, and cheaper feeling. The bride in bright red, and a groom who still had visible bruises and cuts. No family or friends around. Was this the wedding he'd pictured for himself?

No.

To be fair, he'd also never pictured getting married in the first place. So, in the end it didn't really matter to him what the chapel looked like or if the officiant was wearing a wig, because none of that mattered. This wasn't supposed to happen to him—the same thing he'd thought his father was weak for, being so in love that he was constantly at the beck and call of his wife, was the only thing Roman currently dreamed of.

Fucked, that.

But he didn't mind it.

When he parked the car, Karine turned to him. Her eyes were so bright, her smile growing radiant—and now that he thought about it, she hadn't stopped smiling since she got into his car in Vermont. With him, she was happy.

Always.

He kept reminding himself of that.

But there was still something lurking behind her stare, too. It felt like every quiet moment between them was charged with the questions she couldn't seem to bring herself to ask, but he always saw them staring back.

Thing was ... if she couldn't ask them, he didn't know if she could handle the answers. So, he was going to wait. She would have to ask, simple as that. Sometimes, self-awareness was, in itself, a lesson in strength.

He needed her to start figuring out, and *demanding*, what she needed. Whether that was answers, or otherwise ... but not today.

He reached for her, cupping her cheek with his hand.

"Are you sure you want to do this, Karine?" he asked.

There was no pause between his question, and when she leaned between the seats into him, taking his kiss hard from his mouth. Fiercely. Like she owned it; like she owned *him*.

Because she did.

"Let's do this. Let's get married," she whispered against his lips.

Roman already had the car door open.

. . .

Want more of Roman and Karine's story—check for book 3, THE MARRIAGE at www.bethanykris.com/themarriage, to continue the trilogy or …

Here's a sneak peek:

Chapter 1

Roman wanted to touch Karine while she stood across from him—tuck the stray strands of wavy hair that had fallen out from behind her ear—feel the shivers race over her shoulder blade when his fingertips glided down the column of her throat. But he made do with her palms tucked inside his larger hands as the officiant stood at their sides at the little makeshift church. The inside looked even less like an actual church than the outside—signage and proper placement could really do a lot for things.

The man in his robe was reading from a book, smiling at his own words and putting on quite a show. At least, the guy did seem to enjoy his job and some people might enjoy this kind of thing. Although, Roman didn't care about the words, or much for the man speaking them—it was all a means to an end.

And a very beautiful beginning.

He just wanted to be married to this girl—he wanted to be bound to Karine for life. Even if the fraudulent paperwork made the marriage illegal, it was the act itself that couldn't be undone. A bell that would *never* unring.

Besides, it wasn't like following the law had ever made much of a difference to men like him before—it certainly wouldn't matter to Dima to learn Karine had married Roman in a ceremony. Legal or not, that didn't change what it was.

Or what it meant.

If she belonged to Roman, like he was tying himself to her, then nobody, not even Dima would take her away from him. He would die to make it true. There was no cost he would not pay.

The woman who stood close by was also the official witness to the wedding—the officiant's wife wore a bright smile throughout her husband's theatrics. No doubt, it was something she had seen a hundred times.

He was just more interested in Karine than the finer details of the happenings around him. He was fine pretending nobody else existed but him and her. Her in that red jumper, with her silky dark hair laying in messy waves over her shoulders. *Her* with her eyes so bright, and a sweet mouth stretched into the prettiest smile.

Could she feel his racing heartbeats through his fingertips?

Was she as excited as he was?

As *eager*?

They would walk out of there as man and wife—till death did they part. And he still wasn't even entirely sure they were going to make it out of everything else alive, let alone *this*.

But she didn't stop staring back.

And *that* smile ...

Those nerves that he was too proud of a man to show quieted with her in front of him, hands still steady in his. At one point, he had to repeat words after the officiant. Nothing religious, Roman had been quick to specify, not even a single verse. It was the basic, legal wording the officiant technically had to use. Karine repeated the same.

Roman hadn't attended many weddings in his lifetime— the one's he'd been forced to suffer through had been worsened by hangovers and stolen drug-fogged memories. So, he wasn't completely aware of the proceedings. He simply did what he was told until finally the moment came that he'd been waiting for.

The *only* part that really mattered.

"You may kiss your bride."

He lunged at a laughing Karine who had already pulled

her hands from his to reach back for him. Engulfing her in his arms, he pulled her to his broad chest, crushing her there in the hard wall of his hold. Staring up at him, he realized— not for the first time, but certainly in the most significant way—how much smaller she appeared against him, barely toppling five-foot-three without a pair of heels. But she liked it—he saw that in her stare when those hungry eyes of hers locked on his mouth.

She liked being swallowed by him, inside his embrace, close to his heart. Always watching up at him through thick, lowered lashes. There, he thought she felt safe. He hoped it was always that way.

"Well," Karine whispered the moment their lips started to graze, "*kiss me.*"

He made it good, too.

Bruising and breathless.

Undoubtedly uncomfortable for the other two people in the room watching, although he gave them credit for the fact they didn't stop clapping until he finally pulled away from his grinning, new wife.

Karine weaved her fingers in his hair, her lips grazing the side of his stubbly cheek as she said, "This is not how I pictured my wedding day."

"Someday, we'll do it again—exactly how you want it."

He took her hand in his, and brought it to his mouth to give her fingertips the gentlest of kisses.

She shook her head, tugging her fingers out of his to run them over his mouth and chin. "That's not what I meant, Roman."

She, too, had seemed to have forgotten about the others in the room. Or maybe they were just more important.

"What I pictured as my wedding day was going to be the end of my life. What *little* of it that I had. This is not what I was told it would be, and this was perfect."

Well, then …

Never one to be at a loss for words, he framed her delicate face with both palms, and said the only thing that really felt appropriate after her admission. "I love you."

"I love you, too, Roman."

ᵗʰᵉPROMISE

Karine kissed him that time—leaning up to her tiptoes to press her lips to his before nipping at his tongue when he dared to taste her.

His hands travelled down the deep cut in the back of her jumper, the pads of his fingers dancing dangerously low on her silken skin. Enough to make him hard. Just to know he was touching his *wife*. This was his wife. The baser part of his nature reveled in the idea that she was his to adore, spoil, enjoy however he wanted to, and there wasn't anything anyone could do about it.

The rational side of Roman reminded him there were still people watching, and he didn't care to let them see what came next.

"Come on, let's get outta here," he said, groaning the words against Karine's teasing kiss.

With the very last of his control …

She at least took mercy on his soul.

• • •

Roman carried Karine over the threshold of the room he'd booked for their honeymoon—it only seemed fair to keep *some* traditions. Even if they were being silly, it made her smile and laugh. That's all he wanted.

Karine was beyond fascinated with Las Vegas, and as things were going well—there were no apparent dangers—Roman felt like they could do anything. Within reason. If anything, maybe for a few days, the two could live like nobody was watching.

Wouldn't that be something?

He had booked them one of the best suites at The Venetian Resort with a view some people would have killed for. More than anything, he just wanted to give Karine everything her heart could possibly desire while they still had the chance to enjoy it.

She kept her arms locked around his neck when he carried her in. Tipping her head back to look up at the intricately engraved ceiling of their suite, she marveled at the many details covered in gold leaf.

"I don't think I have ever seen anything as beautiful as this," Karine remarked.

"No, I haven't, either."

When she met his stare again, he'd not once looked at anything but her.

Karine's smile bloomed instantly, her next words bubbling out with a laugh. "You keep saying you don't know anything about weddings, and yet you know exactly what to do to make it all perfect."

Roman spun a slow circle in the middle of the large room with her still cradled in his arms. "I don't know much about weddings—that doesn't mean I don't know anything about loving you the right way. I've had some great examples of love in my family."

He put her down, but Karine clung to him sinking into his body. Never too far away, he knew. She didn't like that at all. His hands traveled down her back until he cupped her ass.

"Your mother and father, you mean?"

"My grandparents, too," he added. "Not that I ever really understood it before you. That's okay, though. I'm not sure I was supposed to."

She nuzzled her face in his chest, breathing deeply like she was sucking in the very scent of him directly to her lungs. He stroked her hair, staring out through the glass wall that overlooked the view of the Las Vegas strip. God knew he had better things to consider, but he couldn't ignore the sinking of his stomach.

Karine wouldn't know he dared to do it.

That he let his mind go *there*.

For a few moments, he allowed himself to think about the fact that this was not forever. This feeling, no matter how good and wanted—like they were invincible and their journey together would be easy just because they had each other—none of it was permanent.

Or even real.

Their current circumstance was not forever. The truth was harsh, and too concerning for him to put the weight on Karine's shoulders when he was sure she already had enough to handle. Roman didn't know what the future held for them. Everything could go tits up tomorrow, and that alone stayed like a heavy lump of cement deep in his gut.

Never far from his mind.

Not that he wanted it there.

Not now.

So, he took Karine's face in his hands and gave her another deep kiss, letting the seconds tick by them in silence as the taste of her on the tip of his tongue chased away those bad thoughts he shouldn't have let ruin their moment.

Ending with a kiss on the tip of her nose, Roman winked, saying, "Time for an important decision. You have to decide whether you want me to fuck you right now, or go shopping."

Karine's laughter really was infectious. There was never a time when he wasn't amazed at how happy she was. The way her whole face beamed was truly a sight to behold, and for some reason, he was the person who could make her do this.

How had that happened?

Love was *crazy*.

"That's probably the hardest choice a girl has to make," she replied through a wide grin.

Roman only shrugged.

It really *was* up to her, though he had a side he was leaning toward if he was being honest. Who could blame him?

The very tease that was Karine in her sexy, red jumper-dress, the low dips in the back and front showing off just enough to make his mouth water, hadn't been far from his mind all damn day.

It was a good thing his wife—he still couldn't believe that she was his *wife*—seemed to be able to read his mind as she let her fingers graze the red straps and lower down the deep dip along her chest. Her breasts heaved. When she slowly parted her lips, he knew what her answer was going to be.

"Fuck me," she said.

• • •

"I can't decide which is the better view," he said, smirking at her.

Karine stood with her back to the glass wall of windows facing the bright lights and a city that never slept. She had stripped down to nothing but her bright red thong. A good choice, even if it did tempt his control, for their wedding night.

Roman couldn't take his eyes off her, so his statement had been a false one nonetheless. Nothing in the world was more beautiful than her.

"Tell me how to make it a better one," she told him, dragging her teeth over her lower lip. "The view, I mean."

"It's already perfect, but I still want you to touch yourself, Karine," he said, a cigarette burning between his fingers. The smoke rose up to the ceiling, clouding his vision as it passed his face, but he didn't look away from the sight of Karine letting her thumbs drag over the peaks of her firm, pink nipples. "Imagine it's me touching you, the way you shiver when the rough side of my thumb slides down the center of your stomach."

She did, her soft gasps coming out shaky and high. Then, he took a long drag off his cigarette, making the end burn with a bright, orange glow. His cock was thick and hard in his pants, and he did nothing to hide the visible line of his erection already bulging.

Karine's hand dipped beneath the lace waist of the thong, her pleased whine letting him know she was wet and already tender to the touch. She rubbed her clit, and then slipped a finger into herself the way Roman would have done.

But he was sure it wasn't enough.

Not quite like his touch.

Her tits shuddered as desire coursed through her body, the delicate line of her shoulders falling forward with her breathy moan. When she thrust another finger into herself, she stepped backwards, pressing against the glass.

From Roman's position, it appeared like she was flying. Soaring over sin city. And that was all his patience could take.

It took him less than a minute to shed his own clothes.

ᴛʜᴇPROMISE

She still hadn't managed to get herself off in that time.

A fucking shame.

He flicked the burning cigarette into a crystal ashtray next to the leather bucket chair, and went to her. With some force, he pulled her hand out of her thong, intent on doing the job himself, now. His hands were all over her, cupping her tits, and flicking her nipples with his thumbs until she trembled. His tongue left a wet, hot trail down the center of her torso. Her skin tasted of salt, and his pants of breath had gooseflesh blooming along her stomach.

He would have loved to do this forever.

Feel her.

Taste her.

Have her.

Once more, he was reminded just how fleeting these moments truly were for them—who knew when they'd be able to enjoy time alone like this again. As fast as the anger came and went, he'd still felt it.

It had still been there.

And it wasn't fair.

Roman wanted this with Karine as much as he wanted it for her, too—for her to always be happy like this. Carefree and dreamy when he touched her. He wanted it to last forever.

But it wouldn't.

That's why it also hurt.

He slipped her thong down her thighs. It swished to her ankles as he pressed himself into her until her backside stuck firmly to the glass under his weight.

Could people see them from below? If so, then he hoped they found themselves envious of Karine. Of how beautiful she was on display when she was being loved properly, and fucked well.

He took her face in both his hands, searching her ocean eyes darkened with bliss. She still had that lingering smile—it was like he almost couldn't remember the Karine he'd first met. Perpetually afraid, always tired.

He vowed in that second to do everything he needed so that he would spend the rest of his life with *this* Karine.

His Karine.

When he lifted her up against the windows, Karine wrapped her legs around his hips. She was featherlight in his arms, and already shifting her hips to get even a brush of his cock along her slit. As she did finally sink down on his length, he was lost to the slick, silken heat encompassing his dick when he plowed in.

Her arms rested on his shoulders while her fingers toyed with the back of his neck, weaving in and out of his hair. He swallowed her soft moans with kisses, settling his cock deeper into her with every thrust until she was shuddering with each one.

Neither seemed to notice the thudding sounds they made—Roman drove himself into Karine, making her body rock against the glass window with a rhythmic beat. One of the only beats he knew how to keep, honestly.

He could see the sprawling Vegas city over her shoulder when his lavished attention at the spot on her neck that she loved for him to kiss, and for a moment, they were on top of the world.

What was he thinking about before he started fucking her? He couldn't even remember, his mind was already too hazy from the whimpering sounds his wife made in his ear as he brought her closer to her sweet release. It was a glorious place to be.

"*Roman …*"

Her whisper of his name fell like a prayer between them. She watched him through lust-hooded eyes with pouty lips swollen from his kiss.

"Tell me anything," he murmured.

He didn't stop, never once breaking his pace while her breaths came out fast, and ragged. She struggled to form the words, but when she did, he hadn't been ready for them.

"Promise me you'll never leave me."

Because everybody did, he knew.

In one way or another, everybody left her.

Roman couldn't look away from her, but if he said those exact words, they would be a lie. Life wasn't that simple, and certainly not the one he chose to live. He still wasn't going to lie to Karine—or make promises he couldn't keep.

"*Promise me.*"

That time, she spoke sharper.

Desperate.

"I promise I'll never abandon you, Karine," he said, cupping her chin and dragging the pad of his thumb over her trembling lower lip. "Those are still different things."

And he knew it wasn't what she wanted to hear.

Not that she showed it.

Throwing her head back, she moaned louder, bounced harder in his arms, her cunt so tight around him that it already felt like she was milking him dry. With every thrust, she was closer to the edge and so was he.

As wet as a lake between her thighs, even the clenching of her pussy wasn't enough to stop his cock from stretching her open and stuffing her full. That's really what she'd wanted when she was against the windows, touching herself and thinking of him.

She wanted to be *too* full.

Good and used.

Fucked in the only way he could do to her. The only way she *wanted.*

"Come for me, babe," he urged, husky and breathless, already feeling the way her inner muscles were starting to spasm around him when he fucked her a little harder. "You're gonna feel this for a week, Karine."

"God, that's what I want."

Yeah, he knew.

When his hand circled her throat, and he could feel the fast flutter of her heartbeat against his palm, her final cry was loud and broken. She came with a shout, and it only took feeling the gush of warmth around his cock to make Roman empty his balls while he held Karine firm, and deep.

It was the pulsing jerk of his cock inside her that had Karine smiling like the cat who had gotten the cream. There was nothing that turned her on more than his seed filling her; he bet he could make her beg for it, even.

It was only once the two had crashed to the floor together—in a heap of satisfaction and happy laughter—that

Karine used their mingled fluids as lubrication to keep his painfully hard cock very much alive and well. There was a sharp stab of pleasure that came with every jerk of her hand down his length, but goddammit ...

He wanted more.

Karine straddled him, the slick sliver of her pussy all pink and still hungry for him hovering over his cock that she handled with two hands for a moment. "Again?"

Roman leaned up, tucking the hair behind her ears.

He wanted her insatiable.

Undeniably his.

And she was.

"One more time," he told her, his smile growing sinful along with hers as she slid down his length again, slow and tender, "and then we're eating."

Karine winked. "Deal."

XO,
BK

ABOUT THE AUTHOR

The author of too many novels to count, Bethany-Kris is a Canadian, lover of much, and mother to four sons, a glaring of cats, and a pack of dogs. A small town in Eastern Canada where she was born and raised is where she has always called home. With her boys under her feet, a snuggling cat, barking dogs, and a spouse calling over his shoulder, she is nearly always writing something ... when she can find the time.

Find where to follow BK and stay up to date with all her books news at www.bethanykris.com.